PRAISE FOR
LIFE, LOVE, & LAUGHTER:

"These two women have written a bag full of entertaining short stories, mostly filled with wry humor reminiscent of O. Henry. Very well done, filled with fun characters, and the best part is, you can fill any short waiting period with entertaining reading that ends in just a few pages. Definitely a book worth having close at all times." —George A. Bernstein, Amazon Top 100 Author of *Trapped, A 3rd Time to Die, Death's Angel,* and *Born to Die*

"A fresh and exciting collection of short stories. Humorous and surprising, a real whodunit treat." —Fred Lichtenberg author of *Deadly Heat at The Cottages: Sex, Murder, and Mayhem, Hunter's World, Double Trouble,* and *Retired, Now What?*

"Brilliant short stories by two talented authors—kept me on the edge of my seat anxiously awaiting the imaginative surprise endings." —Richard Brumer author of *The Chemist's Shop, Meeting Max,* and *The Last Sunrise*

"Authors Littlefield and Menear have once again woven their unique abilities to combine humor and suspense into stories that are sure to please the most discriminating readers. Every minute is a worthwhile investment in reading pleasure."
—Frank E. Lamca, author of *The Gypsies and the Devil Hound*

"The *50 Short Stories* are wonderfully creative writings for adult readers of any age. Littlefield's and Menear's plots and characters are at times laugh-out-loud funny and goosebumpy at others. Perfect for readers who want to read a short story in one sitting or enjoy hours of entertainment." —Tina Nicholas, author of *Condo Crazies* and *Affair in Athens*

Dedicated to Dottie's Brothers and Sharon's Uncles,

Robert and George Metz

LIFE, LOVE, & LAUGHTER:
50 SHORT STORIES

S.L. MENEAR
D.M. LITTLEFIELD

Black Stallion Publishing

LIFE, LOVE, & LAUGHTER: 50 SHORT STORIES

Copyright © July 2016 by S.L. Menear & D.M. Littlefield

TRADE PAPERBACK & DIGITAL EDITIONS 2018

Black Stallion Publishing
1281 N. Ocean Blvd., Suite 149
Singer Island, Florida 33404

All rights reserved. Black Stallion Publishing supports copyright. Copyright promotes free speech and fuels creativity. Thank you for buying an authorized edition of this book and for complying with
copyright laws by not reproducing, scanning, or distributing any part of it in any form without permission. You are supporting writers and allowing Black Stallion Publishing to continue publishing books for every reader. Printed in the United States of America.

ISBN-10: 1-943264-05-8
ISBN-13: 978-1-943264-05-6

10 9 8 7 6 5 4 3 2 1

Cover Design by Victoria Landis
Cover Re-Design by Patti Roberts of Paradox Book Covers

This is a work of fiction. All names, characters, places, and incidents either are the product of the authors' imaginations or are used fictitiously, and any resemblance to actual persons living or dead, businesses, events, companies, or locales is entirely coincidental.

Black Stallion Publishing

LIFE, LOVE, & LAUGHTER:
50 SHORT STORIES

S.L. MENEAR
D.M. LITTLEFIELD

TABLE OF CONTENTS

1. Silent Thrills by SLM & DML 1
2. When Time Stood Still by DML 19
3. Deadly Rejections by SLM 25
4. Surprised Delivery by DML 31
5. The Golden Years by DML 36
6. Sky Gods by SLM 38
7. Winter Wonderland by DML 42
8. The Magic Button by DML 47
9. My First Solo Flight by SLM 49
10. Secrets by DML 53
11. Sleuth Hounds by DML 55
12. My First Ocean Dive by SLM 67
13. Sleep Deprived by DML 71
14. Aerobatic Lessons by SLM 75
15. Meadow Muffins by DML 77
16. Flowers by DML 81
17. Holiday Greetings by SLM 83
18. Stuck in an Elevator by DML 89
19. Catatonic Snifferitis by DML 94
20. Sibling Insanity by SLM 96
21. Girl Talk by DML 100
22. The First Pilot by SLM 103
23. Eavesdropping by DML 105
24. Mall Critics by DML 107

25. Virtual Sex Flight Instruction by SLM 111
26. Chili and Hugo by DML 118
27. Expensive Mistake by DML 123
28. Betrayed by SLM 125
29. Once Upon A Time by DML 126
30. Killer Scots and Hot Cubans by SLM 130
31. Ouch! by DML 134
32. The Boys by DML 136
33. Guinevere's Lance by SLM 138
34. Clem's General Store by DML 159
35. Side Effects by DML 163
36. Sink or Swim by SLM 165
37. Unbelievable by DML 170
38. What's Going On Here? by DML 180
39. Cruise Capades by SLM 184
40. Melanie by DML 190
41. Wife Wanted by DML 194
42. Semper Fi by SLM 199
43. The Rattled Hunter by DML 201
44. Monsters by SLM 203
45. My Unconscious Muse by DML 207
46. Stressed Out by DML 209
47. The Fairies' Godmother by SLM 213
48. Dumpster Diving by DML 214
49. The Word Artist by DML 217
50. Lunar Madness by SLM 220

Authors' Note: Silent Thrills includes six true stories with personal insights from both authors. Although they participated in the same adventures, their individual experiences were quite different, so they included both points of view for your enjoyment.

SILENT THRILLS

S.L. (Sharon) Menear and D.M. (Dottie) Littlefield

HOT-AIR BALLOONING

Dottie: The predawn silence was broken by blasts of flame from the propane burner in the hot-air balloon. I never dreamed I'd be doing something like this in my fifties. As we clung to the large wicker basket attached to the glowing multi-colored balloon and waited for liftoff, I was as excited as a ten-year-old girl about to experience her first roller-coaster ride.

Sharon: After several fact-finding phone calls back in the olden days of 1981, before the Internet, I decided on an early morning launch for our first hot-air balloon ride because the wind would pick up after sunrise and carry us on an exciting journey. An evening launch required waiting until the wind died before inflating the balloon and would've resulted in a dull, stagnant flight.

The center of my grass runway on Sky Classics Farm near Hershey, Pennsylvania was the ideal place to inflate and launch the seventy-foot balloon. Empty fields flanked the runway, but an enormous tree towered halfway up the hill between the runway and my home's backyard.

I assumed the balloon would ascend vertically from the takeoff site, and we'd have restraints to tether us to the basket.

Wrong.

The sides were almost four feet high, and the basket was open except for the burner in the center. Passengers could walk around and peer over the sides. No belts, harnesses, netting, or parachutes.

I inherited my father's fear of heights—actually, a fear of falling from high places. I had no problem piloting a jet airliner at 35,000 feet because it was impossible to fall out. The cabin was pressurized, and the plug doors opened inward. I was accustomed to wearing a five-point seat harness in the Boeing cockpit.

Our seven-story balloon had to be inflated with a big fan before dawn in calm wind. Once the balloon was filled on its side, the burner added hot air to lift it upright. We launched with four passengers and the pilot. I expected a slow steady ascent, but we rose a few inches, bumped back down, and continued like that as we drifted toward the sole tree.

The pilot blasted staccato shots of hot air from the burner. Nothing happened. New to ballooning, I didn't expect such a delayed reaction. A few feet from the tree, we shot up like a rocket to two hundred feet. I grasped the corner support in a white-knuckled embrace as our basket brushed past the tree.

Dottie: What a thrill! I yelled, "Whee!" as I leaned out and grabbed a fistful of leaves on the way by. I smiled and showed them to my daughter, who had a death grip on the support arch. Although she was one of the first female airline captains in the world, standing in an open basket soaring high above the ground made her uneasy.

Heights didn't bother me, but I wasn't fearless. My participation in somewhat dangerous activities usually followed watching Sharon go first or having her accompany me, like today.

Sharon: I didn't scream, but I thought, dear God, don't let me fall out of this freaking basket! When the balloon stabilized at altitude, so did my heart rate.

Mom kept saying, "Sharon, come over and look at this! Ooh, look at that!" I was glued to a corner post, a captive of Dad's phobia, but Mom ran from side to side like an excited child. That's what I loved most about her.

Dottie: Occasional blasts from the burner were the only sounds as eerie fog shrouded the rural landscape below, hugging the lowlands, rivers, and streams. The early morning breeze quickened when the sun inched above the horizon. Soon, the fog dissipated in the wind, and our balloon picked up speed.

I savored my bird's-eye view as we glided silently two hundred feet above the Earth. I leaned over the basket and saw an owl dive from a tree and catch a rodent. When a deer jumped over a fence, I spotted a pheasant nearby running through tall rows of corn. Trees dressed for autumn in bright splashes of orange, yellow, and red dotted the countryside.

Sharon: I told Mom, "I can see fine from here." There was no way I'd release my grip, but I still enjoyed a safe panoramic view of the Susquehanna Valley. The wildlife had no idea we were flying above them until a burner blast broke the silence. Pigs and cows looked up in terror and stampeded to the barn.

Sound traveled upward. People chatting two hundred feet below sounded as if they were in the basket with us. Although a strong wind whisked us across the vast valley in record time, we didn't feel the wind because we were traveling inside it—a unique experience. How was that possible? Wind is a moving air mass, and our balloon was carried along as a part of it.

Dottie: As we sailed over people, we surprised them by yelling down. A school bus with curious children pulled off the road. The kids scrambled out and cheered.

A chase car followed the flight to assist with the landing and to drive us home. Our landing in front of the kids in the brisk wind was bounce ... tip ... bounce ... tip ... bounce ... tip. We hung onto the basket's inner cables as it was dragged along for several seconds before stopping. As we climbed out, the van driver greeted us with flutes of Bollinger Champagne.

Sharon: When the pilot told us to brace for the landing, he wasn't kidding. We were moving horizontally about 20 mph when we touched down in a plowed field and carved an extra-large furrow as the wind caught the deflating balloon and dragged the basket on its side.

The ground crew grabbed the trailing ropes and wrestled the balloon to a stop. They appeased an angry farmer with a bottle of Bollinger Champagne, a slice of quiche from their picnic basket, and a certificate assuring him a balloon landing on his land was a rare honor that would bring him good fortune. It was clear the crew had mastered how to deal with these situations. We toasted the farmer and left him smiling.

Since then, I've taken four more balloon rides, but I always held on to a corner post.

***

SUBMARINERS

Dottie: When I was sixty-five, I accompanied my daughter in a two-passenger research submarine in Grand Cayman. We sat behind the glass-bubble nose of the quiet, battery-powered sub and watched the scenery change as we silently descended eight hundred feet into the abyss.

Sharon: My mother and I share a love of animals, adventure, chocolate, and writing. My father and I share a fear of dark closed-in spaces and falling off high places. A rare chance to descend along the seven-thousand-foot Cayman Wall into the depths of the Caribbean Sea was too exciting to pass up, so I ignored the claustrophobic trash talk spewing from my subconscious.

Mom trusted me to ensure that whatever conveyance I convinced her to ride in was as safe as possible. She also assumed I could take over in an emergency and save everyone. I blamed the movie industry for her unrealistic expectations. We were on vacation, not in a *Die Hard* movie.

I chatted with the sub pilot about systems and fail-safes.

"What happens if the propulsion unit fails or the battery dies?" I asked. "If we sink all the way to the bottom, we'll be too deep for a rescue."

"The pressure at seven thousand feet would crush the sub anyway, but no worries. If we have a failure, I'll blow the ballast tanks, we'll return to the surface, and our support ship will find us."

"Are you sure?" I crossed my arms. "This sub looks awfully heavy to be offset in an emergency ascent by such a small volume of interior air."

He patted the thick steel hull on the chubby little eggplant-shaped sub. "She's never let me down." He chuckled. "Down …. Get it? Heh, heh!"

"Hilarious. Do we get in before or after they drop this tub in the water?"

"We'll board before the ship winches us over the side. Wouldn't want you pretty ladies to get wet." He winked.

Great, our pilot thought he was a comedian *and* a Don Juan.

Dottie: Colorful coral and plant life were abundant as a myriad of multi-colored fish swam in front of our large porthole. They disappeared as we plunged deeper into the black void. At eight hundred feet below the surface, our spotlight illuminated a large barnacle-encrusted freighter resting on a ledge. The sub pilot circled the freighter so we could observe it from every angle—such an eerie sight buried in a dark, silent world.

Sharon: All the pretty stuff was in the shallower depths where the sunlight fed the reef. A giant sea turtle glided past us as brilliant fish darted around him. Too bad the sharks steered clear. I would've liked observing them from our sanctuary. The varied sea creatures had banished my claustrophobia until we descended into a pitch-black Stygian death trap. I felt like the jaws of an obsidian vise were crushing our sub.

I took a deep breath and glanced over my shoulder at the pilot seated above and behind us. "Now would be a good time to turn on the external lights," I said as my voice ascended two octaves.

"Lights? What lights?" he said, then grinned.

I unbuckled my seatbelt, stood, and turned. My five-foot-four-inch frame wasn't intimidating, but my intense glare spoke volumes in the dim cabin. I enjoyed comedy as much as anyone, but hundreds of feet beneath the surface was no place to fool around.

"No need to get up!" He pointed. "See? The spotlight is on. Look at the big sunken freighter."

"Uh huh. This isn't a search-and-destroy mission. Keep the freakin' light on!" I glared a moment longer—a hint he might have to contend with a claustrophobic crazy woman if he didn't shape up.

The sunken ship looked ghostly, caught on a ledge jutting from the rock wall. Creepy eels slithered out through broken windows in the crew quarters. What had happened to the crew? Did they escape or were they entombed inside? I took a deep breath and glanced at my watch. How much battery power was left in our submarine?

Dottie: As we started our ascent, I was sad to leave the strange, dark world of the abyss. It wasn't long before we were winched aboard the surface ship. That part of the trip felt like an amusement park ride.

At the end of our thrilling excursion, we were each given a video record of the deep dive and a fancy certificate confirming we had descended to eight hundred feet in the submarine, which was only two hundred feet less than the normal maximum depth for military nuclear subs. Not many people can say they did that. For me, it was another exciting adventure with my daughter.

Sharon: The crew on the support ship greeted us with Dom Pérignon Champagne. Although I prefer still wines, especially reds, I downed two glasses before the ink was dry on our submariner certificates. My problem was that I knew too much about what could've gone wrong to fully enjoy the experience. The crushing depth and darkness closing in on us gave me some tense moments, but it was a thrilling experience I'll never forget.

When I'm old and look back on my life, I'll only regret the things I didn't do.

***

SOARING

Dottie: Like my daughter, my son, Larry, was a pilot. He flew all kinds of aircraft and gave me a ride in a sailplane, also called a glider, the same year as my sub adventure. Sleek and motorless, the glider had extra-long wings, a glass canopy, and tandem seats. I sat behind him.

A single-engine airplane towed us to three thousand feet. After the towline was released, we glided in big circles and rode the air thermals like the high-flying birds I've always envied. Once again, silence enveloped us as we soared above the Earth in a thrilling dance with our feathered friends.

Sharon: My brother was eleven months older and had always felt very competitive with me. I blamed my father for orchestrating competitions between us when we were young. In high school, I finally realized competing with boys was a bad idea. Winning killed any chance for romance, which probably had been my father's strategy.

Although my brother started flying in his early teens and soloed when he was legally old enough at sixteen, I earned my private pilot license first at twenty-three. By then, Larry had been flying eight years. He'd been too busy (lazy) to study for the written exam he had to pass before taking the flight test and earning his pilot certificate.

When Dad told him I had earned my private pilot license,

he bought a four-seat Cessna Skyhawk and rushed to acquire his private pilot license, commercial pilot license, and instrument rating. Seven years later, his competitive nature kicked in again when I was hired to fly jet airliners with US Air (later renamed US Airways and now American Airlines). He earned a flight instructor certificate, airline transport pilot certificate, multi-engine rating, helicopter license, glider rating, and seaplane rating. He even explored getting a blimp license. Geez, what would he have done if I'd been an astronaut?

Larry convinced me it would be fun to get a glider rating, so I traveled to the ideal location for training: Arizona in the summer, where there was plenty of hot rising air known as thermals.

When I signed up for the course, I had to show my airline transport pilot certificate.

"If you can fly airliners, you can get your glider rating in no time," the young instructor said.

Right, I thought, because light little gliders are so similar to big heavy jets.

Bright and early the next morning, a Cessna 180 pulled us into the sky. At three thousand feet, I released the towline, and we sailed through the calm morning air in silence. It was too early for thermals to lend lift, so we circled the runway during our gradual descent and remained aloft longer than I expected. The silence relaxed me.

Flying a glider was nothing like flying a jet. It was simple and easy. Planning ahead was important because there was no engine to keep us aloft. I soon learned to estimate the glide distance from various altitudes, always have more altitude than needed for final approach, and use the spoilers on the wings to kill the lift to descend to the runway. The landings were always fun.

Right before my solo flight, my instructor said, "If you have to land somewhere off-field, remember those big cactus trees are as hard as concrete. Steer clear."

I glanced around during my glider solo and noticed "those big cactus trees" were everywhere. No way would I land off-field unless the tow plane exploded at low altitude on takeoff. No concrete trees for this girl. Besides, I knew every man on the field was judging me. That never changed.

Nothing unusual happened during my solo flights, a welcome change from some of my other adventures. Later that day, my instructor took me up in their sleek, high-performance, aerobatic glider, which was way more fun than flying the sluggish glider trainer.

When we caught a thermal, we kept a tight bank to remain inside the narrow column of warm, rising air and shot up to six thousand feet—plenty of altitude for loops and rolls. We transited from one thermal to another, air hissing across our canopy the only sound as we put the sailplane through its paces. I loved everything we did except our last climbing spiral inside a late-day thermal. Pilots who had finished their work day joined the fray. Gliders were everywhere—above us, below us, beside us.

Clear canopies and panels in the floor allow glider pilots to see above and below them. I saw way too many sailplanes. One or two would've been okay, but not ten or twenty. It reminded me of a World War I dogfight with airplanes diving, climbing, looping, and rolling all over the place.

I'm not one for showing off or senseless competition. The only female in a gaggle of competitive male pilots, I decided to land while we still had both our wings, so I called an audible and told the instructor I needed a pit stop. Problem solved.

***

HORSEBACK RIDING

Dottie: I lived with my son for a while after my husband died in December of 1988. His home was about an hour drive east of Pensacola, Florida. When Sharon flew in to visit for a few days, we decided it'd be fun to ride from a nearby stable that featured a scenic, four-mile shaded trail. My children and grandchildren enjoyed speed, so I made sure I got a gentle old mare that wouldn't run if her tail was on fire.

Sharon: My mother, brother, and way too many people, had the ridiculous notion that I could do anything because I flew jet airliners. That was why I never told anyone what I did for a living unless it was absolutely necessary.

The airline pilot mystique had been a recurring theme, often adding terror to my adventures, like the time I went horseback riding with my mother, brother, and his teenage daughters. I wasn't an experienced rider and hadn't been on a horse in ten years.

After watching my family mount their assigned horses, the stable boy realized all their good horses were taken. He called his boss over to where I waited and said, "We're short one horse. The stallion is the only one left."

My brother looked down at him. "No problem. Sharon's an airline pilot."

"Well, little missy, if you can fly airliners, you can ride Satan," the stable master said. "Saddle him up, Billy." He waved the kid toward the stables.

I didn't want my brother and nieces to think I was a wuss. How bad could Satan be? After all, rental horses usually had to be threatened with a stick to get them moving faster than a slow walk.

"We're going to get started, Sis," Larry said. "You can catch up on the trail."

"Okay, I'll find you in a few minutes, but keep your pace slow until I get there."

As they disappeared into the tree line, Billy led a large black stallion toward me. His neck was arched, his ears were perked to full alert, and his eyes were wild with eagerness.

Uh oh.

He danced around when Billy tried to quiet him while I mounted.

Billy looked up at me. "Keep a tight rein on him or he'll run away with you."

"Tight rein" my ass! It took all my strength to restrain him to a fast trot. When my arms got tired, and I eased up a fraction of an inch, he bolted. We caught up to my family in seconds. Their horses blocked the trail, and Satan slid to a stop. I had one hand on the horn and one on the back of the saddle to save me from being launched over his head during the sudden stop.

"Oh, good, you're here," Larry said, clueless. "We've been waiting for you so we can go fast. Yee hah!" He took off in a canter.

My stallion from Hell took that as his cue to lead the pack. Despite my iron grip, Satan pushed past the horses and left them in the dust. I held on and ducked under the branches. He covered the four-mile circuit with the same zeal as a race horse in the Kentucky Derby, his snorts and pounding hooves the only sounds.

I didn't even have the energy to scream. Hanging on required all my strength. It was a miracle I was still aboard when the stables emerged beyond the trees.

Satan slid to a sudden stop at the water trough, launching me over him headfirst into the four-foot deep water. I climbed out as the devil horse guzzled. Every muscle in my body ached, my legs wobbled, and my hands looked like shaky claws.

When Larry returned with Mom and the girls, he said, "Geez, Sharon, you shouldn't be such a showoff. You could've fallen and hurt yourself." He cocked his head. "Wait a minute, how did you get soaking wet?"

***

HANG GLIDING

Dottie: I was sixty-eight when I got a chance to hang-glide over Biscayne Bay in Miami. As we headed out into the bay in a large speedboat, the big kite-like contraption with pontoons rested on an aft platform. As usual, I asked Sharon to go first, and she survived. When it was my turn and the boat was about a mile from shore, I was secured face-down in a sling harness six inches above the glider pilot.

After the boat accelerated to 35 knots, the pilot yelled, "Clear!" We instantly shot up as the towline rapidly unspooled. At 1,500 feet, he released the towline. Gliding over the bay, I spotted huge manta rays and other large fish. The pilot maneuvered us to the shoreline to ride the air currents above the high-rise condominiums, and I waved to the sunbathers below. Afterward, we made a smooth water landing on the pontoons. I never even got wet.

Sharon: My brother, Larry, had several years of experience hang gliding off mountains when he invited us to try out the new company in Miami that launched hang gliders from a boat.

I'd never been hang gliding, except for a pre-flight lesson on a small hill in New Jersey years before. That was supposed to have been a ground-handling lesson, but the kite was too big for me, and it lifted me into the air after a few running steps. I found myself looking down at my instructor from thirty feet above, my legs still in motion after the unexpected trip aloft. His panicked expression told me this had never happened before.

He shouted instructions, but it was too late. The big glider had rotated horizontally, and the wind was behind me. Instantly, the kite dove straight down, and the pointy end stuck in the ground. Harnessed in, I swung around harmlessly under the kite's framework. My instructor pulled me out, and I walked away without a scratch, but I was filled with enough adrenaline to power a freight train.

Despite that debacle, I thought hang gliding over water would be fun, especially with no chance of diving into dirt. Larry had his hang-glider certification, naturally, so he would go solo. I expected a relaxing tandem flight with a professional glider pilot.

When it was my turn, Larry said to the pilot, "Sharon's an airline captain. You should let her fly it."

I glared at my brother. "Are you crazy? I'm not going up in that kite alone!"

The hang-glider pilot stepped in. "It's okay. I'll put you in the pilot position, and I'll strap in above you in the passenger slot and talk you through it. This'll be easy for someone with your experience."

Right, because hanging under a kite in the sky is exactly like flying a jet.

I scrutinized the pilot—fit, muscular, and six feet. Big enough to control the hang glider and avoid a New Jersey repeat.

A 30-mph wind from the east and hot sun caused a bumpy day aloft. When the launch boat accelerated to 35 knots, the operator released the winch, and we shot up into the sky. In seconds, our boat looked like a tiny water bug from the end of the 1500-foot towline.

"Pull the tow release," my instructor said.

When I did, we seemed to pause. Then the kite banked sharply to the left, and my heart almost jumped out of my chest. My fear of heights/falling flooded me with adrenaline. I had a white-knuckled death grip on the control bar as air turbulence buffeted us up, down, and sideways.

Holy hell, what have I gotten myself into this time?

"Compensate by moving the control bar toward the turn," the instructor yelled. "That will shift your weight away from the turn."

When I moved the control bar to the left, we rolled into a right turn. After several banks back and forth, I finally managed to stabilize the hang glider for a few seconds. Then the turbulence upset the balance again. I'd never flown anything so sensitive to the pilot's slightest movement. Even helicopters aren't that crazy.

Experienced hang-glider pilots anticipated glider responses, made constant small adjustments, and kept the kite in a stable glide. A terror-stricken person with a falling phobia, who for the first time ever was hanging out in the open 1500 feet up, couldn't be expected to do that.

"Relax your grip on the control bar," the instructor yelled.

"That's not going to happen," I shouted in a squeaky voice. I was harnessed to a tippy, squirrelly kite soaring over Biscayne Bay, and he expected me to be rational and relax my grip on the only thing I had to hold onto.

"Reach down with your big, strong arms and take control of this friggin' kite!" I yelled. I could care less if I spoiled his high opinion of airline pilots. Survival trumped ego.

I had prepaid for three flights on the death kite, and sibling rivalry kept me from admitting my fear. By my third lesson, I had adjusted to hanging in space high above the water, so I was able to relax and enjoy it. The view was fabulous, and the kite gave me a bird-like sense of freedom I'd never experienced in any type of airplane. I was glad I'd pushed past my phobia and learned a new skill. And the hot instructor was another plus.

***

HELMET DIVES

Sharon: Snorkeling on the surface while looking down at the underwater world wasn't the same as being *in* it. I'd been a scuba diver since 1999 and wanted Mom to experience the beauty and freedom of an ocean dive without having to contend with the hazards of breathing compressed air at depth. At eighty, she was too old for a scuba class, but an underwater park in a St. Croix cove offered glass-bubble helmets fed by surface air—the perfect solution.

Dottie: Our guide explained that our thick Plexiglas helmets on shoulder mounts would hold us down so we could walk on the ocean floor. Long hoses fed air from a surface pump into the helmets. The heavy weight on my shoulders became light underwater as I slowly descended the ladder into a silent world thirty feet below.

When I reached the bottom, I plodded along as if in slow motion, holding onto the rope lining our path. The colorful Caribbean dive park seemed to explode with schools of brilliant fish in color combinations of red and gold or electric blue and yellow. They hovered, encircling my head. Vibrant coral reefs teemed with exotic life. As the sea plants swayed in the current, I cherished my journey through that beautiful underwater world.

Sharon: The bubble-helmet dive with Mom was quite different from the antique hard-hat dive I experienced in Dutch Springs, Pennsylvania more than thirty years ago, which was long before I knew anything about scuba diving. A pilot friend was a member of the North American Chapter of the Historical Diving Society, and he invited me to their annual hard-hat dive. When I arrived, I was surprised I was the only woman included in their gathering.

The hundred-foot-deep lake had been transformed into a dive park with sunken airplanes, boats, buses, and other objects to view on the bottom. Years ago, the spring-fed crystal-clear lake had been a quarry with ledges at varying depths.

Putting on the diving apparatus known as a diving dress was quite a production and required the assistance of two crewmen. The one-piece dive suit was made of rubber between layers of tan twill. After they wrestled the suit onto me, I plopped down on a bench and slipped my feet into thirty-four-pound dive boots. Then the team joined a copper-and-brass breastplate to my weighted suit. The final piece was a copper helmet with brass fittings. The surface team bolted the heavy helmet onto the breastplate, imprisoning me in the suit.

There was no way I could've taken off that helmet, or the rest of the suit, on my own. My fate was entirely in their hands. After a check to ensure the dive master and I could hear each other via the communication line, the crew bolted the faceplate to the front of my helmet.

Now I was dependent on the air hose to feed compressed air into the helmet. Timing was critical. They couldn't turn on the air until I was underwater because it wouldn't be safe while surrounded by the lesser outside surface pressure. The small volume of air trapped in my helmet had to last during the trudge down the eight steps into the water.

But first I needed help to struggle up off the bench. My dive gear weighed 176 pounds, and I weighed 120 pounds. The math was not in my favor, especially on land. Thank God for the big, strong men who pulled me up and guided me to the stairs. I was instructed to back down the stairs so I wouldn't get tangled in the air hose, communication line, and safety rope. Worried I'd run out of air, I hurried down the steps into the water.

What a relief to hear the hiss of compressed air entering my helmet. The dive master told me to continue walking backwards into the lake so I could return without tangling the lines. As I worked my way down the underwater slope, I expected the water to be as clear as air. Instead, I was entombed in a claustrophobic nightmare. The divers before me had stirred up the bottom silt, and I couldn't see my hand in front of my faceplate.

"How's it going down there?" the dive master asked.

"I'm in zero visibility," I said, trying not to sound panicky.

"Oh, it's stirred up from all the previous divers near the steps. Keep going until you reach clear water."

I was disappointed I couldn't see anything, and after the complicated ordeal of merely getting the suit on and entering the water, I didn't want to forgo the underwater park. "All righty, I'll keep going."

Walking on the bottom was probably a lot like wearing a spacesuit on a planet with twice Earth's gravity—cumbersome and exhausting. I was still blind in the silt cloud when my right foot slipped over a ledge.

In a desperate attempt to stop from tumbling backwards into the depths, I made breast-stroke motions and fell onto my knees. Almost falling terrified me. I crawled away from the ledge and focused on controlling my breathing. The dive master must've heard me gasping for air through the voice-activated microphone.

"What's happening? Are you okay, Sharon?"

"I almost fell off a ledge, and I still can't see anything." I was frightened, but also bummed I missed viewing the submerged aircraft and other interesting things.

"That ledge is at a depth of fifty feet. You should've reached clear water. Walking blind near those ledges isn't safe."

"No kidding! This isn't fun. I hope I can find the steps."

"Relax and get your breathing back to normal. Then follow the safety rope forward to where you started. You'll be okay."

His voice was comforting in the midst of nothingness. I was walking blind. Except for his occasional comments, the only sound was my breathing—torture for a claustrophobic person. I pushed the fear from my mind and concentrated on reaching the steps.

After what seemed like an eternity, I bumped into the staircase. "I'm at the steps now."

"Okay, this is the hard part. You'll have to climb the steps under all that weight, and we'll have to turn off your air before you reach the surface to avoid exploding the helmet (*and my head!*). If you don't reach the platform before you run out of air, you'll pass out and fall into the lake. Then we'll have a bitch of a time getting you out and reviving you."

"Are you kidding me? I'm not freakin' Superwoman!"

"You'll be fine. Your friend told me you're an airline captain."

Sonofabitch! That airline pilot nonsense is going to get me killed!

I steeled myself and started up the steps. Damn, those boots were heavy!

When I was halfway up to the platform, I heard him say, "Turning off air now. Keep going."

Each laborious step felt heavier. When I was two steps from the top with most of my body out of the water, the diving dress felt like it weighed five hundred pounds. As I struggled to lift my right foot to the next step, my vision blurred, and I lost my balance.

Terror gripped me as blackness closed in. Strong hands grasped the front of my suit and yanked me up, saving me from a disastrous fall. The men hauled me to the platform and opened my faceplate. When my world came into focus, I couldn't wait to get that damn helmet off.

I discovered later the only reason they had allowed an untrained person like me to do the hard-hat dive was because I was an airline pilot. I've no clue why that should've made a difference unless it was because pilots tend not to panic. In any case, I'll never forget that dive, and I'll always be grateful for strong men.

Note to self: Remind relatives and friends to keep their big mouths shut about my pilot career.

***

Dottie and Sharon: We hope you enjoyed our silent adventures, including Sharon's silent screams, and that we proved silent activities can be filled with thrilling moments.

WHEN TIME STOOD STILL

D.M. Littlefield

Wilbur, an old dilapidated Wichita truck, had been abandoned on the prairie hill for many years. With each passing year, the morning dew penetrated deeper into his rusty green body, but at least the hot Texas sun warmed his aching steel frame. Wilbur gazed down at the highway, exhaled a lonely sigh, and blinked his headlights, recalling the glory days of the East Texas oil boom that had started in 1930. If only he could go back to that time and remain there forever.

Of all the buildings on Kilgore's main street, the gas station and oil-well-supply store were the most vivid in his memory. During the Great Depression, the discovery of rich oil deposits transformed tiny Kilgore into a bustling boomtown. Twenty-four oil wells inside one city block yielded the richest acre of oil in the world.

Production of new wells increased from seven wells every two weeks to seven wells a day, then to one hundred wells a day and more. Regular gasoline was sixteen cents a gallon, and ethyl was eighteen cents. People looking for work flocked to Kilgore from all over the country. The streets were crowded with horse- or mule-drawn wagons and cars and trucks made in the 1920s and early 1930s.

Kilgore was where Wilbur met Lily, his long-lost love. Wilbur remembered that wonderful day like it was yesterday. He was in front of the oil-well-supply store when she parked near him—the prettiest white pickup truck he'd ever seen. He almost blew a gasket, trying to build up his courage to speak to her. Then a shiny black Ford sedan parked between them. The sedan's motor idled softly as his headlights roamed over Lily's lovely steel body.

"Hey, oil patch bumpkin, pay attention," the sedan whispered to Wilbur. "I'll show you how a slick city sedan makes out." He honked his horn at Lily and said, "Honey, they call me handsome Harry. I'm the slickest, fastest sedan in East Texas. Why don't we take a little drive up through the hills and find a nice secluded place to park?"

Wilbur was so steamed over Harry's crude proposition to Lily that he had to hold onto his radiator cap to keep it from blowing off. Lily wasn't one of those Tin Lizzies that Harry usually parked close to ... the hussies that parked in front of the saloons at all hours of the night.

Lily's cold glare should have deflated Harry's tires, but his ego was as big as an oil derrick. He assumed she was just being coy. When her driver returned from the store, she backed into the busy dirt street, muddy from a long stretch of rain. Lily cautiously accelerated around a mule-drawn wagon stuck in a big mud puddle. Beside the wagon, she sank into thick mud up to her lovely hubcaps.

Handsome Harry's driver jumped in and drove him up behind Lily. "Don't worry, honey," Harry said. "I'll have you out in a jiffy." Harry eagerly pressed his bumper against hers and tried to push her out. Lily shook with indignation as Harry raced his engine and pushed harder. Soon, he was stuck deeper in the mud than Lily.

When Wilbur's driver returned, he took charge of the situation and backed up Wilbur behind the embarrassed sedan. He hooked a tow chain to his bumper, and Wilbur easily pulled Harry out of the mud to the top of the hill. After the tow chain was unhooked, the humiliated sedan drove off in a huffy puff of exhaust smoke.

Wilbur snickered. An oil field bumpkin like him may not be handsome, but he knew how to handle a sticky situation. He hurried back to help Lily. His driver nosed him up to her front bumper and attached the tow chain. When their headlights met, Wilbur felt a massive jolt of electricity, like a jump start from a lightning bolt. He quivered with excitement as he gently pulled her to firm ground.

Lily demurely dimmed and blinked her headlights at Wilbur. "You're the most powerful truck I've ever seen. Thanks for rescuing me. I hope we meet again." She reluctantly drove away.

Lily obviously liked him, even though he wasn't a handsome sedan like Harry. He was built in 1926 to do heavy oil field work. No fancy frills, just a powerful motor, a winch, and a strong bed that could carry three tons.

Lily's compliment elated Wilbur. As he watched her drive away, he sighed with happiness. Her molded steel curved in all the right places, and her headlights—wow! When she gazed at him with her demure little blink, she fogged up his windshield and almost melted his transmission.

The next day, Wilbur was thrilled to see Lily parked at his driver's drill site. Nervous, his motor sputtered when he drove up beside her. "I was hoping I'd see you again, Lily. This is where I work."

"Wilbur, it's wonderful to see you again too. My driver is the new supervisor, so I'll be here with you every day."

Each day, Wilbur parked next to Lily. Soon they were roof over wheels in love. Deep down in their motors they knew they had found true love. Their happy days seemed to fly by until the work on the drill site was finished.

"I heard my driver say we're going to another drill site far away. We might never see each other again! Good-bye, Wilbur. I'll always love you and be true to you. I hope and pray we'll be together again someday." Tears glistened on her headlights.

Wilbur choked out the words, "I'll always love you, Lily, and I'll never stop looking for you." He felt like his engine block would crack from sorrow. He watched her drive away until tears blurred his headlights.

***

Wilbur never saw Lily again, except in his memories. Those happy reflections were the only things that made the long, lonely years bearable.

A mockingbird perched on Wilbur's rusty winch and chirped a sweet song, interrupting his reverie. Wilbur sighed and listened to the bird, which had weaved its nest into his caved-in roof. His torn, ragged seat harbored a family of field mice. Wildflowers poked their pretty heads through the spokes of his rusty wheels as he watched vehicles speed by on the highway below.

Over the years, Wilbur had witnessed the dirt lane below become a gravel road, then a paved two-lane road, and finally a four-lane highway. Years of accumulated prairie dust on his headlights had dimmed his vision, but he diligently looked for Lily every day. He marveled at the speed of modern vehicles. Wilbur's top speed had been 18 mph when he was in top condition.

He was surprised to see a shiny red Chevy pickup drive quietly up the hill and park in front of him. Two men circled Wilbur, inspecting him. They decided to ask his owner if they could haul him away. He watched them walk down the hill toward his owner's house.

"What do those men intend to do with me?" Wilbur asked the new truck.

The arrogant truck looked disdainfully down his shiny chrome grill at Wilbur and sneered. "I've never seen a truck as old as you, all rusted and falling apart. You can't be good for anything. They'll probably dump you in a junkyard with derelicts. Why they'd even bother to haul you away is beyond me, unless it's because you're such an eyesore."

Humiliated, Wilbur was too hurt to respond. This truck was young now, but time would catch up to him sooner than he thought. One day, he'd be old and unwanted too.

The men returned and drove the young truck away. Wilbur sadly searched the traffic, perhaps his last chance to find Lily. He dreaded what tomorrow might bring.

The next day, the men loaded Wilbur onto a flatbed truck and hauled him away. He squinted through his dirty headlights, surprised at how much the towns had grown. Finally, his long journey ended, and he was unloaded. He glanced around for other derelicts, but the warehouse was empty.

Alone again.

On Saturday morning, a group of men entered with all sorts of tools. An old Ford Model A drove in. Wow, it looked good for its age! A sign on its door was a clue: East Texas Vintage Auto Club. Its driver walked over to inspect Wilbur.

"Old-timer, they don't make 'em like you anymore, but we'll do our best to restore you," he said, patting Wilbur's hood.

The men sanded and scraped Wilbur all day. It felt wonderful, like a deep massage. They returned the next day and every weekend for months. He thrived on their company and attention.

Finally, Wilbur's restoration was complete.

He no longer hunched over from his caved-in roof. Now, he proudly stood tall with a new roof, new seat, new glass, and repairs too numerous to list. His coat of shiny green paint made him look young again. He felt grateful these men cared about him. And the best part? For the first time in fifty years, he could see clearly. His headlights shined with happiness. *I wish Lily could see me like this.*

The men were admiring Wilbur and taking lots of photos when they heard a horn. They walked outside to investigate. Moments later, they pushed a pretty pickup into the warehouse and parked it in front of Wilbur.

Wilbur blinked his sparkly headlights in astonishment. Could his headlights be deceiving him? Was it really Lily? His long-lost love was right in front of him—just as young and pretty as ever! She had a happy gleam in her headlights and a flawless coat of white paint.

A man snapped photos of them together. "If these two could talk, they'd have some mighty interesting stories to tell."

The other men agreed as they gathered their tools and departed.

The happy old couple chatted all through the night,

recalling the good old days and catching up on the many years they'd been apart. They were thrilled to be together again and wondered why they'd been restored.

The next morning, Lily was loaded onto a trailer while Wilbur watched, resigned to whatever fate had in store. Then he was loaded onto a flatbed truck that followed Lily's trailer. Wilbur strained his headlights to keep Lily in sight as they drove through town. They parked next to a large building with a big oil derrick in front. Lily was unloaded and pushed inside the building while Wilbur waited apprehensively.

Soon, the men pushed Wilbur inside too. Wilbur couldn't believe his headlights. He found himself back during the oil boom. Did this building have magical powers? He was on the main street in Kilgore with all the old familiar buildings, just as he remembered. The movie *The Great East Texas Oil Boom* was still on the theater's marquee. Even handsome Harry was there, handsome as ever, but stuck in the mud again. The mule-drawn wagon was mired in the muddy street too, just like long ago.

Wilbur's headlights beamed with happiness when he saw Lily. She was up to her lovely hubcaps in mud, like she'd been when they met so many years ago. As Lily's motor hummed like a contented purring cat, Wilbur knew they would always be together now. His wish to return to this special time had been granted.

The kind people who'd made his wish come true had his and Lily's motor-felt thanks forever. In the East Texas Oil Museum in Kilgore, time will always stand still for Wilbur and Lily.

Author's Note: "When Time Stood Still" is based on the Main Street display inside the East Texas Oil Museum that depicts antique vehicles stuck in the mud during the Great East Texas Oil Boom. The museum is located in Kilgore, Texas, where I used to live.

DEADLY REJECTIONS

S.L. Menear

Sir Clive Pierpont adjusted his gold cuff links emblazoned with the family crest and pressed the elevator button for the hotel's tenth floor. The doors were closing when a hand with blood-red fingernails gripped one of them. A middle-aged woman built like a fireplug barged in.

Clive focused on her frizzy brown hair and black polyester pantsuit, shiny from wear. *Typical, frumpy American. Hideous hair. Hope she doesn't try to converse. Why is she staring?*

She moved closer. "I saw your picture in the brochure for the Mystery Writers' Conference. You're that literary agent, Clive Pierpont, aren't you?"

"It's *Sir* Pierpont to you."

"This is America." She thrust her hands on her hips. "We don't use titles here."

"Americans aren't worthy of titles." Clive lifted his chin and adjusted his silk tie.

She glared at him. "You're just as snotty in person as you are in your letters."

Clive raised an eyebrow. "I beg your pardon. Do I know you?"

"Frieda Frobisher. You rejected my brilliant cozy—called it a 186,000-word monstrosity best suited for burning."

"Frobisher ... ah, yes, you could've fit three cozies in that word count. Worst writing I've ever read—used it as fire starter in my fireplace—lasted six months. You haven't a clue how to write properly."

"Shows how much you know. Friends and relatives said my novel, *The Butler Didn't Do It*, was the best murder mystery they'd ever read."

"Oh, *really*?" Clive sneered. "How many of them are literary agents?"

"None, but they're avid mystery readers."

Clive stepped out of the elevator at his floor and turned to face her. "I shall mimic your detestable writing as I slowly and stealthily creep down the ominously dark hallway to my luxuriously appointed, highly-priced suite." He shouted through the closing doors, "Don't quit your day job!"

Later that night, Clive was startled awake when someone injected something into his silk pajama clad backside. He blacked out before he could roll over.

***

"If the Devil wears Prada, her evil twin, literary agent Priscilla Penthouser, wears Chanel." Prissy Penthouser deleted the disparaging quote a rejected author had posted on her Facebook page and checked the time on her iPhone. She tapped her Montblanc pen on the table and turned to the coordinator for the agents' panel. "Where's Clive? Our panel starts in five minutes."

The harried woman glanced around the crowded room. "I called. No answer on his room phone or cell. I'll ask someone to check the men's room."

"Good, I'll have time to powder my nose." Prissy adjusted her Chanel suit and strode into the restroom, her Manolo spiked heels clacking on the tile floor. She applied fresh red lipstick and smoothed her short, salon-styled black hair. While gazing into the mirror, she noticed a thin, gray-haired woman exit the stall behind her.

The woman squinted at Prissy. "You're Priscilla Penthouser, the literary agent." She held out her wrinkled, liver-spotted hand. "I'm Lily Whimple, and I'd like you to represent me. My cozy is sure to be a best seller."

Stepping back, Prissy recoiled as though Lily's hand was infected with leprosy. "We may not be a good fit." She turned up her nose at her cheap pantsuit and worn sneakers. "I only represent high-end clientele."

"My cozy is very high end. You'd love it." She moved to block the door.

Prissy blew out a sigh. "Give me a brief description."

"My novel, *Dead Divas Don't Sing*, is a 197,000-word, twisty-turny, suspenseful, murder mystery."

"I thought you said it was a cozy."

"That's right, it's my first novel. You should pitch it to Hollywood. They'll want to make it into a movie. We'll be rich. What do you say?"

"Forget writing. Try basket weaving." Prissy pushed past her and strutted out.

When Prissy entered the meeting room, an anxious conference volunteer pulled her aside.

"Top secret: Clive was murdered in his room last night," she whispered. "Don't tell. We don't want to upset anyone."

Prissy's jaw dropped. "What happened?"

"Someone sedated him, connected a portable printer to his laptop, printed out several rejection letters he'd written, wadded them up, and stuffed them down his throat. He suffocated."

"Oh, that's awful!" Prissy smoothed her skirt and glanced at the wall clock. "We should begin the panel, don't you think?"

The volunteer looked across the crowded room and sighed. "Yes, as they say, the show must go on."

***

After listening to droning amateurs in afternoon pitch sessions, Prissy ordered a bottle of Montrachet chardonnay at the conference cocktail party. Distracted by conversation, she felt a sharp prick when someone bumped into her back. She assumed it was just a protruding ring on the person's hand and didn't bother to turn around.

It wasn't long before she felt drowsy and excused herself. Back in her room, she kicked off her shoes in a chair facing the door and leaned her head against the wingback. Comfortable, she closed her eyes and dozed off.

She woke when she felt a sharp object pierce her neck, severing her left carotid artery. Without thinking, she yanked the Montblanc pen from her neck. As blood spurted from her wound, she spotted her executioner standing in the shadows with a small crossbow.

***

Veronica Vixenne greeted her fellow agents at the power table for the Mystery Writers' Banquet. Two seats were empty. A rotund middle-aged man in a too-tight suit sat in the open seat beside her and dabbed his sweaty forehead with a linen napkin.

"Veronica, I enjoyed my pitch session with you earlier today. You're my first choice to represent my 168,000-word international thriller, *Tubing Down the Ganges*. You remember me, Rupert Finch, from this afternoon?" he asked.

Veronica sighed and drained her glass of cabernet. "Yes, Rupert, I remember you."

"My novel is a literary tour de force any agent would die for. I bet you're glad I picked you." He sipped a double whisky on the rocks.

Veronica flagged a passing waiter. "A bottle of Chateau Montelena 2012 cabernet sauvignon, right away, please."

Rupert yelled, "Put it on my tab." As he grinned at Veronica, tiny bits of dark nuts studded his teeth. "So," Rupert leaned forward, squeezing her arm, "where should I send my manuscript?"

Veronica recoiled. "Toss it in the incinerator."

"I thought you liked my thriller set in India." He slumped back.

"Puhleeze, the Ganges River is a slow-moving, shallow cesspool about as thrilling as a trip to a toxic waste dump."

Rupert's face reddened, and he fled the ballroom. Veronica drank her wine in peace.

After the banquet, she retired to her room and savored a hot bath. She was half-asleep in the tub when she heard the door to her room open and close. "Who's there?"

Moments later, someone entered the bathroom, plugged her laptop into the electrical outlet, switched it on, and tossed it into her bathwater.

***

The next morning, Detective Lou Manly looked at the portly matron in the tub and sighed. "This mystery conference is turning out to be a murder fest," he said to his partner. "It was supposed to be a conference for writers, not murderers."

"Three murders so far." His partner pulled out his notebook. "I interviewed the president of the Florida chapter hosting the event. After the first murder, she found a website called PoeticJustice@AgentsWhoDeserveToDie.com, run by some guy called Freddy the Fixer. The dead agents are among those listed on the website."

"Get me a list of all the writers who posted complaints about them."

"They got hundreds of angry letters."

"Match them with the list of conference attendees."

"Already did. Only three matches."

"Great! Round 'em up. I'll interview them individually in a small conference room."

***

After completing lengthy interviews with the three suspects, Lou stared at his notes. "They all have airtight alibis," he said to his partner. "What are we missing?"

A foul-smelling police officer blotted with garbage stains entered the room. "Detective Manly, I found this buried in the trash." He held up a small crossbow. "Could have been used to fire that pen into the vic. It's been wiped clean."

"Excellent work, Officer Santiago. Get this to the lab." Lou turned to his partner. "I hope we're dealing with a lone wolf." Lou checked his watch. "The conference ends in two hours. Lock down the hotel. No one associated with the conference leaves."

Conference attendees were held in the ballroom.

"I searched the rooms of Frieda Frobisher, Lily Whimple, and Rupert Finch," Lou's partner said. "Nothing."

"Each writer has an alibi for the murder of the agent who rejected them," Lou said.

"Yeah, but not for the other agents."

"No reason to murder agents they didn't know." Lou shook his head. "I have to release them."

***

When Frieda, Lily, and Rupert checked out, they had one identical room charge: a pay-per-view fee for Hitchcock's classic movie, *Strangers on a Train*.

SURPRISED DELIVERY

D.M. Littlefield

Ralph, the seventeen-year-old delivery boy, stomped through the Pizza Palace's back door with a bloody handkerchief to his nose and his clothes splotched with red. "This is a dangerous job. I'm not sure I want to do this anymore."

His boss, Enzo, glanced at him while taking a pizza out of the oven. He did a double take and wiped the sweat off his swarthy face with his apron. "What happened to you?"

Ralph heaved a sigh and leaned against the counter. "My first delivery was Mrs. Harris, and her twin brats had their squirt guns filled with red Kool-Aid. They nailed me. On my next delivery, Mrs. Bank's terrier jumped up and bit my butt." He turned around and looked down over his shoulder. "Did he take a chunk out of my jeans?"

Enzo shook his head and lit a cigarette.

"I just came from the Lopez house. Mrs. Lopez answered the door in a sheer negligee. I couldn't help staring at her, so her husband punched me in the nose. I ain't ever going back there again. I took this job to save up for a car, but it looks like I won't live long enough to buy one."

"Kid, everybody has bad days. Working in a hot kitchen is no picnic either. At least you get to enjoy cool air while driving all over town in my new delivery car. You think you've got it bad? When I owned a big pizza place in Chicago, I had to pay protection money to the mob. I grabbed the first offer I got, sold it, and moved fifty miles down here to our quiet little town of Dumpling Falls."

Enzo exhaled smoke. "I'll call Mr. Lopez and tell him we won't deliver his pizzas anymore. Don't quit. Start defending yourself. Get a squirt gun and shoot back at the brats and dogs."

Ralph wiped the remnants of blood off his face and sighed.

Enzo checked his list. "You have one more delivery tonight—the last living relative of our town's founder."

"Oh, you mean Tillie Sparks."

"Yeah, she said she left the kitchen door unlocked and to come right in. She can't hear you knock with her television on full blast. Try to relax on the long drive, okay?"

Ralph ran his hand through his red hair and moaned. "Okay, give me her pizza."

Enzo checked his watch. "By the time you get there, *Dancing with the Stars* will be on. Wait for a commercial before you talk to her. She's a fanatic about that show and won't want to be interrupted."

On the drive over, Ralph thought about how much he liked the feisty old lady, the town celebrity. Even in her nineties, she was sharp and tipped well. Her fat male bulldogs, Starsky and Hutch, named after an old TV detective show, were her constant companions. He thought they should have been named Tweedle Dumb and Tweedle Dumber.

In Tillie's driveway, Ralph parked behind a beat-up Toyota Corolla he'd never seen before. When he got out, he noticed a man entering Tillie's kitchen. Who was he? Ralph went in and closed the door. The stranger spun around and pointed a gun at him.

Ralph froze.

The dogs barked.

"Take the money from my purse!" Tillie shouted over the blaring television and woofing. "It's on the counter. Bring the pizza in here."

The gunman, a stocky man with olive skin and dark hair, pressed his finger to his lips and scanned the room. He spotted the purse on the opposite counter.

Transfixed, Ralph watched the stranger, who was so focused on the prize he was oblivious to the pool of water on the linoleum floor around the dogs' water dish. His feet flew up in the air when he slipped, and he landed on his back. His right elbow slammed the floor, which triggered his gun with a deafening bang. The bullet ricocheted off the stove's steel hood and struck the man in the forehead. Dead.

"Ralphie? What happened?" Tillie yelled.

Ralph was rendered speechless as blood pooled around the motionless man on the floor.

The dogs bolted in and sniffed the body but soon turned their noses up to the pizza box in Ralph's hand.

Tillie hobbled in, wearing pink plastic curlers and fuzzy bunny slippers with part of their ears chewed off. She glanced at Ralph and poked the body with her cane. "Who's the dead guy?"

His lower lip quivered. "I … don't know. I … I … thought you knew him."

"Nope." Tillie glanced at her watch. "Bring the pizza in by the TV. The commercial's almost over."

"Wait! Aren't you going to call the police?"

"He's not going anywhere. I don't want to miss *Dancing with the Stars*. I'll call when it's over."

Before Ralph could respond, two thugs burst in with guns drawn. Ralph leaped over the body to Tillie, his eyes wide with fear.

"Hands up!" the taller man yelled.

Ralph dropped the pizza box and raised his hands. The dogs tore it open and started devouring the pizza.

Tillie looked down in disgust. "There goes my dinner." She glared at the intruders. "This is your fault."

"Hands above your head, ya old biddy!" the other man shouted.

"That would be a miracle. I'm ninety-four. I haven't been able to raise my hands that high since I was eighty-five."

He shook his head and reached for the gun next to the body. "So who knocked off Eddie da Mooch?"

"Not me. I was watching my favorite TV show," Tillie said.

The goons glared at Ralph, who was teetering on shaky legs.

"Don't look at him. He just got here." Tillie glanced at her watch again. "Can we wrap this up? Maks is dancing next. He's my favorite."

The taller man scowled. "We had a contract for the hit on Eddie, so we're takin' the credit." He turned to his partner. "Vito, take Eddie's picture. The boss'll want proof."

Vito squatted for a good angle. "The damn dogs are in the background."

Tillie stamped her cane. "I don't allow swearing in my home!"

The tall thug rolled his eyes. "Just take the shot from the other side," he said, waving his gun in front of Tillie and Ralph.

Ralph trembled as he stared at the gun. He felt a warm liquid trickling down his pant leg and glanced down, hoping he hadn't lost control. A dog was lifting his rear leg toward him with a satisfied look. Ralph grimaced and closed his eyes.

Vito stood next to the body and focused the camera phone on the dead man's face. He hesitated and sniffed. "What the …?"

His partner stepped away from the dog and the boy. "Geez, Vito, take the damn picture. Let's get the hell outta here!"

Tillie stamped her cane again. "I said no swearing!"

He waved her aside with his gun. "Go watch yer stupid show already."

***

Later, the coroner's van and two police cars parked at Tillie's house. She sat on the sofa with her dogs while a deputy questioned her. Ralph leaned against the wall, staring into space and mumbling.

The deputy spoke on his cell phone. "Sheriff, a pizza delivery driver noticed a body on his customer's kitchen floor and asked her to call us. Yes, sir, Tillie Sparks. She admits she waited until her TV show was over. She claims two mafia guys armed with handguns made the hit and came back to take his picture for proof."

One of the dogs jumped off the couch and trotted over to Ralph. The dog sniffed Ralph's pants, lifted his leg, and covered the other dog's scent in fresh pee. He took one more sniff before prancing back to the couch with his head held high.

"Yes, Sheriff, Mrs. Sparks is fine." The detective smiled at Tillie as he held the cell phone to his ear. "The pizza delivery guy? Hang on, I'll ask."

The detective walked over to Ralph. "Hey, kid, you all right?"

Ralph sucked in his breath and yelled, "No! I quit!"

His shoes squished as he stomped out.

THE GOLDEN YEARS

D.M. Littlefield

Ray and Abby Morris finished their waltz and sat next to each other, facing the dance floor at the Senior Center. With their walkers handy, some of their friends enjoyed refreshments at tables as they watched the dancers swing and sway to the big-band music of the 1940s.

Ray knew Abby loved to dance and considered it good exercise. Although he felt golf was enough of a workout for him, he liked dancing because the music brought back memories of when they were young, and it eased them into a romantic mood. Now in his late seventies, Ray's aches and pains diminished amorous thoughts. No matter the mood, his chances were slim until he tried the magic sex pill his buddies bragged about. Now he was frowning less and smiling more.

Abby's response surprised him. She no longer stayed up until the wee hours of the morning watching classic movies. As soon as he said he was ready for bed, she was too, and she began flaunting sexy nightgowns. Ah, yes, life was good again.

Ray smiled, anticipating the evening's romantic climax after they arrived home. A frown quickly replaced his smile. *Damn! I forgot to refill my sex prescription.*

He felt Abby's hand on his thigh but stared straight ahead as he nudged it aside.

She grabbed his thigh again, clutching it in earnest with pleading eyes. "Ray, I need you ...," she whispered.

Red faced, he tried to push her hand away. "Abby, please control yourself. You're embarrassing me in front of all these people."

She glared at him. "Is sex all you think about? I need help. I'm feeling dizzy, and I don't want to fall off the chair!"

SKY GODS

S.L. Menear

A month after my twenty-first birthday, I began a career as a Pan American World Airways flight attendant based at JFK International Airport in New York City. I flew to eighty-eight countries spanning the globe.

Those were the glory days of the airline industry, and Pan Am was the premier international carrier. Their pilots were revered as sky gods, and their stewardesses were treated like movie stars. People stopped me on the street and asked me for my autograph—no idea why. We cooked gourmet food to order in first class and served baked Alaska flaming. Heads of state, Hollywood legends, and international tycoons were frequent passengers.

My flight attendant career began long before the existence of the internet, debit cards, and smart phones. Pan Am's hiring standards for pilots and cabin crew were the most stringent in the industry. All the pilots had military backgrounds, and many were former U.S. Navy because Pan Am's first aircraft were amphibious flying boats. Those were long before my time.

All Pan Am flight attendants were required to speak at least two languages, but three or more languages were preferred. Consequently, many more Europeans were hired than Americans. Back then there was no such thing as fairness or political correctness. All cabin crew had to meet strict appearance standards and weight limits. White gloves, makeup, and nail polish were mandatory as were nylons and heel heights on uniform shoes. Flight attendants had to pass weight and appearance checks before every flight sequence.

Trainees had to pass an extensive course that included far more than pointing out the location of emergency exits and serving food and beverages. We had to memorize a world map and then fill out a blank map with the names of every country and all the cities Pan Am served in their proper locations.

Coach passengers purchased alcoholic beverages, rented headsets for music and movies, and paid for them with cash from any country, so we had to learn the currency and exchange rates for all eighty-eight countries in our route system. The bartending course covered all mixed drinks, premium beers, lagers, and extensive knowledge of the best wines and how to serve them properly.

The biggest challenge was learning how to cook gourmet foods in blower ovens. Rack of lamb, roast beef, filet mignon, filet of sole, chicken cordon bleu, and Cornish game hens were a few of the many foods on the menus. Eggs to order for first-class breakfasts were the most difficult to prepare. They too had to be cooked in blower ovens. If eggs were left in the ovens a moment too long, they turned a grayish green color that was quite repulsive looking.

We had to learn the customs of many countries to avoid giving offense, as well as how to address their heads of state, and how to recognize all the various military insignias from around the world. We were also required to dress appropriately for whatever country we stayed in during our layovers. Pan Am flight attendants were expected to be above reproach and represent our employer positively at all times.

We also received extensive medical training as well as training for a variety of aircraft emergencies, including bombs, inflight fires, crashes, water landings, and dealing with hijackers and terrorists.

I didn't mention everything taught in the training school, but suffice it to say it wasn't an easy course, and many trainees failed and were sent home.

After passing the new-hire course, my travels with Pan Am

included many exciting adventures most people experienced vicariously in books or movies.

In a country full of brunettes, my blond hair helped save me while shopping in the bazaar in Tehran, back before the Shah was deposed, when rebel factions opened fire with automatic weapons. A shop owner herded me and two blond friends into a back room, down a stairway, and into a dark escape tunnel. He ushered us to safety under the glow of an oil lantern. The other shoppers had to fend for themselves.

In 1972, our crew overnighted at the Intercontinental Hotel in Managua, Nicaragua where Howard Hughes resided in the penthouse suite. That night, a major earthquake destroyed almost every building in the city, except our pyramid-shaped hotel.

HH flew out in his private jet before the aftershocks ruined all the runways and trapped our Boeing. The sky gods drove us south out of the burning city to the international airport in San José, Costa Rica. We thanked God for our sky gods.

Throughout my Pan Am career, I endured many earthquakes, rebellions complete with bombs and bullets, KGB agents following me, lots of crazy people, and famed international criminals on my flights. Way too many adventures to mention here.

I helped with the evacuation of Saigon during the final days of the Vietnam War. The Pan Am cabin crew carried Department of Defense cards with military officer ranks in case we were taken prisoner. The pilots retained their commissions as former flight officers in the U.S. military.

The evacuation flights were chaotic and tension filled with mobs of people crowded into every open space in the cabin, including sitting in the aisles and beside the doors. Safety rules were ignored during the extreme emergency, all of which could've been avoided if the populace had heeded the warnings and left a week or two earlier. Our huge B747 was in danger of being targeted by an enemy missile as we struggled into the sky with our heavy load of human cargo.

I and the other flight attendants trusted the pilots with our lives. *We* called them sky gods because they always brought us home safely, no matter what.

In the mid 1970s, I transferred to Miami and joined the Pan Am Flying Club. Three months later, I earned my private pilot license. The Pan Am sky gods were kind to me. They let me fly a Boeing 707 for two hours over South America on a flight with few passengers and good weather. I also savored the thrill of flying a Boeing 747 en route from JFK to Frankfurt, Germany. The jumbo jet felt as steady as flying a big house.

That was my light-bulb moment: I wanted to fly jet airliners. During my free time, I concentrated on earning the necessary pilot certificates and ratings. In late 1978, I quit Pan Am to work as a flight instructor and charter pilot, eventually landing a job as a commuter airline pilot.

Two years later, I was the first woman hired as a copilot with US Air (later changed to US Airways), bypassing the flight engineer position to fly right seat in a BAC 1-11 jet. After six years flying the BAC 1-11, B727, DC-9, and B737, I earned my fourth stripe and joined a handful of female captains worldwide.

I had achieved my impossible dream and transformed myself from stewardess to sky god. The view from the left seat in the cockpit of a Boeing airliner is the best view in the entire world.

Thank you, Pan Am!

WINTER WONDERLAND

D.M. Littlefield

An old man was slumped on a bus-stop bench as the snow silently floated down around him. He seemed unconscious, and I wondered if he was all right. I nudged him upright and caught a strong whiff of alcohol. He squinted up at me through bloodshot eyes and murmured. I dropped my luggage and brushed away the snow on the bench.

"I understand, buddy," I said as I sat beside him. "If I had to live here, I'd stay drunk too. I'm on my way back to sunny Florida where I can golf and fish all year."

The old man blinked. "Ta Florida?"

"Yeah, I moved there after I retired, but my wife developed a fear of hurricanes after we endured three in one year. She began yammering about moving back to Michigan to be close to her sister and free of hurricanes. I let her drag me here just to stop her nagging, but I kept our Palm Beach condo."

"Condo ... Palm Beach." The old man sighed and sagged against me, a captive audience.

"It snowed here the day after we moved in. I admit I felt peaceful watching the fluffy flakes slowly drifting down on the trees and landscape.

"We awakened to a winter wonderland, everything covered in a beautiful white mantle. The wife and I built a snowman in the front yard. She made hot chocolate for us while I shoveled our sidewalk and driveway. For the first time in thirty years, I enjoyed shoveling snow."

"Ugh, snow," the old guy grumbled.

"Later, a snowplow blocked our long driveway with a foot-high strip of compacted snow from the street. The driver smiled and waved. I waved back and shoveled his deposit, assuming he didn't mean to block our drive. These things just happen.

"That night, it snowed an additional five inches, and the temperature dropped to ten degrees. Branches littered our yard, broken off from the weight of heavy ice and snow. After shoveling our driveway, the snowplow blocked us in again. The driver smiled and waved. My hands were too frozen to wave back or shovel more snow."

"Huh, damn snowplowsssss!"

"I started my car and rammed the narrow two-foot snow ridge like a mad man. The front wheels went up the hard-packed snow and crashed down on the other side, leaving the rear end dangling an inch above the ground. It took me an hour to shovel it free. The cost of snow tires for both cars set me back a bundle."

"Yeah, a bundle," he said, burping.

"The next day our guesspert weatherman said it was much warmer. Hah! He doesn't know what warm is. That night, the temperature dropped with more snow. That didn't deter my wife from daily shopping trips that always ended with her car in a ditch and me hauling it out."

"Wimmen drivers!"

"I decided to save myself some grief and buy her a heavy-duty four-wheel-drive Range Rover. I should have bought her a surplus army tank. It takes a supreme lack of driving skills to get stuck in a Rover. But my wife proved to be quite adept at ramming the Rover into mountainous snow drifts, so I insisted on being the designated driver.

"A few days ago during breakfast, she announced she would spend the day baking for her family's Christmas Eve dinner. She reminded me to shovel off the entire driveway to make room for her relative's cars. When I stood on the drive, I looked up at the roof on the house and garage and decided to shovel it first, starting over the garage."

"Roofs ... too high fer me."

"I backed up the Range Rover to make room for the snow I'd shovel off the garage and used a safety rope tied to a tree in the backyard while I stood on the front of the slanted roof. After shoveling a mountain of snow, I went down the ladder and retrieved the safety rope. I tied it to the front bumper of the Rover and carried the ladder behind the garage.

"I was halfway through shoveling the back of the roof when I heard the Rover's engine roar to life. Before I had time to react, I was yanked up the roof's peak and down the front side. I had a death grip on my shovel as I dug it into the shingles in a vain attempt to delay my nosedive. My wife couldn't hear me scream as I landed face-first in the mountain of snow and plowed through it."

"Plowed ... hah!"

"My wife was looking over her shoulder while backing out and didn't see me. I lost my shovel in the snow pile, and a wad of wet snow gagged me when I tried to yell. I was emerging from the mound when she finally spotted me. Her look of horror was little consolation as my heated profanity melted my snow mask."

"Hah, swearing ...!" He nodded.

"Apologizing profusely, she brushed the snow off me while explaining she ran out of eggs and couldn't find me to drive her to the store. I had a bruised body and a mountain of snow to shovel before the family arrived, so I told her to drive carefully and started searching for my shovel. Merry Christmas my ass!"

"Merry Christmasssss!"

"The next day, we got another eight inches of the white crap. The expensive new Rover was covered in salt and brown crud. That damn snowplow came by twice, and I was beginning to think the driver was giving me the finger instead of waving. It was hard to tell because of his thick gloves."

"Hah, the finger!" He struggled to sit straighter but slumped back down.

"That night, it snowed again before the temperature plummeted. The next morning, I dressed in several layers to brave the fierce chill and staggered through three feet of snow to our frozen mailbox. In an effort to pop it open, I pounded it so hard I left a dent the size of my fist."

"Dent," he mumbled.

"While I was fighting with the mailbox door, the snowplow buried me waist deep. My legs felt like they were encased in frozen concrete. That SOB was lucky I couldn't move. Otherwise, I would've bashed him in the head and buried him in the mountain of snow next to my driveway. Nobody would've found him until the spring thaw."

"Yeah, bash him good!" He belched a whisky scent as he looked at me.

"Then we got six more inches of the white crap with sleet on top. We haven't seen the sun since the day we moved here."

The old drunk began to snore.

I nudged him awake. "More snow was on the way. The power went out, and the toilets froze. I decided to keep us from freezing to death with a roaring fire in the fireplace, but the only wood available was from the broken tree branches wet with snow. So I soaked them in lighter fluid. When I lit them, the explosion transformed my eyebrows, eyelashes, and mustache into kinky black curly cues on a bed of angry red skin."

"Oooo, hic, flames, hic!" he said, more alert now.

"Burning twigs were scattered across the room, and my clothes were smoldering. Our Christmas tree erupted into a flaming torch that lit the curtains on fire. My wife ran screaming into the room and dragged me outside. She rolled me in the snow and called the fire department. Then she pulled me up and shoved me into the car."

"Strong woman, hic!"

"My wife's frantic attempt to rush me to the hospital ended with our Range Rover sliding across solid ice and crashing through the ER's entrance. That was the final chapter in the Rover's short but suspense-filled life."

"No more Rover." He shook his head.

"So here I sit, waiting for the airport shuttle bus to head back to sunny Palm Beach. Divorce is a small price to pay for paradise." I elbowed the old man as the bus approached. "You might want to give Florida a try."

He straightened. "Thas why I'm waiting for the bussss."

THE MAGIC BUTTON

D.M. Littlefield

My best friend, Brenda, and I lived in a gated retirement village for people fifty-five and older—friendly and safe for widows.

Brenda's next-door neighbor called me early this morning and asked if I knew why an ambulance had taken her away late last night. I didn't know, so I hurried to the hospital.

I was shocked to see how pitiful she looked with stitches in a gash on her forehead, her left arm in a sling, a bandage on her nose, and two black eyes.

"Brenda!" I gasped. "What happened?"

She looked up at the ceiling and frowned. "Well, Alice, I tried to recall what caused this and wondered if my big boobs did it when I leaned over to take off my shoes."

"I don't understand."

She sighed. "I remember I came home in a high-spirited mood because of all the drinks I had at the dance. To prolong the feeling, I set a stack of long-playing big-band records on the phonograph and hummed along to the music as I undressed and waltzed into the bathroom. Then I sat on the toilet-seat lid, leaned over, and removed my shoes. I remembered to take out my hearing aids before I took a leisurely shower. After I toweled myself dry, I inserted my hearing aids and sang along to the music."

"I enjoy singing along to the old songs too," I said.

"Wonderful memories."

Brenda smiled with a dreamy look. "I remember my youth like it was yesterday. During World War II, men our age were scarce on the home front. My girlfriend and I went to USO dances to meet guys in uniform. Back then I was a pretty twenty-year-old, dancing every dance with our service men on leave. Last night, I was reliving those extraordinary days as I waltzed into my bedroom to the mellow music of Tommy Dorsey with Frank Sinatra and the Pied Pipers singing 'Dream.'"

"That all sounds nice, but how in the world did you get hurt?" I asked.

"Apparently, my alcohol-fogged brain, combined with my vivid imagination, produced a hallucination of two handsome hunks standing in the hallway by my bedroom door. Mesmerized by the magic moment, I felt like I was twenty again as I twirled around and winked at them.

"One of the men cleared his throat and softly said, 'Mrs. Brown, we're the paramedics you called by activating the emergency call button you're wearing around your neck.'

"I blinked, gasped, and gaped down at the call button wedged between the huge, sagging boobs on my naked eighty-year-old body. Mortified, I fainted and fell face-first on the tile floor."

"Oh, you poor thing!" I took a moment before I asked, "So, um, just how good looking were those paramedics?"

MY FIRST SOLO FLIGHT

S.L. Menear

The following story is true and happened exactly as written. Looking back on my life, I've noticed a recurring phenomenon I call the First Experience Anomaly. On many occasions when doing something for the first time, I encountered unusual circumstances that never happened again when I repeated the same activity. Thank God!

On a warm summer morning in 1973, I arrived at the New Tamiami Airport in South Florida, renamed Miami Executive Airport in 2014, shortly after dawn with an excited smile on my face and a knot in my gut. I was ready for my first solo flight in an airplane one week after my first flying lesson in a two-seat Cessna 150 trainer. The weather was calm and sunny with a few puffy white clouds dotting the blue sky—a perfect day to fly. The scents of aviation fuel, engine oil, and wet grass hung in the air.

I wore old cutoff jeans and my least favorite shirt. Although I was fairly certain I'd survive, I knew the back of my shirt wouldn't. It would be cut off and pinned to a wall in the flight school.

My flight instructor, Joe Gleason, tried to look serious, but I saw the smile in his eyes. Only twenty-one, he'd been flying since he was fourteen. A blond, blue-eyed Steve McQueen look-alike, he was the son of an airline pilot and an excellent flight instructor. I was a young Pan American World Airways stewardess. Working with a handsome instructor was fine by me.

Joe explained he'd accompany me on a few circuits around the traffic pattern. If I flew as well as I had on the previous lesson, I'd stop to let him out and return to the air alone. Time seemed set on fast-forward as I completed several touch-and-go landings.

Joe exited the airplane.

As I taxied to the runway, I noticed a crowd had gathered—my boyfriend with his Nikon camera and telephoto lens, all my pilot friends, and lots of airport people I barely knew. Everyone wanted to see the *girl* fly solo.

After being cleared for takeoff, I pulled onto the runway and selected full throttle. My little Cessna was aloft in a few seconds. As if he were still beside me, I imagined Joe's voice: "Right rudder. Keep it straight."

Adrenaline pumped through my veins as I flew around the traffic pattern. The fear every pilot feels while being scrutinized by his peers churned my stomach. I didn't fear dying in a fiery crash; I feared messing up in front of the pilots—a fate far worse than death for any self-respecting flyer.

I was paralleling the runway in the traffic pattern on the downwind leg when the controller asked me to extend that leg to accommodate two aircraft waiting to takeoff. I glanced down at the runway to my right and then looked up into the frightened yellow eyes of a great horned owl.

Giant owls weren't included in my solo briefing.

Somehow, I managed to avoid a collision, which could've made a nasty dent in the leading edge of the wing or a hole in the windshield followed by a bloody feather facial.

My heart was pounding like the drum solo in "Wipeout" when the controller cleared me to land.

As I lined up for the first solo landing, my hands were sweaty, my mouth dry. My brain barely registered the sensation of wheels touching down as I gently braked and took the first turnoff to taxi back for another takeoff.

One full-stop landing down. Two to go.

My heart rate was in sprinting mode as I barreled down the

runway for takeoff number two. When I turned downwind, I noticed dark clouds towering in the distance.

The controller informed me I was number seventeen for landing. Did I mention there were ten flight schools on the field? I was instructed to extend my downwind leg ten miles to allow space for the landing traffic.

As I neared the threatening clouds, the controller warned, "Caution all aircraft in the pattern. A tornado has been reported on the extended downwind."

Tornadoes weren't covered in my solo briefing.

I flew through green air, spotted the tornado, and opted to leave the area until the twister disappeared. Joe must've been chewing on Rolaids, wondering where I was.

Twenty minutes later, I worked my way back into the landing pattern. Soon, I completed heart-pounding landing number two.

One more.

Worried Joe might try to stop me, I didn't even look at him as I hurried back for my last takeoff. I needed three takeoffs and landings together to get the solo signed off in my student logbook. I think my hands might've been trembling on that last takeoff, mostly fearing Joe's wrath rather than more terrors aloft.

I was lined up for my final landing when a frazzled flight instructor allowed his student to leave the downwind leg without a landing clearance. They turned and cut me off. I banked and climbed to avoid a midair collision as the controller yelled for me to go around.

Pilots' stupidity wasn't covered in my solo briefing.

After another nerve-racking circuit around the airport, I landed and taxied to the ramp. Joe waited with crossed arms. Everyone else smiled.

"Not bad for a girl," Joe said. "Now turn around."

I lifted my long blond hair and felt the back of my shirt pull away from my skin as he cut away the fabric.

"Time to christen the new pilot!" the men yelled.

They carried me to the infield pond and tossed me in. I grinned as I waded out drenched in slimy water.

Everyone cheered.

After fifteen thousand hours of flying and twenty years as a jet airline pilot, I've forgotten many flights, but I'll never forget my first solo.

SECRETS

D.M. Littlefield

Howard and Joyce sat at the breakfast table in the kitchen as she rambled on about him not socializing enough in the four months since they had moved to a huge retirement community in Central Florida called The Villages.

"I don't know why you don't want to play golf or tennis or do any of the numerous activities with the men. I've met very interesting people here, and I'm enjoying the lifestyle. Today I'm having lunch with the girls, playing cards afterward, and attending a play later. I'll be home around nine. If you get hungry, heat up a frozen dinner from the freezer.... Don't look at me like that! You knew I didn't cook when you married me, and I don't intend to start now."

He nodded and sighed as he poured more milk on his cold cereal. A retired English professor, he kept busy doing research on the book he was writing. He spent most of his time at the community library and taking long walks.

What would he do if he knew she was having an affair? She'd thought moving to a dynamic community would put the spark back in their marriage, but it hadn't. That was why she was meeting Jerry Flynn at the Tower Hotel again after lunch with the girls.

"What are your plans for today, Howard?"

"I thought I'd walk to the library and do more research on my book."

"You do that every day. Why don't you do something different?"

"Maybe I'll try golf after I finish my book."

"You're sixty-eight. By the time you finish your book, you'll be too old to play golf. Wake up! Get a life for Pete's sake."

She leaned down for his perfunctory kiss on her cheek, picked up her handbag on the hallway table, and walked out the front door.

***

Howard smiled, anticipating his research. He would have a delicious home-cooked lunch with the widow, Mary Sloan. Then research.

At five, he was due at the widow Carmen Rivera's home for a delicious Italian dinner. And more research.

His book title: *The Uninhibited Sex Life of Women after Menopause.*

SLEUTH HOUNDS

D.M. Littlefield

My name is Spike. I'm a K-9 German shepherd. My squad lives in Rosie's apartment building with our retired police officer masters. They don't know we're still active in police work. Rosie is the widow of Officer Tim O'Grady. She gives us drool-worthy treats from her restaurant on the ground floor. We love Rosie and include her huge Saint Bernard, Dudley, in our covert missions even though he's never had K-9 training. He's not too bright, but he's loyal and obeys my orders.

This morning as I walked to the park with my master and a hyperactive Jack Russell terrier, our leashes became tangled. We had to stop more than once for my master to untangle us. I knew Fritz and Max, my German shepherd team members, wouldn't put up with the new dog's annoying antics.

My squad wagged their tails, welcoming me. I waited for my master to remove my leash as he struggled with the annoying terrier's leash because the fool dog wouldn't stand still.

"Awwww, why'd you bring that runt?" Fritz whined. "He'll drive us nuts, he's so squirrely."

Dudley's floppy ears perked up. "Squirrel?" He jerked his big head right and left, flinging drool. "Duh, uh, where's the squirrel, Fritz? Where's the squirrel?"

Fritz sighed. "There's no squirrel, Dudley. It's just a figure of speech."

Max nudged Fritz. "Be careful what you say around Dudley, or he'll trample us looking for a squirrel. He must've been dropped on his head when he was a puppy."

"Listen up, boys," I barked. "This is JJ. He belongs to Rosie's niece, Lyn. They're moving into the vacant apartment on our floor. Rosie said if we aren't nice to JJ, she won't give us juicy leftovers from her restaurant."

My squad gave JJ a disgusted glance and groaned. We jerked our heads from side to side, trying to avoid the jumping terrier.

Fritz slammed his big paw on JJ's head and snarled, "Sheesh, runt, sit!"

JJ trembled. "Okay, okay, okay, I'm thrilled to meet the famous K-9s. I've heard you've officially retired along with your human partners, but you secretly bring criminals to justice on your own time now. I want to join your squad."

"No way!" Max growled. "We don't want a mini-dog on the Sleuth Hound Squad."

"What about dimwit Dudley?" JJ barked. "He isn't a K-9."

I raised my hackles and glared down at JJ, curling my lips back to show my big fangs. "Don't ever call him that! He's Rosie's dog and our loyal friend."

JJ cowered. "Okay, okay, okay, I'm sorry. It'll never happen again. Please, please, please, let me in your famous squad."

"Humph. What could a runt like you do?" Max snarled.

JJ squirmed out from under Fritz's paw and trembled in front of me. "I could be your snitch. Lyn's a detective. She tells me all about her cases."

Fritz faced the street. "Hey, look who just arrived!"

We fell over one another to watch a stretch limousine pull to the curb and panted in eager anticipation as the chauffeur opened the rear door.

"Hey, turn around and listen," JJ whined. "I have important information."

We ignored him and stared with open-mouthed admiration. JJ walked underneath Dudley to see what held our undivided attention.

A beautiful, standard white poodle with polished nails and ribbons on her ears stepped daintily onto the sidewalk. We sniffed the air to capture her alluring scent. I could tell JJ was smitten too because he didn't notice Dudley drooling on his head.

After the poodle spent a few minutes in privacy behind a bush, she pranced past us salivating dogs. She gave us a dismissive sniff and stuck her nose up. Her jeweled collar sparkled in the Florida sunshine as she jumped into the limousine. The chauffeur smiled and waved at us before driving away. We let out a collective groan as we sank to the ground in a euphoric state.

JJ barked for our attention and then jumped up and down like a bouncing ball.

We bobbed our heads, trying to maintain eye contact.

"Stop jumping or I'll have Dudley sit on you," Max growled.

"Okay, okay, okay." He paced between us. "Listen, listen, listen, a drug pusher Lyn arrested has been set free because of a legal loophole. He used to hang out in this park and sell drugs to kids. Some of the kids died. Maybe he's in the park now."

I looked down at JJ. "Can you describe him?"

"If I tell you, can I be a member of your squad? Please, please, please?" He was about to jump up again, but I glared at him. He paced instead, waiting for an answer.

I sighed and looked at my squad. "Should we give him a chance?"

Fritz lifted his hind leg to scratch his ear and smirked. "Sure, let him make a fool of himself."

Max looked at JJ in disgust. "How did you get a stupid name like JJ?"

"It's short for Jumping Jack." JJ jumped up and performed a back-flip.

"That figures," Max grumbled.

JJ paced again. "The drug dealer has dark skin, a mustache, and is as tall as Spike's master."

I nodded. "I saw a man fitting that description enter the

park."

Fritz nudged me. "Spike, do you have a plan to catch the scumbag?"

"While our masters are busy playing cards, we'll sneak away and sniff for drugs. Bark once if you find him. JJ, stay close to Dudley. Everyone fan out. When we locate him, we'll chase him through the woods to the highway."

"Why the highway?" JJ whined.

"We'll let the traffic snuff him out," I barked.

Dudley nodded. "Duh, yeah, sniff him out."

Fritz gently corrected Dudley. "You mean snuff him out, big buddy."

"Duh, yeah, snuff him out."

"Road kill." Max grunted his approval. "I like it."

I found the man JJ had described leaning against a tree in a deserted area near the woods. As I wandered nearer and lifted my rear leg to water the bushes, I caught the scent of drugs on him and barked once to alert my squad.

When the man called a young boy over to him, I followed the boy and nonchalantly sniffed the ground while eavesdropping.

"Kid, I'll give you a really good deal. This blow will make you feel like Superman. I usually sell it for fifty dollars a pop. I'll let you have it for twenty-five if you get your friends to buy from me. I'll give you the discount every time you bring me a new customer. You in?"

The kid shifted his weight from side to side. "I'm saving my money for a skateboard."

"Forget about the skateboard. You'll be flying high without it. Here, try it." The man offered him a tiny baggie.

"Well ... okay."

Before the boy could take the baggie, I growled and moved between them with my fangs bared.

The man backed away. "Hey, kid, call off your dog!"

"He's not my dog," the boy yelled as he ran away.

My squad converged on the drug dealer. We snarled and bared our bone-crunching fangs. The man ran through the woods as if hell hounds were chasing him. Low tree branches scratched his face, and he stumbled over tree roots as he glanced back at us. Fritz and I lunged at his backside and tore his jeans.

"Save a piece for me," Max snarled.

We fell back to let Max nip at him.

Dudley lumbered along on the perimeter with JJ alternately running alongside, beneath, and in front of him.

The man veered away from my planned route to the highway. "Dudley, chase him to your left ... no, no, your other left ... good boy!" I barked.

JJ darted out from underneath Dudley and locked his jaws on the man's right pant leg. The man plunged into the drainage ditch beside the highway, and JJ tenaciously hung on as the man waded through deep water. My squad stopped at the edge of the ditch, panted, and snarled. JJ ran out of air and sputtered to the surface. The man grabbed JJ's neck and held him underwater as he waded toward the highway.

We leaped into the water and swam after him, bent on saving JJ. The man let JJ's limp body sink and clawed his way up the embankment onto the highway. He dodged a car and turned to look at us. He never saw the eighteen-wheeler that mowed him down.

"He's flat as a Frisbee!" Max softly woofed.

"Road kill," Fritz grunted. "He deserved it for killing those kids."

Dudley stuck his head underwater and grabbed JJ by the scruff of his neck. He swam back to the woods, bounded out of the water, dropped JJ on the ground, and gently pushed his big paw on JJ's chest. Water squirted out of the little guy's mouth. Amazed, we circled Dudley and watched.

"I didn't know Dudley knew CPR," Max barked as he shook off water.

"Maybe it's instinctive. You know how soft-hearted he is," I barked. "He tries to comfort injured creatures he finds in the park. I've seen him hold them between his big paws, lick them, and let them go. Not that they go very far on wobbly legs after having been scared to death."

When JJ opened his eyes, Dudley held him between his

front paws and licked him.

JJ coughed and squirmed to get away. "Okay, okay, okay, big boy! You can stop with the licking now. I'm fine."

Our squad formed a circle, bumped noses, and wagged our tails—our equivalent to human high fives. As we headed back to our masters at the picnic table, JJ ran alongside me.

"I did good, didn't I? Huh, didn't I? Am I in the squad now? I proved I'm an asset."

Max turned to Fritz. "Well, he got the ass part right."

"Humph. Good one, Max."

"How about it? Am I in the squad now?" JJ yapped.

"You did okay, except for almost drowning. I hope you figured out you can't breathe underwater. We'll give you a chance on one more case before we decide."

JJ was so pleased he performed back-flips the whole way to the picnic table. We arrived wet and muddy, much to our masters' displeasure. We rolled in the grass, shook off, and rolled some more before relaxing.

***

As our daily routine, we gathered beside the park picnic table the next day. Our masters unleashed us so we could catch the Frisbees they threw. They also took turns throwing Dudley's big rubber bone. Later, they played cards while we romped in the park.

On her way to work, Lyn left JJ with our masters. He rushed over to us, trembling with excitement.

"Listen, listen, listen! Lyn told me a child molester she arrested was released from prison. She's concerned he might be in this area. He has light skin and hair and is the same height as Max's master."

"That description fits the scumbag I tracked five years ago," Max snarled. "He kidnapped and tortured a little girl. When I found him, he was digging a hole to bury the unconscious child. I savored biting his arm when he tried to hit me with a shovel."

"We must find him before he hurts another child!" I

barked.

"If he's in the park, he'll be at the playground looking for another victim," Max growled.

"If we spot him, let Max take the lead," I ordered.

I stationed my squad around the playground and stood by the water fountain. Fritz waited by the sandbox, while Max sat by the slide. Dudley and JJ stood by the seesaws. JJ kept close to Dudley ever since he nearly drowned.

A little boy fell off the slide. His mother left her toddler in the stroller and rushed over. Distracted, she didn't notice her child climb out of the stroller. The little girl walked unsteadily down a curving path to a pond.

A gray-haired man took her hand. Instead of leading her back to her mother, he walked her away from the playground. Max followed close behind them to take in the man's scent. We ran to catch up as they walked around a bend hidden by bushes.

When the man bent over to pick up the child, Max leaped at him. The man fell and struck his head on a boulder and lost consciousness. His gray wig slid over his forehead and exposed his light hair.

"He's the same kidnapper I caught a few years ago," Max growled. "I'll never forget his scent."

When the toddler began crying, Dudley licked her face to comfort her.

"Dudley, help me drag this child molester into the pond," I barked. "Max, you and Fritz take the girl back to her mother. JJ, you go with them. We'll catch up later."

Fritz guarded the child's right with Max on her left. JJ coaxed her to follow him by performing back-flips. She trundled after him as he led her back to her mother.

Dudley and I hauled the unconscious man into the water. When we reached the middle of the pond, we released him and treaded water to watch him sink. Much to my dismay, he floated.

"Dudley, climb on top of him and hold him underwater until no air bubbles come up."

"Duh, okay, Spike." Dudley's huge body covered the man

as he stared into the water, watching for bubbles. After a few minutes, he looked up. "Duh, all done. No more bubbles."

"Good work, Dudley. He can't hurt more children. Let's haul him back to shore for the police to find him."

As we swam back with the body, a cyclist saw us. "Look, those brave dogs are trying to rescue someone," she shouted, pointing.

People who had gathered on the shore helped us drag out the pedophile and tried to resuscitate him without success. Police units, an ambulance, and television crews arrived on the scene. The television crew filmed us for the evening news. When they finished, we slipped away to our squad at the playground. An alert reporter followed us.

Excited, the toddler's mother told the reporter my squad had led her lost girl back to her. The reporter's cameraman filmed the mother, her children, and my squad. The reporter praised our protective instincts. I barked a farewell and led my squad across the park to where our masters were calling us. We settled around the picnic table and relaxed.

It wasn't until our masters watched the evening news that they learned of our heroic deeds. Rosie was so pleased she gave us big juicy steaks.

***

The next day at the park, JJ told the squad about Lyn's new case. "She's concerned because the thief seems crazy. He robs stores and restaurants at gunpoint in broad daylight. Then he runs out to his car and grabs a stick of dynamite. He lights it and throws it at the front door of the building. Then he speeds away in his car. He has injured and maimed a lot of people. Two have died. We must stop him."

"JJ, we're not allowed to cross the street," I barked. "We'll stand watch over our block from the park. If we see the thief, we'll alert our masters and let them handle it. I'll watch Rosie's restaurant. Fritz, watch the bank, Max, the drug store, and Dudley and JJ, the flower shop."

We took our assigned places in the park every morning

after we played Frisbee, and Dudley played his fetch game. After two weeks of boring surveillance work, I noticed Dudley had lost patience and was pestering our masters to play fetch. They took turns throwing his rubber bone. After a while, they pretended to throw it and then hid it in the cooler so they could get back to their card games. Dudley sniffed everywhere for it.

A convertible with the top down pulled into the No Parking Zone by the mailbox in front of Rosie's restaurant. Unusual. My squad looked at me, waiting for a command to alert their masters.

"Let's wait and see what he does," I barked.

The male driver entered Rosie's restaurant. A few minutes later, he ran out holding a paper sack and dropped it on his front seat. Sure enough, he grabbed a stick of dynamite. I barked the command to alert our masters to the impending disaster across the street.

My squad went berserk barking and grabbing our master's clothing, pulling them to their feet. To my surprise, JJ wasn't jumping and barking. Instead, he assumed a classic hunting-dog stance with his tail and foreleg raised and his head pointed toward the thief. Our masters looked across the street and gasped when they saw the man light the long fuse on the dynamite and throw it against the glass door of Rosie's restaurant.

Dudley's ears finally perked up. Flinging drool in the wind, he galloped across the street. We watched in horror as he zeroed in on the lit dynamite, thinking it was his rubber bone.

The thief was about to drive off when a mail truck stopped at the mailbox and blocked him. He yelled and raised his fist at the mailman before jamming his car into reverse and ramming the car parked behind him. Frantic, he checked for traffic as he jerked his car forward and back, trying to escape before the explosion.

Dudley picked up the dynamite, carried it to the convertible, leaned his big head over the rear door, and dropped it on the back seat. He trotted back to us as the convertible sped off.

Half a block away, the car exploded and rattled the

windows of nearby buildings. Thankful he didn't get hurt, I was amazed by Dudley's actions. A hero, he saved Rosie's restaurant and all the people inside.

Dudley's picture appeared on the front pages of newspapers and on every television news channel. During a ceremony, my squad watched the mayor award him a medal for bravery. Rosie was so proud she named a sandwich after him: The Dudley Delight.

***

The following day, our Sleuth Hound Squad returned to the park with little JJ.

I looked down at him. "Dudley saved not only your life when we chased the drug dealer but also all the people in Rosie's restaurant. I hope you understand now why we never call Dudley a dimwit."

JJ nodded. "Yeah, he's my good buddy too."

The bank alarm sounded. Our masters sprang up and looked across the street. A masked man ran out of the bank with a large cloth bag in one hand and a gun in the other. He rushed across the street, threw his mask into a trash can, and raced into the park.

Our masters yelled the attack command, which filled me with joy. I felt young again as my squad chased the perp through the park with our masters following.

We dodged his bullets as he ran to the woods. As we closed in, he stopped at the base of a big tree, shoved the money bag inside his shirt, and aimed his gun at us.

"Hit the ground!" I barked.

We all hugged the ground except Dudley, the biggest target. I heard a shot and Dudley's yip as he fell to the ground, motionless. The man pocketed his gun and jumped for a branch, trying to climb above our reach. I ordered my squad to nail him while I rushed to Dudley's side.

"I'll get him!" JJ barked. He raced to the tree, jumped on Max's back, and leaped into the air.

The perp wrapped his arms around a branch and hooked

his right leg over it. He was about to lift his left leg up when JJ grabbed his pant cuff and jerked his little head from side to side. The gun slipped out of the man's pocket and dropped to the ground.

"Let go!" The man yelled as he tried to shake JJ off his dangling leg.

JJ growled as he swung back and forth.

Fritz picked up the gun and waited for his master, who arrived out of breath. He wrapped the gun in his handkerchief.

Dudley lay on his side, panting and bleeding. I leaned down and licked his wound, trying to comfort him.

My master pulled out his cell phone and took a deep breath. "I'll call the police and our vet. Rosie will be heartbroken if Dudley dies." He petted me. "That's good, Spike. You take care of him while we wait for the vet."

"Hang in there, buddy. Help is on the way," I whined.

Dudley blinked his sad, trusting eyes at me and snuffled.

I heard police sirens wail in the distance.

Detective Lyn and two police cars arrived. She ran up and kneeled beside Dudley.

"Our vet was only a mile away on another call," my master said. "He's on his way now."

She cradled Dudley's big head and looked into his eyes. "I know you're big and brave, but you're Aunt Rosie's loveable, furry child. She mustn't lose you."

The vet parked his van and rushed out with his medical bag. "Good, Spike, I see you're taking care of my patient."

I barked hello and moved out of his way.

The vet examined Dudley. "Just a flesh wound; the bullet grazed his shoulder. I'll cleanse it, stitch it, and give him a shot of antibiotics and pain medication. He'll be fine. I'll give Rosie some antibiotic pills and instructions on how to take care of her big boy."

After the vet finished, Dudley limped toward the man hanging in the tree and snarled. Fritz's master handed the perp's gun to Detective Lyn. Smiling, the humans rested their hands on their hips and gazed up at JJ swinging back and forth from the man's pant leg.

The thief had a death grip on the branch as he looked down at us snarling K-9s. We drew our lips back and bared our fangs.

"Get those dogs out of here! I might fall!" he yelled.

"Good, maybe we should leave you with the dogs," Detective Lyn said. "You shot their best friend." She turned to our masters. "Gentlemen, your K-9s taught my dog how to catch criminals. JJ has a good grip on the perp. I think we can all agree this is his collar."

We watched JJ as Max barked, "You've got to give the little runt credit. He really hangs in there."

"Yep, he's an official Sleuth Hound now," I barked.

MY FIRST OCEAN DIVE

S.L. Menear

I earned my deep-water scuba certification in October of 1999 in an Arkansas lake with a depth of over two-hundred feet. In April of 2000, I was ready to explore Florida's fabulous coral reefs. My brother, Larry, with forty years of dive experience since age ten, accompanied me. The Atlantic Ocean and its inhabitants were new to me. This was another of my First Experience Anomalies, which I referenced in the story about my first solo flight.

I beamed with excitement as the dive boat ploughed through five-foot rollers on its way to the offshore reef. This would be my first venture into the ocean in scuba gear. I tightened my buoyancy-compensator vest straps as the captain put the engines in idle. My next move was to roll backwards over the side while holding my mask in place, which was far easier than trying to walk to the aft platform while wearing the heavy tank and dive weights.

The warm waters of the Atlantic Ocean along Florida caressed me as I descended in water as clear as air, my bubbles sparkling like diamonds in the sunlight. I dived to a depth of ninety feet off the Palm Beach coast, where brilliant fish darted over a rainbow-colored coral reef three miles offshore from The Breakers, an iconic grand hotel built in the 1920s.

A longtime surfer and boater, I had always thought lovingly of the sea as Mother Ocean. I was about to learn she had a dark side and suffered from occasional PMS.

My eager eyes roamed over the magical undersea world on the way down. When I reached eighty feet, Larry pointed under a coral ledge. I swam in for a closer look and recoiled as an eight-foot long, neon-green moray eel greeted me.

Holy crap! I wasn't expecting a sea monster right out of the gate!

As a woman, I had a God-given fear of snakes that traced back to Adam and Eve. Moray eels looked like giant snakes. I swallowed half my air when it opened its mouth and showed me its razor-sharp teeth.

Cornering the huge, potentially dangerous eel didn't seem like a wise move.

I retreated, my heart hammering as the frantic flutter of my fins telegraphed my terror.

My breathing was barely under control when Larry tapped his tank with his dive knife to draw my attention. He waved me over to where he hovered in front of a large hole in the reef and pointed at something inside.

Silly me, I still thought I could trust my brother, so I swam to the hole and looked in.

When my eyes adjusted to the darkness, I noticed two large yellow eyes glaring at me. A head the size of a basketball opened its enormous mouth full of scary teeth. My heart rate skyrocketed as I sucked in too much air and looked for Larry. He was farther along the reef, poking the tail of the fifteen-foot monster moray eel facing me so it would lunge out of the hole and give me a better view. *Nice.*

I panicked, gulped more air, and backpedaled like crazy in a cloud of varied bubbles of my own making.

As I tried once again to get my breathing under control, the dive master waved me over to show me a deadly stonefish that blended into the reef. His hand gestures meant *never touch this.*

Like I would ever do *that.* With the fire coral, stone fish, and nasty critters waiting to dart out and bite my hand off, no way would I reach in or touch *anything*!

The bright light of a flash camera drew me to a ledge where

two eight-foot nurse sharks slept on the sand underneath. They looked like giant catfish. Their eyes popped open and radiated anger the moment I arrived.

I gulped even more air.

Holy hell! What had happened to benign Mother Ocean?

This was like swimming through a living minefield! I wish I'd had a chance to acclimate to the extraordinary underwater world before encountering all the scary stuff. Then maybe I could've managed my air consumption better—and my heart rate.

My anxious breathing had depleted my air supply down to the reserve air, so I had to return to the dive boat long before the experienced divers. On my way topside, a dark shadow glided in overhead, blocking the sun. It was a fish as big as a submarine and covered with white spots. This time I stopped breathing and tried to become invisible.

My body vibrated with chills, despite the warm water, as I prayed the massive shark wouldn't notice me. He meandered away, uninterested in my quivering body.

Thank God!

When I surfaced, the swells had grown to ten feet. Clearly, I had picked a bad day to visit Mother Ocean.

Every time I reached for the dive platform on the back of the boat, a huge wave would lift it high above me and then send it crashing down. It was exhausting trying to climb aboard without being crushed. I was almost out of air, and I couldn't use the snorkel because the swells breaking on my face kept filling it with water. It was then that I understood how it was possible for a person wearing a mask and snorkel to drown.

When I finally grabbed the hinged platform, Mother Ocean took pity on me, and a wave flung me onto the deck like a dead fish. The crew helped me remove my heavy dive gear, and I crawled to a seat and collapsed.

Later, my brother surfaced, swiftly mounted the platform, and strode onto the deck like the boat was parked on concrete. He made it look so easy. I envied him.

That night, I learned on the TV news that the gargantuan

fish I'd encountered was a sixty-five-foot whale shark rarely seen in local waters. It only ate plankton ... unless its Volkswagen-sized mouth inadvertently inhaled an unlucky diver.

Larry told me the fifteen-foot moray eel, named Gretchen, was accustomed to local divers feeding it. He explained moray eels breathed through their mouths, so they weren't trying to scare me with their array of pointy teeth.

Why hadn't he told me that *before* the dive?

SLEEP DEPRIVED

D.M. Littlefield

I parked my car and pulled down the visor mirror to check my face. There was lipstick on my front tooth. Why couldn't I be like my best friend, Sarah? Picture-perfect, pretty, and petite at almost five-feet.

We'd known each other for over thirty years and were neighbors in Golden Lakes Village in West Palm Beach. Two times a week we met at Dunk the Donuts early in the morning, followed by a trip to the library while our husbands golfed.

It was almost eight when I walked to our favorite booth at the back of the doughnut shop, where Sarah was looking out the window.

"Good morning!" I said as I slid into the booth and laid my purse down.

She turned and scowled. "What's good about it?"

Dark circles under her bloodshot eyes shadowed her face, devoid of makeup. Small white feathers blanketed her messy hair and clothes. Her sweater was crooked because it wasn't buttoned right.

Dumbfounded, I leaned in. "What happened?" I whispered.

Sarah sipped her coffee and blew out a sigh. "I'm thinking about a divorce."

My eyes widened. "But just last week you celebrated your forty-eighth anniversary. You and Ed have been our best friends for years. When Ed retired and you moved to West Palm Beach, we missed you both so much we moved here too. Please don't get a divorce."

She shook her head. "Eileen, I didn't say I was getting a divorce. I said I was thinking about a divorce." She looked up at the ceiling. "Hmmm, if I were single, I wouldn't have to wear earplugs to bed because of Ed's snoring, and I'd have complete control of the TV remote."

The breeze from the ceiling fan dislodged one of the feathers in her hair, and it floated onto the table. "Don't worry, Eileen, I won't get a divorce." She rolled her eyes. "I still love the big lug." She brushed the feather off the table and took another sip.

"What's with all the feathers?"

Sarah sighed. "You know I have insomnia. I lie awake for hours, sometimes till dawn, trying to sleep. About five this morning, I finally got to what I call my twilight zone—just before the sleep zone. That means I'm drowsy, about to drift off. I have to be very careful not to disturb my twilight zone.

"I was almost asleep when I needed to pee. I kept my sleep mask on and didn't scrounge for my slippers. Barefoot, I felt my way to our master bathroom, where I lifted my nightgown and fell into the toilet."

I gasped and covered my mouth. "Oh, Sarah, no!"

"They can put a man on the moon, but they can't get a man to put the toilet seat down. My legs flew up as I hit the cold water. I yelped when I banged my head against the lid, and the seat fell down around my neck. It pushed my sleep mask down and uncovered my right eye.

"I struggled to grip the slippery toilet rim and push myself up. But I couldn't, so I grabbed for anything within my reach and accidentally flushed the toilet. The water rose up to my armpits and overflowed. I yelled for Ed but didn't hear him. Then I remembered to remove my ear plugs. When I lifted my arms to remove them, I sank lower in the toilet."

"That must've been awful." I tried my best to sound sympathetic and not crack a smile.

"I heard Ed shuffling to the bathroom, thank god. He

turned on the light, rubbed his hand over his face, and leaned against the door frame with an incredulous look."

"What the hell are you doing in the toilet? he said."

"I growled, 'What do you think I'm doing, taking a bath?'"

"He scratched his head and said, 'I use the tub.' Then he raised his eyebrows and shook his head. 'I think you're losing it, baby doll. Why didn't you turn on the light?'"

"I shouted, 'You know why I never turn on the light! Help me up! If you'd put down the toilet seat, I wouldn't be in this pickle!'"

"He said, 'Don't you mean you wouldn't be in this toilet?'"

"Ed bent down to grab my hands, but then he backed away. He pointed at me and said, 'Don't move! I'll get the video camera. We can win ten-thousand dollars for this on Funniest Home Videos!'"

"I shrieked, 'Hell no!' Then I narrowed my uncovered right eye and hissed, 'Not if you want to live!'"

"He rolled his eyes and said, 'Tsk ... tsk! You do get cranky when you fall into the toilet.'"

"I hollered, 'You're the reason I'm in the damn toilet, and that's where our marriage is going if you don't shape up!'"

"He finally pulled me up, handed me a towel, and said, 'When I was little, my mother taught me this rhyme: If you sprinkle when you tinkle, lift the cover when you hover. Because I'm neat, I always lift the cover.' He looked at me with a silly grin as he patted the top of my head."

"I hate it when he pats my head. It makes me feel so short. Seething in anger, I mopped up with the towel.

"Ed ambled off to bed and said in a condescending tone, 'You could've avoided all this by just turning on the light.'"

"I went berserk and ran up to him, pushing him face-first onto the bed. I whacked him over and over with my feather pillow while he covered his head with his hands. The pillow ripped open, but I didn't let up until it was empty. Our bedroom looked like a blizzard. I threw my wet nightgown on the floor and got dressed.

"He rolled around on the bed, roaring with laughter and holding his belly. I was looking for something else to hit him with when he fell off. I smirked and flashed him a vigorous two thumbs up for payback. Then I grabbed my purse and slammed the door on my way out. I could still hear him laughing, the devil."

Suppressing a laugh or even a smile, I swallowed hard and glanced out the window.

"Ed's in for a big surprise. I ordered an electric toilet seat. If the seat is raised, it automatically returns to the down position after one minute. Problem solved and marriage preserved." She grinned and sipped her coffee.

A feather floated down and landed on my doughnut.

"Um, Sarah, where can I buy one of those electric toilet seats?"

AEROBATIC LESSONS

S.L. Menear

He wasn't the best husband in the world, but he was one hell of an aerobatic pilot, and I wanted him to teach me some of the stunts I'd seen at air shows. We both flew jet airliners for a living. Our home was attached to a grass-strip runway near Hershey, Pennsylvania, and our favorite toy was a 1947 *Bücker Jungmann* biplane. Our German antique aircraft was equipped with a modern engine and was fully aerobatic.

My problem? A fear of falling. Most people call it a fear of heights, but it's really a fear of falling off high places. The *Bücker's* open cockpit triggered my fear during inverted maneuvers. Even though I was strapped into a five-point harness and wearing a parachute, the powerful negative g-force made me feel like I was being pulled out of the airplane.

Irrational fear compelled me to grip the steel-tube fuselage rail as if my life depended on it. So, of course, my demented husband insisted I fly inverted straight and level and hold my hands over my head "to overcome my fear." I did it, but instead of conquering my fear, it gave me extreme tunnel vision.

He said, "Keep the ridge line on your left and the valley on your right."

I said, "All I can see is a narrow tunnel with the nose of the aircraft at the end. No freaking ridge! No freaking valley! My eyes feel like they're about to pop out. Screw this! I'm rolling right side up."

"You need a distraction," he said, as I rolled the airplane upright.

He was seated directly behind me in the tandem-seat biplane and reached into the narrow space on either side of my seat to pull my belts extra tight. Whenever he did that, something scary always followed.

That time it was an extreme stunt called a *Lomcovák*, invented by an insane Czech with a death wish. A violent snap roll flowed into an end-over-end forward tumble that ended in an inverted spin. I was confident the wings and tail would remain attached to the German-engineered biplane. I was not so sure about me.

He claimed his slow-motion version of the *Lomcovák* was tame and fun. The only difference with his kinder, gentler version was the snap roll didn't bang my head into the side rail hard enough to bruise me.

I eventually learned how to do what I considered the fun stunts, but I never mastered a roll on top of a loop. My husband's laughter was my main clue that I had messed up the timing and something bad was about to happen. He would chuckle first. All-out laughter always accompanied our entry into an inverted spin.

I failed to see the humor.

We're divorced now.

MEADOW MUFFINS

D.M. Littlefield

While driving to my granny's ranch alone at night on a deserted country road, a deer leaped in front of my car. I swerved and skidded on the wet road toward a deep drainage ditch.

I slammed on the brakes. The car stopped with one front wheel hanging over the edge and the rear wheels stuck in the mud. Frustrated, I pounded the steering wheel. Oh, that hurt! I had forgotten about my scraped knuckles from changing a flat tire earlier.

It had been exhausting driving through heavy showers all the way from Houston. I saw Granny's ranch lights in the distance on the other side of the ditch that separated her land from the road. Instead of walking the longer winding road, I decided to cut across her property.

I retrieved my penlight before locking the car. I needed my hands for holding the barbed wire fence apart, so I plunked my car keys into my large handbag and tossed it into the trunk alongside my suitcase. As soon as I slammed the trunk lid closed, I cringed, realizing I had locked myself out of the car. Meadow muffins!

I shined the penlight on the ditch and decided it was possible to jump across it with a running start. After backing up to the road and taking a deep breath, I raced toward the ditch and leaped. I landed on the slippery slope.

Sliding down the wet embankment, I clawed the ground and broke six fingernails. My penlight was covered with mud when I came to a halt. I looked up for something to grab and clutched a branch on my right with both hands. Oh, that hurt! It was a thorn bush. With painful grunts, I managed to crawl to the top of the ditch.

I wiped the mud off the penlight and my clothes. Clenching the light between my teeth, I ducked my head while holding the barbed wire apart. The sleeve of my new red pantsuit ripped when I reached up to free my long black hair from the barbs. Now my scalp was minus some hair. Meadow muffins!

Such a klutz! Why couldn't I be more like Granny? I'd seen her shoot the head off a rattlesnake from fifty feet with her Colt 45 six-shooter. She was as brave as her hero, John Wayne, but she looked like Sophia on *The Golden Girls* and was just as sharp and witty. Since childhood, I enjoyed spending my summers with her. Even now, at twenty-six, I cherished my visits.

When I was ten, I walked on top of the pig-pen fence and fell in. Angry and frustrated, I shouted the four-letter S-word I'd heard the hired hands use when they were angry. Granny stormed out of the barn. She said no granddaughter of hers used potty-mouthed language like that, and I should say meadow muffins instead. She said it meant the same thing but was more ladylike. I never used the S-word again.

As I tramped through the fields it began to drizzle, or as Granny would say, "It's spittin' outside."

At the next barbed-wire fence, I stretched my leg through first so my hair wouldn't get caught again. This time, the back of my pantsuit ripped. Meadow muffins!

A cowbell clinked, so I shined my penlight toward the sound. Elsie, Granny's cow, was ambling toward me. Thanks to Granny, I learned how to milk Elsie and the goats.

I enjoyed riding Granny's horses and remembered never to squat with my spurs on. It was fun caring for her ranch animals. One of my favorites was Aflack, a thirteen-year-old duck. He was my constant companion, just as Lady, the German shepherd, was hers.

Granny's Billy goat, Elmo, liked to show off by butting things. We had to be careful not to bend over when he was nearby.

Lost in memories, I stepped into one of Elsie's soft, stinky, meadow muffins. It oozed inside my shoe as I tried to pull it free. My foot came loose, but my shoe stayed stuck. I bent down to retrieve it and wham, I was airborne. I landed face-first onto the muddy ground and puffed a strand of hair away from my eyes to look behind me. Elmo. As I wiped the mud off my face with one hand, I groped for my penlight with the other.

Elmo's happy bleating called the rest of his herd to come marvel at his talent. I didn't know goats had such good night vision. My rear end must have been too tempting. His groupies surrounded me as they bleated their praises to Elmo.

I stood up and glared at Elmo before hopping on one foot to retrieve my shoe stuck in the stinky meadow muffin. I reached down and shook most of the poop off my shoe, hoping that walking through the wet grass would finish the job. If not, a creek awaited at the bottom of the hill.

Elsie, Elmo, and his groupies followed me to the creek and waited on the bank to see what other amusing entertainment I might provide. Beyond the opposite bank, the outdoor light on Granny's barn lit up her barnyard and the creek I had to wade across.

After rolling up my pant legs and holding my shoes and socks in my hands, I slowly waded in. The creek was usually shallow, but recent rains brought it up to my thighs. Halfway to the other side, I stepped into a hole, twisted my ankle, and fell back into the water.

Struggling to pop my head above water, I lost my shoes and socks while frantically splashing. Finally, I managed to sit up in the strong current, coughing and sputtering in water up to my neck.

My audience on the creek bank mooed and bleated their appreciation for my performance. My hands searched the creek bottom and found only my shoes. Meadow muffins!

After wading out, I limped up to the barnyard, leaned

against a tree to put on my shoes, and looked back at my attentive audience. Elsie mooed. Elmo and his groupies bleated, hoping for an encore. I bowed and limped toward the house, leaving them wanting more.

My soggy shoes squished as I walked up the porch steps to the kitchen's screen door and inhaled the mouthwatering aroma of bread baking.

Lady walked to the screen door, wagging her tail and whining.

Granny gaped at me. "Betty Jo! Land sakes, you look like a tattered tea bag that's been dunked way too many times." She held the door open and patted my back. "Bless your little pea-pickin' heart. Come on in. What happened?"

Lady sniffed me, which triggered a sneezing fit. She crawled under the kitchen table and covered her nose with her paws. I guess I'd overloaded her sniffer.

I heaved a sigh and explained. Then I rolled my eyes. "This trip couldn't have been worse."

Granny looked up at me and took my hand. "Oh, it could've been a lot worse! Good thing you didn't cut through the northeast pasture."

"What do you mean?"

"That's where I keep Bulldozer."

Puzzled, I frowned. "What? You bought a bulldozer?"

"No, I bought a mean bull and named the ornery varmint Bulldozer. Check him out after sun up. And don't bend over unless you want to be butted into the next county."

FLOWERS

D.M. Littlefield

I sprang up in bed when I heard loud banging and yelling. Rubbing my eyes, I looked at the clock. Three in the morning. *Is the house on fire?*

I struggled into my robe and ran barefoot downstairs where I squinted through the front-door peephole. I groaned in disgust.

When I yanked the door open, I stubbed my big toe. "What are you doing here? You'll wake up all the neighbors," I said, hopping in pain.

Ben, my ex-husband, leaned against the door frame, drunk. He held a pitiful bouquet of pansies ripped from my window box. Clumps of dirt on their roots dangled as he thrust them at me and almost lost his balance.

"Here, you can't say I never gave you any flowers," he said, slurring. His breath reeked of alcohol as he leaned in.

I backed away, fanning my face.

"I have a question. Why'd you divorce me?" He asked. "We were married over twenty years, and I think I deserve an answer. Was it the drinking, the drugs, or all the cheating? Or was it something else? Tell me, I have a right to know!"

I rolled my eyes and clenched my jaw, knowing he wouldn't remember anything I said. "It was everything you just said and more."

He gazed at me, bleary-eyed, with a lopsided grin. "Well,

that makes me feel better. I thought maybe you were mad at me for some other reason."

I took a deep breath. "You're drunk, Ben. How did you get here? Did you drive?"

He tried to straighten up and almost fell over. "I drive better drunk than most people drive sober."

A police car with flashing blue lights pulled into my driveway. Two officers inspected a car stuck in my lawn and then looked Ben over, shaking their heads.

One officer said, "We're responding to a disturbance call. Do you need assistance?"

Ben waved his arms and bellowed, "I don't need your ... your stance ... ass stance." He fell down the steps and sprawled at their feet.

The officer's partner pushed his hat back from his forehead, crossed his arms, and glared down at him.

The other cop looked at me. "Lady, do you know this man?"

I sighed. "He's my ex-husband. This is only *one* of the reasons why we've been divorced for five years."

The officer pointed at the dented car on my front lawn. "Is that his car?"

I focused on the car stuck in my beautiful red bougainvillea bush. It had carved deep ruts in my lovely flower beds and lawn. I closed my eyes and nodded my head.

"I haven't seen him in a long time, so I don't know what he's driving, but chances are that's his car."

"Several mailboxes are knocked down along the street. The dents and paint from his car match the damaged property. We'll take him to jail and impound his car. Do you want to press charges?"

I gazed at Ben with pity and was about to say no. Then I recalled all the years of stress and mental abuse he had put me and our children through. I glanced down at the poor little wilting faces of my uprooted pansies.

I felt years of pent-up rage burst forth. "Hell yes, I'll press charges! Lock the drunken loser up and throw away the key."

I returned to bed and slept soundly for the first time in years.

HOLIDAY GREETINGS

S.L. Menear

Dear family and friends,
   What a year! In January, I dated a man named Mike, who I met at the Safari Club on Golden Oldies Night. He was sixty, tall, almost handsome, and still had all his hair.
   Mike was quite the sportsman and convinced me to go on a dive vacation with him and two of his friends.
   He chartered a 102-foot yacht, and we headed for some prime dive locations along the Grand Cayman wall. His friend, Tom, brought along his twenty-something girlfriend, Kimberly. She was the poster girl for Airheads Anonymous and satisfied Tom's most important criteria—big boobs. Why did I care? I got stuck with her as my dive partner so the men could do a little hunting and gathering with their spear guns.
   Nothing like blood in the water to add excitement to a dive. At a depth of eighty feet, Kim and I were admiring the colorful coral and pretty fish when she erupted in a heavy menstrual flow. Her thong bikini wasn't sufficient to stop the blood from leaking into water that was clear as air. A dark cloud swirled around Kim's hips.
   I knew what would be coming next, but I didn't expect it to be so big.
   I looked down the edge of a wall that descended straight down into an abyss several thousand feet deep. The men were trying to spear a huge grouper about twenty feet beneath us.

They didn't notice a dark shadow rising under them and rapidly growing in size. I banged my dive knife against my tank to get their attention, but the hunters were too focused on their prey.

Things happened pretty fast after that. Clueless Kim swam beside me to see why I was signaling. Her blood cloud encircled us just in time for the pelagic predator to get a good whiff and zero in on its prey—us.

I didn't think tiger sharks could grow to twenty feet. I spied its tell-tale stripes as it streaked past the men the moment they shot their spears into the grouper. With one look at the giant shark, they released an explosion of bubbles (not just from their mouthpieces), dropped their spear guns, and bolted to the other side of the reef, leaving us to fend for ourselves.

I'd been told sharks won't attack if you're facing them; they prefer to strike from below and behind. Dive partners should position themselves back-to-back so someone is always facing the shark. That seemed reasonable until a monster the size of an SUV was bearing down on me. What if the face-to-face theory only applied to smaller sharks?

So I decided, the hell with this! I put as much distance as possible between me and sister shark bait.

Not really, but I was tempted. I spotted a crevice in the reef just big enough to admit Miss Disaster Cloud and me. I shoved in Kim and squeezed into the narrow cleft. The biggest set of teeth I'd ever seen missed me by inches. Kim's blood cloud drifted out and whipped the shark into a frenzy. It rammed its big head repeatedly against our hideout.

It was difficult not to gulp air as giant jaws with rows of sharp teeth snapped at my face. If we were lucky, our air would last twenty minutes, assuming we stopped sucking it in. But then we still had to swim up eighty feet and climb into the yacht without the monster eating us. I prayed for a miracle.

We got one in the form of a physiology lesson.

Turns out when a menstruating female is in life-threatening peril, adrenaline shuts down all non-essential functions. Kim's blood cloud dissipated into the vast ocean. The monster circled over us and then targeted the wounded grouper, thank God. The spear guns were still dangling from their tethers connected to the spears embedded in its bloody sides.

We made a break for the boat while the shark shredded the grouper. It took major self-control to not rise faster than our bubbles. I had to restrain Kim. Even so, our survival depended on skipping the customary five-minute safety stop.

Kim and I climbed into the boat just in time to hear the captain call in our deaths to the Cayman authorities. *Nice.*

Needless to say, that was my last date with Mike. Kim couldn't understand why. Being an airhead isn't easy, poor thing.

In February, I enjoyed the Daytona 500, which is always on the same weekend as my birthday. My brother, Larry, flew me to Daytona Beach in his airplane with three of his friends and his drop-dead gorgeous thirty-five-year-old daughter, Hollie. She bought my race ticket for my birthday.

I love watching live NASCAR races. The air is literally filled with testosterone, fuel vapor, and electromagnetic energy. The race is like a mighty battle involving multiple aircraft carriers. The race-car drivers are the fighter pilots. The spotters are combination radar intercept officers/snipers, positioned on the highest point above the track to call out targets (nearby race cars) and warnings.

The crew chiefs are like CAGs (carrier air group commanders), perched atop their pit boxes, planning battle strategies and directing drivers and pit crews. The pit crews work in dangerous environments similar to the decks of aircraft carriers, striving to change four tires, fuel their race car, and adjust the chassis, all in less than twelve seconds, while cars speed past inches away.

The race isn't just about speed. The fastest car with the best driver may not win. NASCAR racing is cerebral, and often the smartest crew chief wins with the best pit strategy.

Men should consider bringing dates to the races because after women breathe in all that testosterone for hours, sex is all they think about when the race ends.

The pre-race had a party atmosphere. Hollie and I strolled

through the race market where we bought cute T-shirts and sipped frozen margaritas in the warm sunshine. While waiting in line for the next tram to our grandstand, I complained that the shirt buttons over my bra kept popping open. The men in front of us turned around and said, "Bad for you, good for us!" We all laughed and became fast friends as we sat together on the tram.

They had grandstand seats in our section at the very top and invited us to sit with them. Their jokes kept us laughing all afternoon. They had just sold their business for millions, so they were celebrating. Then we discovered it was the company my brother had started years ago. Hollie brought Larry up to meet them, and they had fun discovering all their mutual friends.

The air traffic after the race was worse than the busiest hours at a major airport. Shortly after takeoff on the flight home, a private Boeing 737 almost crashed into our Piper Aerostar as the jet overtook us and roared a few feet over us in the clear night sky. The controller hadn't allowed enough separation between takeoffs. My heart hammered my chest, and it took a few seconds to recover from the shock of almost getting killed.

Then we were hit with an invisible horizontal tornado, known as a wingtip vortex, generated by the jet that had barely missed us. Good thing my brother was an aerobatic pilot. Rather than fight the violent roll induced by the vortex, he allowed our airplane to continue all the way around and stopped it right side up. Foul odors filled our cabin, and no one spoke during the rest of the flight.

In April, my brother asked me to fly an old biplane to the Sun'n'Fun air show in Lakeland for his friend. "It'll be fun," he said. "The sun on your face, the wind in your hair—you'll love it. The antique engine runs like a top."

I should mention nothing bad ever happened to my brother. That's probably why he feared nothing, except maybe an angry woman with a loaded gun in her hand.

So I set off for Lakeland in the 1938 *Bücker Jungmann* open cockpit biplane with the original engine. Somewhere over no-man's-land in central Florida, the Tiger motor exploded. A cylinder on the right side shot out of the engine like a cannon ball, leaving a gaping, flaming hole. I cut the fuel. The engine stopped, and the propeller seized.

The fire burned out, but the motor was still trailing black smoke. Oil covered the windshield and blocked my front view. I looked down over the side and saw a smooth strip of grass with a windsock, so I circled down and glided to a landing while looking out the sides. I coasted to a stop in front of a small hangar where an elderly gentleman was waiting with a fire extinguisher and ice tea. What a sweet guy!

I called my brother, explained what had happened, and asked him to fly in and pick me up.

"That's too bad," Larry said, "but that old Tiger engine was bound to blow up sooner or later."

Nice.

A few months later, I dared to hang out with Larry again. An airline pilot, powered paraglider and powered parachute instructor, as well as an airplane and seaplane flight instructor, he excelled at flying almost anything. Maybe because he was so good at everything, he forgot that many others were not, including most of his buddies.

Larry took me for a ride in a tandem powered paraglider that we foot-launched from the public beach on Singer Island and flew low over the mansions near the north end of legendary Palm Beach. The view was spectacular. I finally got to see what was behind all those tall hedge walls no one can see over from the road.

After we landed, he asked if I'd like a ride in the powered parachute that weekend. It resembled a dune buggy with an engine and propeller in back and a rectangular chute overhead.

"You can go up with Carl while I give a lesson in mine," he said.

"Isn't Carl the guy who crashes a lot?" I asked.

"He's way better now, hasn't crashed in months. Besides, it has dual controls. You can take over if necessary."

"But it isn't anything like an airplane. I've never flown one of those."

"Don't worry, it's easy. Besides, Carl won't have any problems."

So, I thought, my brother loves me. He wouldn't send me up with Carl if it wasn't safe. *Wrong!*

I never found out how well Carl flew because we never made it off the ground. He crashed us into a drainage canal at takeoff speed when he made an abrupt right turn for no apparent reason. As our flying machine descended the steep bank, the chute overhead continued forward at 25 mph and yanked us upside down into the muddy, icky water. We almost drowned while trying to release our seat harnesses. Then we dropped headfirst into the muck. I was drenched and covered with mud and slime when I climbed up the bank.

Larry waved as he flew over us—*real nice*.

So much for this year's exploits. I hope I've entertained you.

Happy Holidays!
Sharon

STUCK IN AN ELEVATOR

D.M. Littlefield

Katie sat on the hotel bed, prepared to wiggle and contort her body to pull on her pantyhose. This pair was sliding on too easily, though. She looked at the package. *Oh, no, I bought the largest size! Two of me could fit in these with room left over.*

The phone rang. "Katie, where are you? We're all waiting for you."

"I'm ready, except for the pantyhose. They're waaay too big."

"Then take them off. Just hurry."

"No, I have to wear them or my black-and-blue toe will show."

Mike's voice grated. "Okay, leave 'em on. Tie a knot or whatever you have to do to make 'em fit 'til you get here and ask one of the women for a safety pin. Hurry up, honey."

Katie lifted her evening gown to her chest in front of the mirror. She grabbed the large waist of the pantyhose that had fallen to her knees, tied it into a knot, released her gown, and gasped. "No way!"

Her waist looked like it had sprouted a tennis-ball size growth. She untied the knot, gathered the waistband to the side, folded it back over, and tucked it under her gown. It started to slide down. She realized she would have to hold it in place with her right hand clutching that side until she found a safety pin.

She grabbed her evening bag and rushed into the open elevator across from their room. Katie smiled at the sole passenger, a tall handsome man with a sprinkle of gray at his temples, looking elegant in a tuxedo.

He smiled. "Are you a visitor to Dallas?"

Her blue eyes were bright with excitement as she pushed her long blond hair away from her face with her evening bag. "Yes, my husband's a fireman. He's receiving a medal for bravery at the Firemen's Banquet tonight."

"What's your husband's name?"

"Mike Minnelli."

"I'm Mayor John Kincaid. I have the honor of giving our heroes their medals." He reached out to shake her hand. "I'm pleased to meet the wife of our most decorated hero. I understand you're celebrating your first wedding anniversary tonight."

She shoved her evening bag over her right hand, which was clutching her waist, and extended her left hand.

Katie blushed. "Yep, married to me, my husband gets lots of practice being a hero."

The mayor raised his eyebrows. "I don't understand."

She sighed. "I'm Katie K. Minnelli. The K stands for klutz." She looked up at him. "I warned Mike that I'm accident prone, but he said he could handle it. Now he refers to me as his little package of dynamite. He anticipates explosions and says I keep him on his toes and in shape."

The elevator lurched and plunged past the next four floors. Katie screamed, dropped her bag, and grabbed the railing with both hands, allowing her pantyhose to drop to her knees. The elevator jolted and screeched to a halt, sending her pantyhose to her ankles.

The mayor's face was ashen as he turned to her. "Are you okay?"

"My heart's pounding!"

The mayor used the emergency elevator phone to report they were stuck between floors. He smiled and ran his hand through his short brown hair. "They'll have this fixed soon. While we wait, tell me how you met your husband."

She shuffled her feet, trying to turn around in the tangle of pantyhose.

"Did you hurt your legs?"

"Noooo, my feet tingle." *I'm too embarrassed to tell him about my predicament.* "Mayor Kincaid, will you please let my husband know where I am?"

He smiled and imitated John Wayne's famous drawl. "I sure will, little missy, don't you worry your pretty head. The firemen will rescue us."

She managed a weak smile as he called his assistant on his cell phone to notify her husband.

"Now, tell me about your husband, the hero," the mayor said after he hung up.

"Mike is handsome and very strong. Firemen make the best husbands because they know how to do everything. He's even a great cook. My girlfriend is Mike's sister. She introduced us at her family's picnic at the lake. Mike took me for a boat ride and wanted to take my picture on the end of the pier by the boat. He motioned for me to back up a little, but I backed up too much and fell in the lake. That's the first time Mike rescued me. I can't even recall them all."

"Oh, come on, I'm sure you can tell me a few more."

"OK. Well, his sister lived in the apartment next to him. We double-dated often, and one time when I spent the night at his sister's, I got trapped upside down in her fold-up wall bed. I was squashed between the bedding and wall until she ran next door to get Mike.

"That must've been uncomfortable."

"It was. Then on our honeymoon at this very hotel, the revolving door held me hostage. It stopped revolving after I got in. I was trapped again, and Mike rescued me."

Katie puffed out a sigh. "He told me not to go near the twelve-foot ladder he had leaned against our house to clean the upstairs windows. I wanted to surprise him by cleaning them myself because he was busy working on the car. He came to do the windows just in time to catch me when I fell off the ladder."

"That was fortunate."

"Not for him. He got a black eye from being hit with my

bottle of glass cleaner. Last week my big toe got stuck in the bathtub faucet. It's black and blue, and I have to wear open-toed shoes because of the swelling."

"How did that happen?" the mayor asked with a perplexed look.

"I know men have a hard time understanding these stupid things. It was one of those you-had-to-be-there moments. I was relaxing in a bubble bath listening to music and tapping my toes against the bathtub to the beat when I accidentally shoved my big toe up the faucet. I waited two hours for Mike to come home and rescue me. I'm such a klutz!"

The elevator jiggled, and she screamed as it lurched and jerked down to the banquet floor as they clutched the railing. When Katie heard the uproar of the press awaiting them, she panicked and fainted. The *whoosh* of air from the door being pried open woke her, and she discovered the mayor had scooped her up in his arms.

"Hey, Mayor, who's the babe you're holding, your new girlfriend?" someone shouted. "Looks like you made the most out of being stuck in the elevator!"

Katie remained limp and kept her eyes closed. She imagined photos in the Dallas newspapers of the mayor holding her with her pantyhose dangling from her shoes. She heard the press casting more crude innuendos as cameras flashed. She prayed Mike would come to their rescue.

"Move, please! Coming through! Move!" a deep familiar voice bellowed.

"I hope to God you're her husband," the mayor said. "I swear I was a perfect gentleman. Please, can you clear up this mess?"

Mike took a deep breath and sighed. "It's okay, I'm used to it."

She felt him grab her pantyhose from her prized new Mootsies Tootsies shoes with five-inch heels. Her feet were pulled up as Mike peeled off the pantyhose to display the extra-large size to the media.

"I'm her husband. Let me talk!" he shouted. "She bought the wrong size of pantyhose, and they wouldn't stay up. She was on her way down to me to get this safety pin when the elevator malfunctioned." He held the pin up in the bright lights. Mayor Kincaid is a fine gentleman. I'm grateful he took care of my wife through this life-threatening incident."

She felt Mike lay the pantyhose on her lap, transfer her to his arms, and kiss her cheek.

The mayor sighed with relief as reporters apologized and proclaimed him the hero of the day.

"Mike, you know you're *her* hero, don't you?" the mayor said.

"Yes, sir," Mike whispered. "But I've heard you're a man who can knock the socks off women. Bet you never thought you'd be accused of knocking off their pantyhose."

The mayor laughed. "Take good care of Katie. She's one in a million."

Katie opened her eyes and saw Mike roll his eyes and mutter, "Believe me ... I know."

The mayor patted Mike on the back. "It'll be my extreme pleasure to award you your hero's medal tonight. God knows you've earned it."

CATATONIC SNIFFERITIS

D.M. Littlefield

You've been invited to a new acquaintance's home for the afternoon. You knock on the door, and your hostess greets you. As you step in, your feet freeze to the floor while a powerful offensive odor invades your nostrils. An alarm sends an urgent message to the olfactory center of your brain. Your sinuses begin a meltdown worse than the Chernobyl disaster. Your nasal passages clamp shut.

Your sniffer has been snuffed.

Your eyes bulge, blink, and water while you hold your breath in a catatonic stupor. A few seconds ago, your sensitive sniffer was a finely tuned instrument, enabling you to identify a dozen vintage wines in succession with merely a faint whiff of the glass while blindfolded.

But now your brain has activated your body's fight-or-flight defense mechanism. You apologize and gasp that you forgot you left a pot of soup boiling on the stove. You rush outside and gulp in fresh air while trying not to barf up your lunch.

You're experiencing a mysterious malady known as feline-induced Catatonic Snifferitis. That means the cat's litter box has built up so much toxic waste, the Environmental Protection Agency should declare the house a disaster area.

If you're wondering why this appalling condition still pervades in this era of high technology, you'll be pleased to know the scientific world is addressing this repugnant household dilemma. This very moment at the Lame Brain Laboratory of Science in Catnip Junction, Arkansas, my brilliant colleague, Garfield Morris Peeyew, is diligently tackling the problem. He has often been maligned as a crackpot, as have so many great men of science, but Dr. Peeyew has invented a revolutionary new electric litter box that evaporates odor.

You merely plug the litter box into a household outlet, and it evaporates the odor as soon as the urine touches the box. The invention is not quite ready for the market, though. Unfortunately, there's a small problem.

It evaporates the cat too.

Our dedicated research doctor will persevere with his primary project while also investigating the legend of cats' nine lives.

Let's hope we can dispel that old saying, "Cats don't smell bad, their owners do," meaning cats have an acute sense of smell, but their owners' noses have become immune to the reeking, contaminated litter box, having lost all their sense of smell.

I, Dr. Dudley Dimwit, wish you *purrrrrfect* health.

SIBLING INSANITY

S.L. Menear

My brother, Larry, called from the airport in Lantana, Florida. "Hey, Sis, wait 'til you hear about my new flight student. You've never had one like him. Everybody said he'd be impossible to teach, but he's a real natural."

"I'm guessing he's a doctor or lawyer. Their egos usually make them difficult to teach."

"Nope, he used to be an accountant—had to retire after an auto accident. Now he wants some excitement in his life."

"Are you teaching him in one of your airplanes?"

"We're flying my powered parachute."

"Right, the one that looks like a cross between a dune buggy and an airboat. Why not use an airplane?"

"He wants to avoid all the FAA regulations associated with airplanes."

"Is that code for not passing the pilot physical?"

"Yeah, he'd never pass the vision test, but he has an uncanny feel for the aircraft."

"Well, I guess his vision doesn't need to be 20/20. There aren't any instruments to read anyway."

"Some pilots install an altimeter and an RPM gauge, but they're not necessary."

"Do you intend to sell him a powered parachute when he finishes his lessons?"

"No, his wife would pitch a fit. She doesn't approve of his

flight training. If she had her way, he'd never leave the house."

"So I guess he'll rent yours whenever he feels the urge to fly."

"No, he's just aiming for a spot in *The Guinness Book of World Records*."

"Doing what?"

"One solo flight."

"Clearly there's something you're not telling me."

"Oh yeah, did I mention he's blind? Lost his sight in the auto accident."

"*Blind*! Have you lost your mind?"

"It's not as bad as it sounds. He flies by the seat of his pants, smooth as butter. I talk him through the landings, and he greases it on."

"Yeah, but you won't be with him when he solos. He'll literally be flying blind!"

"I have that covered. I'll talk him down on radio headsets."

"Gee, what could possibly go wrong? Radios are *soooo* reliable."

"He'll have his cell phone as a backup. It's just one flight. Think of it. A boring little accountant will go down in history as the only blind person ever to fly solo."

"Oh, he'll go down all right, and your flight instructor and pilot licenses will go down with him. This has to be the dumbest thing ever!"

"Now you sound like his wife. Don't worry. Everything will be fine."

"It's just that I know how much you love flying. I'd hate to see you risk your career so some fool can get in the record books."

"I'd hate to crush his dream."

"So send him on a fake solo flight."

"He'd sense my presence."

"I'm not suggesting a real flight. Mount the rig on big springs, strap him in, fire up the engine, and let him think he's flying solo. Anchor the rig and aim a big fan at him. With the engine powered up behind him and the headset on, he won't hear the fan. He'll feel the wind in his face like he did during his lessons. Give the rig occasional bumps and jolts for realism. Talk to him on the radio like it's really happening. He'll experience the thrill of a lifetime, and you won't risk your career. Problem solved."

"But then he won't get in the record book."

"And you won't go down in history as the world's dumbest flight instructor."

"Sis, you worry too much."

"Uh huh. I've lost count of how many times I've tried to save your sorry ass."

"Yeah, well my intrepid ass has succeeded plenty of times where cowardly asses feared to tread."

"Yes, but not this time. A Guinness representative will need to witness the flight. The scheduled blind solo will be reported to the media, and the authorities will shut you down and yank your pilot certificates before you start the engine."

"His wife's walking him over here now. It's time for his last lesson. I'll think about it and call you back later. Bye, Sis."

***

The next day, as I tapped away on my laptop and enjoyed the view from the deck of the Hilton on Singer Island, I answered my cell. "Hello, brother dear, how's it going with your blind student?"

"Not so good. He was feeling cocky after his final lesson yesterday, so when he got home, he took their rider mower for a little test drive. His wife ran behind him yelling for him to stop, but he gunned it and ended up in the deep end of their swimming pool. Now she has him heavily sedated. Guess his glory days are over."

"Maybe not. Give her a call and explain my fake solo plan. The flight might be even more convincing if you do it before his meds wear off. Tell his wife it's a safe way to satisfy his thirst for adventure and tell him you can't include Guinness because the FAA would find out and end your pilot career. If she refuses, he'll always resent her. My plan is a win for both of them with no risk to your licenses."

"Good idea, Sis. I'll set it up. The sweet old guy deserves his shot at glory."

"Great. Call me when you're ready, and I'll help you. I'd hate to miss a chance to make a blind aviator happy."

***

I wish I could report that we accomplished the fake solo flight, but the blind man's wife vetoed our plan. In fact, she threatened to sue my brother if he ever contacted her husband again.

Oh well, I think all men are a little crazy, but at least Larry had good intentions.

GIRL TALK

D.M. Littlefield

Sue recognized him. It had been fifteen years, but he still had that silly grin she remembered so well. Back when they were teenagers, Ted had asked her advice on girls. He was her brother's buddy and wanted to date her best friend, Linda.

***

As she and Ted sat on her front porch swing, Sue said, "Linda told me she dated Jerry Gates only once because of what he said when she told him she was cold. She wanted him to put his arm around her shoulders. Do you know what the jerk told her?"

He shrugged. "How would I know? I wasn't there."

"I *know* you weren't there!" Sue glared at him. "The jerk told her she would warm up if she chewed her gum faster."

Ted gave her that silly grin. "Did it work?"

"Of course, it didn't work. She never dated him again. So what have you learned from that?"

He raised his eyebrows. "Never tell a girl how to chew her gum?"

She rolled her brown eyes. "No, silly, if a girl says she's cold, put your jacket around her shoulders or put your arm around her."

He frowned. "If I give her my jacket, then I'll be cold."

"Then both of you cuddle under it!"

He smiled. "That's a much better idea."

"Girls like to be complimented. Pretend I'm Linda. Stare at me with a longing look and say, 'Linda, you take my breath away.'"

He squinted, looking like he was in pain. "Linda, you suck the life out of me."

Sue covered her face with her hands. "No, no, you look like you have a severe stomachache. I didn't say, 'You suck the life out of me.' I said, 'You take my breath away.'"

Ted regarded her quizzically. "It means the same thing, doesn't it?"

She shook her head. "What you said is an insult."

Sue tried to think of something he desired or craved. Knowing teenage boys' passion for food, she asked, "What's your favorite food?"

His face lit up. "Nothing is better than a hamburger at McDonald's."

"Okay, then maybe this'll work for you. When you look at Linda, pretend you're looking at a delicious, mouth-watering hamburger and say, 'Linda, you take my breath away.' Pretend I'm Linda and do it."

Sue felt a warm glow flow through her as he gazed at her with longing and said, "Linda, you take my breath away."

"That's perfect! Now practice that in front of a mirror until you're comfortable with it. And remember girls like guys with good manners, so hold her hand and be polite."

His face lit up again. "When can I kiss her?"

"It depends on the girl. When you walk her to her front door to say goodnight, if she leans her face toward you, that means she wants a kiss."

"Why can't girls just say what they want, instead of making guys try to read their minds?"

She sighed. "Because girls think it's more romantic that way."

"Well, it sure would make dating a lot easier for us."

"Okay, rule one: What to do when things are going great, but she becomes quiet. Ask her if something is wrong, and if she answers *nothing*, that means *something* is wrong.

"Rule two: Let's say you're having a lively conversation, but have a difference of opinion, and she ends it with *whatever*. That's what girls say instead of *screw you*."

Ted's eyes widened. "My mother says that a lot to my dad."

"Rule three: Let's say you want her to go to a ball game with you, but she wants to go to the movies instead, and you say, 'I'm going to the ballgame! You can go to the movies.' She may say, 'Go ahead.' But don't misunderstand. She's not giving you permission; she's daring you. Do *not* do it. You'll live to regret it."

A muscle clenched along Ted's jaw. "I don't know if I can remember all this stuff, and it may not be worth the trouble."

***

Sue smiled, recalling their conversation all those years ago. Now, here she was standing in line at the bookstore for Ted to sign his latest bestseller. She placed his book on the table in front of him.

"To whom shall I dedicate this book?" he asked, not looking up.

"To Sue, who taught me how girls think."

Ted started to write then jerked up his head and stared at her. He jumped up and leaned across the table to hug her.

"Sue! I owe you for my success as a romance author. I wanted to see you while I'm in town on tour." He lavished her with that longing look he had mastered as if yearning for a hamburger. "Please, have dinner with me?"

She couldn't resist smiling. "I'll be waiting for you at McDonalds."

THE FIRST PILOT

S.L. Menear

He was a bastard, literally, in a time when that mattered. His mother was a commoner with poor judgment while his father was a wealthy man with no conscience. He grew up fatherless, nameless. During his sixty-seven years of life, he was a genius extraordinaire the likes of which the world may never see again.

For the Catholic Church and wealthy patrons, he created beautiful sculptures and dark, enigmatic paintings worthy of their masterpiece status. His scientific drawings and inventions astound the world to this day.

Although he was centuries ahead of his time, his aeronautical engineering expertise was not well known. He flight-tested his aircraft inventions in secret, reveling in the freedom, solitude, and pure joy of each flight. He knew the populace was not ready to accept his monumental achievements in aviation.

History is still not ready.

After working twenty years as an airline pilot, I studied the drawings of his various flying machines. I read about an exact replica built according to his detailed specifications and the successful test flight. That was big news to the aviation world—proof that his glider could fly, but not that he had ever flown it.

I was certain he had flown it. For me, the most compelling evidence was something he wrote that demonstrated his personal, intimate familiarity with flight.

"Once you have tasted flight, you will forever walk the Earth with your eyes turned skyward, for there you have been and there you long to return." *Leonardo Da Vinci, 1452-1519*

EAVESDROPPING

D.M. Littlefield

Joe heard the phone in their insurance office ring while his wife, Jenna, was filing invoices. Before she could get to it, he answered it. He noted the telltale click just as he heard a woman speaking.

"Do you have a sex hour in your place of business?" she asked.

Joe took a deep breath, knowing his wife was listening in. "Nooooo, we only have a lunch hour. Do you have a sex hour in your place of business?"

"No, sir, that's why I'm calling you."

His mouth twisted wryly. "I don't take prank calls."

"Sir, this isn't a prank call. I'm with the prestigious law firm of Getcha, Commin, & Goinn. I'm trying to find a man."

He sighed, gazed at the ceiling, and rubbed the back of his neck. "Lady, I wish I could help you, but I don't think my wife would approve."

"No, no, you don't understand. The man I'm looking for is A. Sexhour. That's his name. I think the initial 'A' might stand for Andrew, Adam, or Albert. Do you have anyone by one of those names in your office?"

"No. Uh, how did you get my phone number?"

"Your number is on the list of businesses they gave me to call."

Joe leaned back in his chair, thinking about Ted, his know-it-all brother-in-law, and smiled wickedly. "How late do you work?"

"Until six."

"I know a man who'd be eager to help you. Are you ready for his number? It's 642-1212."

The woman gasped. "Sir, I'm not looking for sex!"

Puzzled, he frowned. "What are you talking about?"

"You said the man could be reached at: Sex for two, want to, want to?"

He rolled his eyes, heaved a sigh, and pictured a bimbo on the other end of the line. "No, no, lady, you've got it all wrong. I gave you Ted's home *telephone* number, 642-1212. He works in the city at a U.S. government office. He'll help you find the man you're looking for. Call him around five-thirty. He's usually home by then. If he isn't, leave him a message." Joe coughed trying to suppress a chuckle. "I'm sure he'll get back to you right away."

"Ooooh, I misunderstood. I'm sorry I snapped at you. You've been very nice. Other people I've called have been nasty and rude. Thank you for your help."

"No problem." He hung up the phone with a smile, turned, and saw his wife with her hands on her hips in the doorway.

She glared at him. "Why did you give her Ted's number? You know how jealous and suspicious my sister is."

Joe crossed his arms. "Jealousy and suspicion are family traits, or you wouldn't know about my telephone conversation." He raised his eyebrows. "Would you, dear?"

Jenna's face reddened. She spun around and stomped back to her office.

Joe leaned back in his chair, closed his eyes, and fantasized about the bimbo caller. He imagined her as a dumb blonde with big boobs, long legs, and a short skirt.

He grinned, thinking he was lucky his wife couldn't eavesdrop on his thoughts.

MALL CRITICS

D.M. Littlefield

Jim and his wife, Gail, walked into the mall corridor toward a bench. They had been enjoying a leisurely lifestyle since moving to Florida from New York after he retired. During their forty-five years of marriage, they had learned to compromise. Jim played golf twice a week, and Gail, a verified shopaholic, demanded equal time, so he had been taking her to the mall twice a week for the past few months.

They had agreed she would shop from ten until one, before lunching together at the Chinese restaurant. He thought the only drawback was that he had to accompany her and drive the car. His wife, a city girl, never learned how to drive. He still hadn't decided if that was a curse or a blessing.

The first time, he made the huge mistake of shopping with her. She led him through every store in the mall from one end to the other until he was exhausted. Thirty-six holes of golf were a breeze compared to that. She, on the other hand, seemed to get more energized.

So he settled on a mall bench, watching people or reading a book.

This was fine at first, but then she began to return later each time. If she was more than a half hour late, he started searching for her. He detested her complete disregard for him. Their mall trips always ended in heated arguments.

Last week, Jim devised an ingenious scheme.

Today, before he plunked down next to an elderly man, he gave his wife a stern look and tapped his wristwatch. "Please be on time. One o'clock! Remember, one o'clock!"

She adjusted the shoulder strap on the handbag that matched her red pantsuit and waved her hand dismissively. "Yeah, yeah, I heard you."

He frowned as he watched his red-headed wife walk away. He knew better than to tell her the red pantsuit on her short, stout body made her look like a fire hydrant.

The man beside him lowered his book and extended his hand. "My name's Fred Watson. What's yours?"

"Jim Morton. Is your wife shopping too?"

"No, she's in the beauty shop getting her hair done. I read while I wait for her."

A group of teen-age girls painted in heavy makeup and tattoos giggled as they strolled by. They wore low-cut tight jeans with skimpy tops and gold rings in their noses, lips, and ears. Their frizzy hair sticking out every which way looked as if they had styled it with a Taser.

Fred shook his head. "I wonder if those nose rings hurt when they have a cold and a runny nose."

Jim grimaced. "It doesn't paint a pretty picture."

The girls were trailed by five teen-age boys, also covered with tattoos and piercings. As they sauntered by, Joe tilted his head to read one of the tattoos. Their pants hanging down around their buttocks exposed their underwear. Jim was tempted to yank up their pants.

Fred arched his eyebrows and shrugged.

"The only good that's come from that idiotic fad is that the apprehension rate on thieves is way up," Jim said.

Fred peered above his reading glasses that rested halfway down on his nose. "Is that so?"

"Yeah, the perps can't run with their pants falling down around their ankles, so they're easy to catch."

Fred chuckled. "Teen-agers never envision their lives past twenty-one. I'm imagining how this group will look when they're seventy-five."

Jim closed his eyes. "I'm seeing all that so-called gold

bling on sagging, wrinkled skin." He shuddered. "What a sad, repulsive sight."

Fred nodded. "You got that right."

They fell quiet until Jim elbowed Fred to check out a couple about their age. "Dead man walking on your right."

The wife gripped her husband's arm like a vise while dragging him along. Her wide eyes had a fixed glaze as she marched triumphantly. The husband's right hand appeared to have a death-grip on the wallet in his pocket.

Jim and Fred turned to see what had mesmerized the woman. There it was in all its glory, a huge sign:

CLEARANCE SALE—SEVENTY PERCENT OFF
RED-TAGGED MERCHANDISE.

Fred sighed, shaking his head. "The poor guy doesn't stand a chance with odds like that."

They lowered their heads to read. Many pages later, Jim looked up to a child's laughter in front of the toy store.

A young mother parked a stroller behind her to examine the large plush animals in a floor bin. Her toddler soon climbed out of the stroller and made a bee line to the massive display near the entrance.

Jim nudged Fred, and they gazed in amazement at the tiny tot's uncanny speed of dismantling the intricate display without any tools. His mother's head was in the bin, hunting for the perfect animal for him.

"That mother should buy her kid an erector set, if they still sell them, or better yet, some power tools," Jim said. "Have his father teach him how to build, not dismantle, or he'll be stripping cars in ten minutes flat by the time he's nine."

"It's mind-boggling to see a tiny child with such incredible skills," Fred said.

The mother finally turned around and spotted her wayward son's project. She threw the animal back in the bin, scooped up her son, and raced out of the store with the stroller.

Jim looked at his watch: five minutes after one o'clock. "Fred, I'm going to have to use my new scheme to get Gail to show up. She's late again."

"Are you talking about an offensive play or an

interception?" Fred enjoyed using football metaphors.

He blew out a breath like a long-suffering spouse. "Noooo, I call it a defensive strategy to prevent a continuing war of words which would stir up my acid reflux during lunch and ruin the rest of my day. I'm going to use Gail's jealous streak to my advantage. Just watch, she'll appear like magic."

Jim looked both ways down the long mall corridor to confirm Gail was nowhere in sight. A pretty, slender woman exited a store and walked toward them. He politely introduced himself and asked her for directions to the Chinese restaurant.

Just then Jim's wife entered the far end of the mall corridor and slowly strolled in their direction with two bulging shopping bags. In between her stops at every store window, she happened to glance in their direction and spied Jim talking to the pretty woman. That did it. In her rush over, she plowed through a group of teenage boys and scattered them like bowling pins.

Out of breath, she marched up to Jim and dropped her shopping bags as she glared up at the tall woman. "Back off, sister, he's mine!"

The poor woman, bewildered, stepped back and looked down at her.

Gail grabbed Jim's right arm and thrust a shopping bag into his left hand. She grabbed the other shopping bag and dragged Jim to the restaurant. When they walked by Fred, Jim grinned and winked.

Fred flashed him a well-deserved two thumbs-up.

VIRTUAL SEX FLIGHT INSTRUCTION

S.L. Menear

Although I loved flying Boeing jets for a major airline, I also maintained my flight instructor certificate and enjoyed taking a private pilot student up for a lesson once in a while on my days off. Last night, a friend who runs a flight school called and asked me to help out with one of his students.

At the crack of dawn, I rode my red Ducati Diavel motorcycle around to the flight-line side at the Lantana Airport and parked in front of the school. Clear skies and calm winds—a perfect day to fly. When I entered the front office/pilot shop, a stocky man in his sixties looked up from behind the counter. His Texas drawl distinguished him from the many northeasterners living in southern Florida.

"Howdy, Sharon, or should I say, Captain?" He bowed and grinned.

I smiled. "Cut the crap, Bart. It's good to see you." I handed him my helmet and glanced around the empty room. "So where's the student with the big emergency?"

"Well, now, here's the thing: He has a private pilot license, way too much money, and ...."

"Let me guess, he bought an airplane that exceeds his pilot skills by a country mile, and he's too rich and arrogant to accept his limitations. Sounds like a dangerous guy."

"Now don't go gettin' your panties in a bunch. I convinced him to take spin trainin' with you so he doesn't kill himself when he plays fighter pilot." He hesitated and cleared his throat.

"Uh, there's one other thing: Sometimes he freezes on the controls in sticky situations. I had to punch him in the face once. Almost broke his jaw. He's afraid to fly with me now."

"Geez, Bart. I thought we were friends. What the hell?"

"I wouldn't have asked you to train him if I thought for one second you couldn't handle him. Besides, I knew you'd get a major charge out of flyin' his airplane. Truth be told, we're all wanna-be fighter pilots at heart." He grinned and winked.

I crossed my arms. "What kind of airplane does he have?"

"He just taxied in. It's right out there." Bart pointed at the airplane as the throaty rumble of its powerful engine rattled the window.

A shiny black Italian-built SIAI Marchetti SF260, like the one in the Bond movie, *Quantum of Solace,* glistened on the tarmac in the bright sunshine. A middle-aged man with thinning hair stood next to the fighter/attack/trainer airplane. Important-looking patches adorned the upper front and sleeves of his gray flight suit. The one-piece jumpsuit was unzipped halfway down his chest, revealing three heavy gold chains on hairy bare skin.

I focused on the airplane. "Do I see machine guns mounted on the hard points under the wings?"

"Yep, he spent a fortune on that airplane," Bart said. "A U.S. senator buddy helped him get the permits so he could keep the wing-mounted guns. It's that plane from the 007 movie. He bought two thousand acres in southern Florida so he can play military pilot and blast away at ground targets. I figured you'd want in on that deal."

"You figured right. Sign me up." I headed for the door. "Come out and introduce me."

A few minutes later, we stood by the sleek Italian fighter known as the Ferrari of reciprocating engine aircraft. Underneath the glass canopy, side-by-side seats featured dual controls with sticks. Unlike most airplanes, the instrument panel was designed for the pilot to fly from the right seat with the copilot or instructor on the left side.

Bart turned to me. "Sharon, meet your student, Grant Garrison." He looked at the man. "Grant, this here's the lady instructor I told you about. She'll get you squared away in the Marchetti. Give you trainin' in aerodynamic stalls and spin recoveries so you don't auger in when you're up messin' around with your new toy."

Grant ran his eyes over my curves and paused a bit too long on my breasts. "Whoa, Bart, how am I supposed to concentrate on flying with a gorgeous babe like her sitting next to me?" He flashed me his million-dollar smile.

"You're not a playboy when you're on *my* clock. I expect you to obey rule number one of Sharon's flight instruction." I locked on his eyes with a don't-mess-with-me expression.

He stopped grinning. "What's rule number one?"

"Never touch the flight instructor."

"Any other rules?"

"If I tell you to do something in the airplane, do it immediately and ask questions later," I said. "Handle the controls as if you're playing a rare Stradivarius or making love to a sensitive, delicate lady. In other words, learn to have what is known in the pilot world as good hands. That pretty much covers it."

"So, if I'm good in bed, I'll be a good pilot?"

"You can learn to apply the same skills to flying, but there's a vast difference between *thinking* you're good in bed and *being* good in bed. I'll know the truth as soon as I see how you handle the airplane." My smug smile warned him he couldn't fool me.

Grant frowned. "Damn, Bart, what are you trying to do to me?"

"I'm tryin' to keep you alive so you can enjoy your new toy. Swallow your pride and do what the lady says." Bart nodded in my direction, turned, and strode to the building.

"Bart said your wing-mounted weapons are operational. Is that true?" I asked.

He shrugged. "I have federal permits for them. My firing range is southwest of here."

"Great, but the weapons aren't loaded now, are they?"

"Yeah, always, but relax, the arming switch has a safety cover. I'll show you where it is." He pointed at it.

We did the preflight inspection, climbed aboard, closed the canopy, and taxied out for the engine and control checks before takeoff. During the takeoff run and climb, it became obvious he was no Don Juan in the boudoir.

He yanked back hard on the stick, and the Marchetti leaped into the sky too steeply. He over-corrected with forward stick, and I rose up against the five-point harness. The turn away from the traffic pattern felt jerky and abrupt. His firm grip on the stick had whitened his fingers.

"I have the airplane." I took the control stick and rudder pedals as Grant released the controls on his side.

Flying the airplane gave him a break and made me smile.

"Sit back and relax while I fly us to the practice area. If you're tense on the controls, the airplane will respond stiffly. Close your eyes and pretend you're a world champion Formula One driver. Every move you make in your race car is accomplished with a smooth, fluid motion as you finesse your way around the race course. The car becomes an extension of your body as you speed over the pavement and hug the corners." I watched the tension melt away on his face.

He smiled and opened his eyes. "I feel calmer. What would you like me to do now?"

"We're at 4,500 feet, so we have plenty of recovery room if you mess up. I'd like you to practice turning right and left so smoothly that I can't feel the turns."

I reluctantly surrendered the controls and closed my eyes. "Don't forget to check for traffic before you turn. Start with shallow-banked turns, then increase the bank angle after you get the feel of it. Remember to ease back the stick to maintain altitude in the turns."

I focused on the sensations from the airplane's movements. It wasn't long before I felt the familiar vibrations of an aerodynamic stall from loss of lift. I opened my eyes and watched the nose fall through the horizon. The monoplane entered a spin to the left.

The ground spun beneath us as we corkscrewed downward

at 1500 feet per minute. My student froze with a deer-in-the-headlights look. Every second brought us closer to death.

I pulled the throttle back to idle. Unable to wrest the controls from him, my next move gave new meaning to the term "joystick" as I employed my virtual sex flight instruction method.

I slid my right hand along the inside of his left thigh—better than dying or stabbing him with my great-great-grandmother's giant hat pin—and yelled, "Grant, stop! You're squeezing me (the control stick) too hard, and I'm falling off the bed. Quick, let go and stretch out your right foot (full right rudder) to catch me. Good. Place your feet on either side of me (neutral rudder). Much better. Relax your hands. Good. Slide your left hand up over my right breast (full throttle) and pull me close to you with your right hand (stick back). Ummm, much better."

We were out of the spin and regaining altitude. Disaster averted by the illusion of hot sex. Male flight students were so predictable, but most flight instructors were men. This method usually only worked with a male student/female instructor. I should patent my virtual sex flight instruction method. Male students would improve their skills not only in airplanes but also in bedrooms. A win-win.

I glanced at Grant—his mouth and eyes were wide open.

I squeezed his knee. "Level off here and throttle back to cruise power."

"What happened? I remember tensing up when the airplane stalled. Must've passed out. I dreamed we were having sex." He wiped his sweaty hands on his pants.

"It wasn't a dream. You froze on the controls during a spin. I had to do something drastic, or we would've died." I pulled out a long antique hat pin from my bag. "If my virtual sex method had failed, you'd have been screaming and pulling this out of your thigh."

He looked horrified.

"Hey, it's better than our airplane becoming a dirt dart."

"Damn, woman, I hope you never have to stab me with that thing. Sex talk is much better." He leaned against the side rail.

"Relax, I only stab students as a last resort." I gave him a friendly jab with my right elbow and winked. "Besides, I'd hate to get blood on the Italian stallion."

He grinned and puffed out his chest. Then he looked confused and turned to me. "I'm not Italian."

"I'm talking about the airplane."

"Oh." He slumped down.

"I'll try to squeeze in a few touch-and-goes when we return to the airport, but first we'll practice aerodynamic stalls, spins, and recoveries until you overcome your fears and feel comfortable with the maneuvers."

I tucked the hat pin into the map compartment.

He covered his left thigh with his hand. "First, I think we should deal with my fear of giant hat pins."

I figured Grant's progress would be slow, so I used a stick-and-carrot approach.

"Whenever you do something exceptional in the airplane, we'll do a strafing run over your snake-infested swamplands."

His eyes lit up. "This'll be fun. I hired an explosives expert to rig ground targets to explode when the Marchetti's bullets hit them."

***

Surprisingly, Grant's skills improved quickly. Soon we were making regular trips to the target area.

I glanced at him as we turned in for another strafing run. "I must admit diving on targets and blowing stuff up is loads of fun, and it pisses off the tree huggers—another win-win." I laughed.

After demolishing a target, he pulled up and executed the victory roll I'd taught him. "Woo hoo!"

"Good thing you're rich. High-caliber machine-gun ammo and ground explosives must cost a fortune." I grinned.

His face filled with joy on every strafing run. So did mine. Fun times. Blowing stuff up was a great stress reliever.

"Hey, Sharon, my wife said my performance in the

bedroom has improved since I began flight training with you." He looked pleased with himself.

"Good hands are good hands, regardless of where they're employed." I turned and gave him a high five.

Another win for my virtual sex flight instruction.

CHILI AND HUGO

D.M. Littlefield

Chili, in the arms of her master, tilted her head and listened, wagging her tail.

"Joe's uncle died and left Hugo in our care," Tina said to Chili. "We're bringing Hugo home today. Be nice to him. He's sad because he misses Uncle Tony. Now guard the house while we're gone."

Joe sighed. "My love, I'll admit Chili understands everything we say. She has the brains, but not the brawn. She's a four-pound Chihuahua with a chili-pepper attitude and the bravado of a Doberman. Instead of telling her to guard the house, teach her to dial 9-1-1."

Tina nodded. "That's a great idea."

Joe rolled his eyes.

After they left, Chili thought, *I'll be nice to Hugo, but I'll let him know right away I'm the boss.*

When her masters came home an hour later, she ran to welcome them. Tina picked her up and hugged her. "I want you to meet Hugo. He's a Saint Bernard." She sat Chili down in front of Hugo.

Chili backed up and leaned her head back to get a full view of humongous Hugo, who must've weighed more than two hundred pounds. Hugo's droopy face looked puzzled as he plopped his massive body down and stared at her. His big nose quivered as he sniffed her and drooled.

Chili raised her hackles and circled his body, barking that he must obey her because this was her territory.

Hugo didn't care who was boss. He'd lost his beloved master. Nothing else mattered.

Joe had hoped acquiring a dog bigger than his brother's dog would stop Tim from hassling him about having an ineffective runt like Chili. Tim was a policeman and patrolled their neighborhood in a K-9 vehicle with his German shepherd partner, Rex. Joe was disappointed Hugo was such a wuss that it appeared even tiny Chili was going to boss him around.

Chili followed Joe and Hugo into the kitchen and slipped in the puddle that had pooled from Hugo's jowls as he lapped up a bowl of water. Chili thought, *I'll teach him not to be so sloppy, but I'll wait until he feels more at home.*

Hugo lumbered to the back door, turned around three times before lying down, and heaved a sigh as he rested his head on his front paws and closed his eyes.

***

A week later, Hugo was still mourning and not eating. Chili worried about him. She took mouthfuls of food out of his bowl and dropped it in front of him. When he ignored her, she barked at him. Hugo closed his eyes and covered his ears with his paws. Chili continued her shrill barking next to his ear until he ate all the food.

Chili whined, "Good boy," and licked his nose.

Eventually Hugo perked up. Chili entertained him with tricks. She sat up, begged, danced on her hind feet, and rolled over to play dead.

Hugo was impressed, so she taught him some of her tricks. Then they showed Tina and Joe as Chili barked commands to Hugo. Chili was proud of him, and Tina and Joe looked happy to see Hugo felt at home now.

A month before Hugo arrived, Chili was attacked by Tiger, the mean tomcat who lived next door. Chili was afraid to walk under the tree in her fenced back yard because the big cat had jumped down from the tree to bite and claw Chili into a bloody mess. Tina had rescued her and rushed her to the vet.

When Chili heard Tiger and his owners were home from vacation, she planned her revenge. After Tina and Joe left for work, Chili softly whined her tale of woe to Hugo and enlisted his help. Hugo shook his giant head, flinging drool, before plodding toward the enlarged dog door.

Chili raced underneath him and pawed Hugo's front leg. "Not yet. You stay here and watch. When I bark, rush out and grab Tiger by the scruff of his neck and shake the stuffing out of him."

Hugo nodded his head and panted, eager for action.

Chili whined, "Good boy." As she pushed through the dog door, she caught Tiger's scent. Chili nonchalantly sniffed dandelions as she ambled toward the tree. The branches rustled as Tiger leaped down a few feet behind her. Chili jumped around to face him.

Tiger pressed his ears flat on his head as he crouched and hissed. His tail slowly twitched back and forth as he prepared to pounce. Terrified, Chili yipped.

Hugo bounded out with his tongue hanging out, splattering drool to the wind. He grabbed Tiger by his neck and shook him. Tiger yowled and clawed the air, trying to scratch Hugo.

"This is a warning," Chili snarled, trembling. "Next time it could be fatal. Stay out of my yard!" Chili looked up at Hugo and barked, "Send Tiger home."

Hugo swung his head side to side gathering momentum and flung Tiger over the fence into his backyard. Chili hopped onto Hugo's back and posed like a queen surveying her domain. *With my brain and Hugo's brawn, we make a formidable pair.*

Hugo proudly trotted around the perimeter of their yard, his tail held high like a victory flag.

That evening they heard Tina and Joe lamenting the daytime burglaries in their neighborhood. Tina worried Chili couldn't defend herself, and Hugo was too gentle to hurt an intruder.

The next day, Chili briefed Hugo on her plan in case of a

burglary.

Hugo panted and looked like he was smiling as he nodded. "Life is more exciting since I met you."

Chili tilted her tiny head and whined, "Are you the strong silent type? I've never heard you growl, snarl, or bark. Can you?"

Hugo growled a deep rumble.

"Good, but it'll be scarier if you snarl, show your big bone-crushing teeth, and then bark. Snarl like this." She curled back her lips, showing her small teeth. "Okay, big boy, show me all you've got."

Hugo looked ferocious as he got in her face, snarling and baring his teeth. He inhaled deeply and let out a powerful roar, like a mighty lion.

She shook off his drool. "Perfect! We'll take turns patrolling the house. I'll go first while you rest. If you hear anything, don't bark. Come and get me. I'll do the same."

Hugo dozed as he waited his turn. Chili heard the glass window in the dining room shatter. She raced to Hugo, shoved her nose under his floppy right ear, and growled. Hugo jerked to attention and crept behind the dining room door where he waited for Chili's attack signal.

Chili hid under the coffee table and watched the masked burglar climb over the window sill with a large sack. She trembled with anger as he snatched Tina's cherished silver wedding tray and started filling his sack with their DVD collection. He took her favorite, *Beverly Hills Chihuahua,* from the bottom shelf, where Chili could fetch it to Tina to play it for her.

Enraged, Chili barked and scrambled to bite him. While the burglar tried to shake her off his leg, Hugo bolted from behind the door and snarled. He looked like Wonder Dog when he slammed the burglar facedown to the floor and smashed his nose. The burglar lost consciousness as Hugo pinned him under his weight. Chili pulled the eye mask off the burglar by breaking the elastic string as she sat on the back of his head.

Five minutes later, Joe opened the back door.

Tina called out, "Chili! Hugo!"

A sharp yip, a deep woof, and a faint moan answered her.

Joe and Tina raced into the living room and stared in disbelief.

Howling with laughter, Joe pulled out his cell phone. "Unbelievable! Tim will need proof to believe this." He snapped a picture of Hugo sprawled over the burglar and drooling on his neck. Chili clenched the mask in her jaws as she perched on the burglar's head, swishing her tail side to side like a windshield wiper.

Joe texted the photo to Tim before calling him. "As you can see, my dogs have caught the day burglar. When you come to get him, bring the paramedics but leave your partner, Rex, in the car."

EXPENSIVE MISTAKE

D.M. Littlefield

After a wonderful fifteen-day cruise from the Port of Miami, my daughter drove us to her home on Singer Island. My throat hurt, my eyes burned, and my head ached, so Sharon asked me to stay with her. I declined, wanting to get horizontal in pajamas in my own bed.

Sharon left my car running to keep me warm while she unloaded her luggage from the trunk. I promised to phone her upon my arrival home.

When I drove into my parking space, I burst into a sneezing frenzy. I reached into my purse for tissues and retrieved my house key attached to my second set of car keys. The cold front's howling north wind forced me to lean forward as I hauled my luggage twenty yards to the house. Sneezing intermittently, I turned on a heating pad in my bed, set the house thermostat to seventy-eight, walked outside for the rest of my luggage, and locked the car with the remote.

I phoned my daughter to report I had arrived home safe and sound. Well safe, but sound was iffy. After donning my warm pajamas and knitted foot warmers at 8:00 p.m., I snuggled under a pile of blankets with only my nose sticking out.

Much later, my sleep-fogged brain heard an annoying, persistent ringing. Oh, the phone. Simply reaching outside my warm blankets to answer the call made me sneeze violently.

I blew my nose and croaked, "Allo."

"Your car is running," a man said.

I turned the light on and blinked at the clock: one-thirty in the morning. I sneezed and blew my nose again.

"My car is running?"

"Yes, ma'am."

That's impossible. I'd never leave my car running.

I sneezed and asked, "Is id a gold Mercury parked in Golden Lakes?"

"Yes."

"And the motor is running?"

The man emitted a deep sigh. "Lady, I'm parked behind your car in a security patrol car with the yellow light flashing. Although I'm not a licensed mechanic, the exhaust coming from the tailpipe is a significant clue the engine is running."

Apparently, he wasn't accustomed to conversing with the mentally challenged. Catching burglars was probably preferable to dealing with a dimwit. I rushed to bundle up and trotted outside.

I thanked him profusely and croaked, "I'b sorry. I'b sick and nod thinking clearly."

My car had been slurping gasoline at $3.59 a gallon for almost seven hours. Instead of carrying my embarrassment in silence, I decided to share it with the world and give others something to smile about and a chance to feel superior.

You're welcome.

AUTHOR'S NOTE: My brother died December 12, 2009, while approaching the runway on Bing Island in the Bahamas. The aircraft veered sharply to the left when he slumped onto the control stick after a heart attack. It cartwheeled across the shallow water beside the runway and broke into three pieces. Larry died instantly. The crash was witnessed by his friends who were waiting for a ride back to Florida.

His loss devastated me. I couldn't write for nine months, and I'll never stop missing him. I felt betrayed. The sky and the sea had always been my two favorite places, but I couldn't enjoy either one after his accident. Pouring my emotions into the following poem helped me start the healing process.

BETRAYED

S.L. Menear

The sea is a cruel mistress
So is her sister, the sky

They killed my brother
I'll never know why

My heart is broken
And always will be

Betrayed by my friends
The sky and the sea

Anchors aweigh, Larry
R.I.P. with valor and glory

ONCE UPON A TIME

D.M. Littlefield

Jack used the tip of his cane to push the elevator button in their assisted living facility while holding onto Ted's walker. "See, my hand/eye coordination is still great. I did it on the first try."

"Hey, you don't have to tell me that. I see your coordination every day as you hold hands with one lady and wink at another." Ted rattled his walker. "You shouldn't have signed me up for this fiasco without my permission. I wanted to watch my favorite TV programs today."

"Quit grumbling. You should mingle more with our neighbors. The women outnumber the men more than twenty to one here." Jack smiled. "It's almost like living in a harem."

"What happened to Mary, your latest love? I've seen you with a different woman almost every evening after dinner."

"We broke up because she wanted a long-term commitment. I like playing the field."

"I can see why you don't want to be tied down at ninety-three, but if you keep playing the field like this, you'll end up planted in it."

"Ted, I see life as a glass half full; you see it as half empty. I'm enjoying what time I have left."

"I was enjoying television until you dragged me to this Adopt-A-Grandparent Day. You owe me big time for this."

Jack and Ted were escorted to big comfortable chairs in separate sections of the library, as were other volunteer residents. They were each handed a book of fairy tales and told to choose one to read to the children.

Ted scowled as the kindergarten teacher brought two boys and two girls forward. "Children, this is Grandpa Ted. He's going to read a fairytale to you. Say hello and tell him your name."

A dark-haired boy with glasses stepped forward and held out his hand. "Hello, I'm Tommy. Are you a professional reader?"

"No, I'm a professional TV watcher." Ted shook his hand and looked into Tommy's inquisitive, bright-blue eyes. *Just my luck to get stuck with little Albert Einstein.*

Tommy sat on the floor and stared at him.

A little girl with red hair and freckles shook his hand. "Hello, I'm Becky. Can you take your teeth out like my grandpa does?"

"No, I still have my real teeth." Ted shook her hand.

Becky tilted her head and focused on Ted's face. "Wouldn't you like some new ones?"

"No, I like the ones I have. Sit down, please."

A little blond boy with big brown eyes stepped forward. "Hello, I'm Jimmy. I like to ride my bicycle. Do you like to ride your walker?"

"I don't ride my walker. I push it."

"Could I ride on it while you push it?"

"Not today. You're here to listen to a story."

"Bummer," Jimmy said as he sat next to Tommy.

"Hello, I'm Emily," a little girl with green eyes and long blond curls said. "I want to sit on your lap while you read the story."

Ted scowled. "I don't think so. Please sit on the floor with your little friends."

"My grandpa let me sit on his lap when he read stories to me before he went to Heaven. Why won't you let me sit on your lap? Don't you like me?" She began to cry.

Just when things couldn't get worse. "Please don't cry. I like you. You can sit on my lap and turn the pages for me." He helped her up. "Everybody listen now while I read the story. Once upon a time—"

"What time?" Tommy said.

Ted frowned. "What do you mean, what time?"

"You know—what time? Was it eight o'clock in the morning?"

"It was long, long ago when they didn't have clocks." Ted sighed. "They had daytime and nighttime. It was daytime. So, once upon a daytime, a handsome prince was riding his horse through a forest when—"

"What color horse was it?" Tommy asked.

"The story doesn't say." Ted raised his eyebrows.

"Make it a white horse," Becky said. "My Barbie doll has a white horse."

"Barbie's lucky. Once upon a daytime, a handsome prince was riding his white horse through a forest—"

"What was the prince's name?" Tommy asked.

"The story doesn't say that either." Ted removed his glasses and rubbed his eyes.

"I want you to name him Prince Ken. Ken is Barbie's boyfriend," Becky said.

"Any other suggestions before I continue?"

"Why?" Emily asked.

"If I keep getting interrupted, I'll never be able to finish the story."

"You sound cranky. Did you have your nap today?"

"No." *Only God knows how much I'd like one right now.*

"Why?"

"I don't take naps."

"If you did, you wouldn't be cranky."

"OK, I'll take naps from now on. ... Once upon a daytime, handsome Prince Ken was riding his white horse through a forest." Ted looked at their bright little faces and waited.

"When can I turn the page?" Emily asked.

"At this rate, maybe never. I've only read one sentence. May I continue?"

They solemnly nodded.

"There were a lot of wild animals in the forest, but Prince Ken was brave and carried a sword to protect him and his horse."

"What's the horse's name?" Jimmy asked.
"What would you like it to be?"
"Blackie."
"You want to name a white horse Blackie?"
Jimmy nodded.
Ted shook his head. "Whatever. Once upon a daytime, handsome Prince Ken was riding his white horse, named Blackie, through a forest. There were a lot of wild animals in the forest, but the prince was brave and carried a sword to protect him and his horse. The prince heard a voice cry out, 'Save me! Please save me!' Prince Ken raced Blackie toward the voice and found a beautiful princess tied to a tree.

"The princess shouted, 'Please untie me before the wicked witch comes back!' Prince Ken untied her and helped her up onto his horse."

"What was the name of the princess?" Emily asked.
"What do you want her name to be?"
"Emily, like mine."
"Good choice. Prince Ken held onto Princess Emily as they rode back to his castle on Blackie, his white horse. They fell in love, married, and lived happily ever after. The end." *Thank God!*

The children waved to Ted as their teacher led them out of the library. He overheard her ask, "Did you like Grandpa Ted reading to you?"

"I think he needs more practice," Jimmy said.

"I like the names he gave everything," Becky said.

"He's probably better at watching TV," Tommy said.

Emily crossed her arms and said, "I think Grandpa Ted needed a nap."

KILLER SCOTS & HOT CUBANS

S.L. Menear

It had been a year since my brother, Larry, suffered a heart attack while flying and died in a crash in the Bahamas. His sudden death at sixty hit me hard.

I missed him every day.

Mom and I needed an escape from the heartache. We loved cruising and didn't want to be home for Christmas with so many memories of my brother, so we took a fifteen-day holiday cruise covering the Caribbean.

We met people from England on our ship who informed us Scots were aboard. Men in kilts had been sighted! I happened to be writing my first thriller, *Deadstick Dawn,* set primarily in Scotland, so I started searching for the kilted men. I, uh, wanted to verify I'd accurately described the Highlanders.

On the first formal night, I found a handsome Scot in a red, green, and black plaid kilt with a black waistcoat that stopped at his trim mid-section, which contrasted nicely with his broad shoulders. As to the debate of what men wear beneath their kilts, he assured me no self-respecting Scot would ever wear anything underneath. A fancy leather pouch, called a sporran, hung from his waist in front, and his patent leather brogues were laced over his white knee socks. I tried to take his picture, but my cursed camera wouldn't work.

The next formal night, I strolled through the casino in my sapphire gown and met the killer Scots dressed in their fancy kilts. They were bigger and broader than the first Scot and looked like real Highlanders. Their daggers, known as skean dhu, were slipped inside their knee socks, as per tradition. Their friends called them the killer Scots because they were always armed.

I thought it was because of their killer good looks. I've no idea how they made it through port security with the daggers. They cheerfully reaffirmed the fact that they wear nothing beneath their kilts.

One of the Highlanders, six-foot-three and quite handsome, said, "Come wie me to my stateroom, lassie, and I'll show ye."

Scots are very friendly. I must've looked like I was thinking it over. My conservative mother gave me her don't-you-dare-do-that glare.

Big sigh.

Another man in their group was a royal historian, who helped me with suggestions for titled characters in my planned short story. It featured descendants of King Arthur and Queen Guinevere in a brief, modern murder mystery set in Palm Beach titled, *Guinevere's Lance.*

Later that evening, romance ignited on the upper aft deck. After a few glasses of Pessimist, a delicious blended red wine, with dinner and the show, I felt daring as I made my way to the top level of the aft deck. My plan was to savor a quality Cuban cigar under the full moon over the sparkling Caribbean Sea after Mom had turned in for the night.

It was quite windy in the designated smoking area of the afterdeck. I stood alone with my back to the wind and inserted the snipped end of the Cohiba between my lips. I held the lighter under the tip and started flicking my Bic. The wind blew it out, possibly saving my long blond hair from catching fire.

Before I had time to decide what to do next, a tall, insanely handsome man with dark hair, tanned skin, and broad shoulders appeared and held his high-tech mini lighter up to my cigar. As I looked into his moonlit electric-blue eyes and the tiny blue flame of his James Bond cigar lighter, I was mesmerized into a pheromone-induced brain fog.

After twenty years of working in the cockpit with handsome airline pilots, I thought I had become immune to their power. Maybe that only applied to American men.

Next thing I knew I was sucking *waaay* too hard on my Cohiba. Cigars weren't meant to be inhaled, especially by non-smokers like me. My cigar was definitely lit, and so was I. When I recovered from my coughing fit, the handsome stranger had disappeared.

Real smooth, Sharon.

So there I was, alone again in the moonlight, windblown hair whispering about my face, when it occurred to me that the smart people must've found a better place to enjoy their cigars. I turned the corner to the non-windy starboard side and saw the handsome stranger sitting alone.

He smiled, introduced himself, and invited me to join him. Renaldo was smoking a cigar and sipping a glass of blended Chilean reds from a bottle of Almaviva wine. He offered me a glass. Nothing goes better with a fine Cuban cigar than an equally fine man and a smooth red wine.

Renaldo lit my cigar—and me—again. Turned out he was from Cuba and a cigar aficionado. He said Cuban cigars were rolled in leaves grown in soil unique to Cuba, which gave them their mild, smooth flavor, and Cohibas were among the very best.

I sipped the sensuous wine and listened to his deep, mellifluous voice as I gently sucked on my Cuban. Moonlight bathed the upper aft deck, which was deserted in the post-midnight hour.

Our mutual attraction caught fire as our cigars burned out. Renaldo kissed me with a fierce passion, and I responded with reckless abandon. We lost control during our steamy lounge-chair sex and ended up in a heart-pounding roll on the deck.

In my fertile imagination.

That man is definitely going in my next novel.

I wish I could report a torrid romance ensued, or at least some hot sex, but no. He was married to dark and exotic Esmeralda. I spied them together in the glass elevator the next day. She was just the sort of wife I would expect a man like him to have. Even so, I'll never forget my Cuban cigar with Renaldo.

I love Celebrity Cruises. Their upscale ships offer enough crew to cater to my every whim. They keep everything so clean and neat I joked if I got up in the middle of the night to use the head, I'd find my bed made when I returned. The food is delicious, the shows superb, and there's a plethora of adults-only havens, such as the indoor solarium pool with soothing music and a gentle waterfall. I wish I could live there.

Our ship, the *Eclipse*, boasted plenty of fancy bars, including the elegant Michael's Club that specialized in fine whisky. Their most expensive single-malt Scotch, Glenglassaugh, was a whopping $170 per shot! Must be very good indeed. I went there to research the best whisky for the rich Scottish laird in *Deadstick Dawn*. At those prices, I was glad I preferred wine.

The cruise ended too soon for me. I was in no hurry to return to reality. If I had unlimited funds, I'd book a permanent suite on that ship.

Alas, now I'm home and missing the ship, the killer Scots, and an extraordinary Cuban.

Oh, well, back to the writing world for me. "*Hola*, Renaldo!" Let the fantasies abound.

OUCH!

D.M. Littlefield

"Ouch! Why did you pinch me?"

"I saw you staring at that young woman. You were undressing her with your eyes."

"I was not!"

"Yes, you were, Tom! I can read you like a book after sixty years of marriage."

"Yeah, well then you must be reading the book upside down. I was looking at her because she was already undressed. She shouldn't show herself like that here in the shopping mall. Her skirt—if you can call it a skirt—barely covers her behind. That girl is showing a lot more skin than fabric, leaving nothing to the imagination. Although she has one thing going for her that is commendable."

"Humph! What's that?"

"You can't accuse her of false advertising. She's up front with everything she's selling."

"Oh, you're an expert on that. On our third date, I remember you flirting with a floozy waitress in a tight skirt. She was up front too. Way up front. I thought her blouse buttons would pop off any minute."

"Awww, geez, Ellen, you bring that up every time we have a disagreement. You can recall what I did sixty years ago, but you can't remember to take your pills every day."

"I just want you to know I've still got my eyes on you. I

don't want you running off with some floozy."

"Humph! I can't run anywhere. I'm in a damn wheelchair."

"Well, Ginny Greenblatt's wheelchair doesn't slow her down. I saw her flirting with you yesterday."

"You're crazy! She was just asking me a question. Who's gonna flirt with a crippled old man like me?"

"A crippled old woman like Ginny, that's who!"

"I'm fed up with your nagging, Ellen. My hearing aids are going in my pocket right now, and then I'm switching my wheelchair to max speed."

"You wouldn't dare do that! You know I can't push my walker as fast as your motorized wheelchair. Hey, wait for me!"

"Eat my dust, Ellen!"

THE BOYS

D.M. Littlefield

Pete Winston settled in a bar stool in the quiet bar. "I need a double Scotch."

The bartender arched his eyebrows. "Rough day?"

Pete nodded. "It was crazy. You wouldn't believe it."

"After years of tending bar, I could tell you stories *you* wouldn't believe. But hey, my job is to listen and take your money. We're alone, so lay it on me."

He gulped his drink and chuckled. "My job is to listen and take people's money too. I'm a marriage counselor. I thought I'd heard it all, but this case was a doozy." He slid his glass in circles on the mahogany bar. "A very attractive woman in her thirties came to see me and said her husband is a prominent building contractor. He objects to how she's raising their adopted three-year-old boys and has threatened to divorce her and take custody of them."

The bartender poured Pete more Scotch. "What does she do?"

He sipped the whiskey. "She talks baby talk to them, says they're so adorable she can't help herself, and thinks her husband is jealous. She said she loves her husband and doesn't want a divorce."

The bartender wiped the bar. "So, what did you tell her?"

"I told her to have her husband make an appointment with me. I saw him the next day. The guy looks like the actor who played Rocky in the movies."

"Sylvester Stallone?"

"Yeah, only her husband is much taller. He said his wife is a former Las Vegas showgirl. He agreed to the adoptions if she let him choose who they adopted. To be fair, he let her name them. He was mad as hell when she picked Reginald and Rodney. He wanted masculine names like Max and Mike."

"The guy has a point," the bartender said, leaning against the polished wood countertop.

"I agreed with him. He thought she was turning their boys into pansies. She paints their nails pink! He threatened her with a divorce when she tied pink lace bandanas around their necks to match their nails. The guy loves his wife, but she's driving him nuts with the boys."

The bartender arched his brows. "So, did you solve their problem?"

"Yeah, I had the whole family come in today. I had to hold a handkerchief over my mouth to hide my laughter when I saw their *boys*." He held up his cell phone.

The bartender gaped at the picture and roared with laughter.

Two black Great Danes with diamond-studded gold collars and pink-lace bandanas matching their pink nails sat together.

"When I recovered, I drew up a legal document. After a lot of heated discussions, they both signed it. It states no nail polish. Only cotton bandannas in a masculine print are allowed. Their gold-jeweled collars will only be worn at home. The dogs will wear their new spiked collars at all other times. Rodney's name is now Rocky, and Reginald is now Rex."

The bartender grinned and gave Pete a high five. "Well done!"

GUINEVERE'S LANCE

S. L. Menear

I was a trust fund baby, but that didn't mean I didn't need my police detective job. Twelve years ago, I was a college freshman at the University of Miami when a murderer carjacked my family. His ski mask exposed only his evil eyes and maniacal grin. He ordered us out of the car and laughed when he shot us. I watched my parents die beside me in the street.

The killer was never caught. Grief transformed me into a crusader for justice. I changed my major to criminology and earned a master's degree in forensic science.

I spent the past seven years on patrol duty with the Wellington Police Department in Palm Beach County, Florida. On my days off, I trolled for the killer in my diamond-white Mercedes roadster with my Glock 40 cocked. The badge was my ticket to justice. The flashy car was the bait. Coworkers assumed I was just a spoiled rich girl. They didn't know what drove me.

Three days ago, I became the newest detective on the force. On Sunday, my day off, I turned onto Pierson Road and glanced at my watch. Uncle Clive and Aunt Elizabeth, the duke and duchess of Colchester, England, had invited me for cocktails and dinner at The Seafood Bar in The Breakers hotel. One of my favorite restaurants, the oceanfront view was similar to a dining room on a posh cruise ship.

The late-afternoon drive from my home near the polo

fields in Wellington to Palm Beach was proceeding ahead of schedule when my cell phone rang.

Detective Rod Malone's slightly slurred voice boomed into my ear. "Gwen, get your butt to the Polo Club pronto. We've got a DB in a Rolls on the southeast side."

My boss since Friday was a man of few words. Just as well, considering he never had anything good to say to me.

I reversed direction, turned into the tailgating area, and spotted a Rolls-Royce Corniche, top down, parked beside the polo field under a banyan tree surrounded by yellow crime-scene tape. An elaborate party tent crowded with elite residents from Palm Beach anchored the site. The aromas of grilled meat and horses filled the air.

I weaved my Mercedes through the tailgaters and parked beside a squad car. An approaching siren overpowered the thundering hooves, drunken revelers, and the loudspeakers booming the play-by-play calls.

After one whiff of Rod's breath, I knew he'd been hitting the sauce. I took a step back.

"What? It's Sunday. I was off duty watching the play-offs when the call came in." He checked out my black Dior cocktail dress and five-inch Manolo stilettos. "Hot date, eh, Gwen?"

I rolled my eyes and walked closer to the handsome guy who appeared to be sleeping in the Rolls. Early forties with a blond crew cut, fit physique, and mirrored aviator sunglasses.

"Are you sure he's dead?" I said without thinking. "Maybe he drank too much." I pulled on latex gloves and nudged his shoulder. Big mistake. His body fell like a rag doll over the center console, and his sunglasses slipped off, revealing dull, sightless blue eyes.

Rod shook his balding head. "Real smooth, Gwen. The ME is going to have your ass. Didn't your fancy finishing school teach you not to touch dead bodies?"

Big sigh. Blushing, I pulled back my long auburn hair and focused on the body and the convertible's interior. No signs of a struggle. No visible marks on the body. No obvious cause of death.

Rod thrust his hands on his hips. "I should've known this

case is too high profile for a newbie. Jet Donley is a Palm Beacher with deep pockets. The press will be all over this."

"Jet Donley? Isn't he the bastard who raped those girls last year?" I Googled him on my iPhone.

"Expensive lawyer got him off." He stared at the body. "Guess too much high living did him in."

When the medical examiner arrived, Rod stepped aside.

The ME pulled on his gloves and opened the car door. He glanced at Rod. "Is this how you found him?"

"Our brand-new detective knocked him over." Rod glared at me. "He was found behind the wheel with his body slumped back against the seat. His guests assumed he was taking a nap. Eventually, they needed to pop the trunk to get to the Champagne cooler. That's when they realized he didn't have a pulse and called 9-1-1."

The short, gray-haired man turned to me. "What the hell were you thinking?" He turned back to the body. "Never mind. Probably natural causes anyway." He pierced the body's liver area with a device that resembled a meat thermometer. "Yep, died two hours ago. Is he high profile?"

Rod nodded. "Jet Donley. Big money. We'll need an expedited autopsy."

Several news vans raced up to be first on the scene. An overeager young female reporter stuck her microphone in my face. "What happened to Jet Donley? Did one of his alleged victims exact justice?"

Rod gave me a let's-see-you-handle-this look, so I jumped into the fray. "Mr. Donley died two hours ago in his car. An autopsy will determine the cause of death. Please step back so the coroner can remove the body. Thank you."

Cameras flashed behind me as the ME zipped the body bag over Jet's face. After he was wheeled away, I turned to my partner. "Where's the crime-scene truck? The Rolls should be swept for evidence."

"I already took lots of pictures. There's no crime here. No sense wasting police resources. I'm heading in to file the report."

After calling my aunt and uncle to apologize for missing

cocktail hour, I searched the Rolls, hoping to find a significant clue Rod had missed. No such luck. I wiped the soft dirt off my heels and fired up my flashy bait car.

Thirty minutes later, I turned onto the stately entrance drive for The Breakers. Majestic royal palms flanked the wide road, which split near the front of the hotel to circle a massive fountain. Under the portico, a valet briskly opened my door and handed me a claim ticket. I straightened my dress and breezed into the magnificent lobby.

The hotel was a picture of Old World elegance with thirty-foot ceilings adorned in unique artistic designs. My heels clacked on the polished marble corridor as I walked south through the lobby and turned east into the hall to The Seafood Bar. My elderly aunt and uncle were at a table overlooking the Atlantic Ocean.

"Auntie Liz and Uncle Clive, it's good to see you." I leaned over and kissed Aunt Liz on the cheek. When Uncle Clive rose to pull out my chair, I hugged him. "How long will you be in Palm Beach?"

My aunt smoothed her elegant white hair. "We're here for the season, my dear Gwen. I do hope we'll see you often. Is your new job keeping you busy?"

"Not until today. A wealthy Palm Beacher died at the polo match. Did you know Jet Donley?"

The waiter poured me a glass of Opus One, a sumptuous red wine blend, and presented the menu. Life was good in the company of a wealthy duke and duchess.

"We sipped vintage Krug Clos du Mesnil in his tent this afternoon." Uncle Clive glanced at Aunt Liz. "We left the match early so we'd have plenty of time to relax and dress for dinner. He seemed fine when we left."

His answer surprised me. "Did you know him well?"

"He was quite the womanizer," Aunt Liz said. "You know the type. I wasn't fond of him, but we fulfilled our social obligation. I heard he raped three girls last year and escaped prosecution."

I sipped the red elixir, savoring the delicious blend from the Rothschild and Mondavi vineyards. "They were merely the tip of the iceberg. He should've spent the rest of his life behind bars. Our legal system failed. At least he can't hurt anyone else now."

My uncle swirled the fifty-year-old Macallan whisky in his glass. "Do you think someone seeking justice caused his demise?"

"Murder?" I bit my lip. "There was no evidence of a homicide."

"Considering his crimes, you shouldn't rule out the possibility someone killed him." He downed his drink.

"Enough about Jet." Aunt Liz patted my hand. "You look fit and fabulous in your little black dress."

"Thanks, Aunt Liz. You and Uncle Clive always look regal no matter what you're wearing." I couldn't help thinking I'd never look good in a bikini again with my ugly scar front and center, courtesy of the killer.

She studied my face. "You're thinking about *him*, aren't you?"

"Sorry, I was thinking about my scar." I took a soothing sip of wine. "I'm looking forward to our opera night at the Kravis Center on Tuesday. *Carmen*, isn't it?"

She smiled warmly. "Yes, dear, we have fifth-row orchestra seats. Plan to meet us thirty minutes before for cocktails."

After a pleasant evening, I returned home and checked my messages. Rod had left an update that Jet's family physician reported he'd been in perfect health.

I went to bed and slipped into my recurring nightmare of the carjacking.

***

I spent Monday researching Jet Donley. Rod and I interviewed the rape victims and their parents. They all had alibis.

Jet's death appeared natural until the autopsy report changed everything. Enough sedative was found in his body to drop him into a deep sleep, and a tiny puncture wound was discovered over the right carotid artery on his neck. No poison. No toxic residue at the puncture site.

Another mystery.

Rod ordered me to spend Tuesday interviewing Jet's buddies, which resulted in multiple passes, lewd suggestions, and no clues to help catch the killer.

After a long frustrating day, I relaxed in a hot shower, dressed to the nines, and drove to the Kravis Center in West Palm Beach.

Opera night with the duke and duchess was fun and festive. I enjoyed a superb glass of Blackstone merlot in the lobby bar before the show and another during intermission. My aunt and uncle knew how to work a room and have a good time. I must admit I enjoyed the celebrity treatment with everyone crowding around us.

After the opera, I returned home happy and relaxed. No nightmares this time, thank goodness.

***

The headline in this morning's paper hit me like a sucker punch. Young Palm Beacher, Bradford "Binky" Worthington, was found dead on the terrace of the Kravis Center last night. Binky died during the intermission, according to the coroner. He'd gone outside to smoke a cigar with his cocktail. No obvious cause of death and no signs of foul play. It looked a lot like the Jet Donley case.

How could I have been at the Kravis and not known? The coroner must have hauled him away during Act Three. I called my boss's cell.

"I'm eating breakfast, Gwen. This better be important."

"A rich Palm Beacher was found dead last night at the Kravis Center. Same M.O."

"Check it out. Could be a connection. I'll see you at the station."

I called the lead detective on the case at the West Palm Beach Police Department.

"Detective Palmer here, how may I help you?" a deep voice said.

"I'm Detective Gwen Stuart from the Wellington PD. I

believe your rich dead guy has a lot in common with my rich dead guy. I'd like to compare notes over lunch today somewhere on your turf. How about E.R Bradley's?"

"Sounds good. I'll meet you there at noon."

Three hours later, I walked into E.R. Bradley's fifteen minutes early and snagged a water-view table. The wide part of the Intracoastal Waterway known as Lake Worth sparkled in the noon sunlight. A balmy saltwater breeze out of the east mixed with the pleasing aroma of food in the open-air restaurant. I ordered an ice tea and gambled on a coffee for Detective Palmer.

Feeling confident I could spot a detective among the lunch crowd, I focused on the only man who surveyed the restaurant like a lion hunting prey. The attractive man in his early forties wore gray polyester pants and a sport coat. I waved.

"Thanks for coming, Detective Palmer. Please, call me Gwen." I gave him my best smile and shook his hand. "I ordered coffee for you. Hope that's okay."

His alert eyes glanced at the coffee and focused on my face. "Thanks, Gwen. Call me John. Been on the force long?" He settled across from me.

I smoothed my hair. "I moved up to detective in the Wellington Police Department last week. Jet Donley is my first murder case."

"The rich rapist?" He scanned the menu. "I heard he was found dead in his Rolls."

A waitress appeared with her pad and pencil ready. I ordered the grilled chicken salad, and John got a burger with fries.

He smiled at the waitress and flashed his badge. "We'd appreciate it if you'd expedite our food order."

I waited until the waitress walked away. "He's like your rich dead guy—a relatively young Palm Beacher in good health with no obvious cause of death. He was charged with several rapes but never convicted. The ME found a pinprick in his neck and enough sedative to put him to sleep. We don't know what killed him, but it looks like murder."

John drained his coffee and waved for more. "Binky also

avoided criminal convictions, but his crimes were white collar. He cheated hundreds of middle-class people out of their retirement funds and got off through legal loopholes. He ruined many lives."

"Has the ME finished his autopsy?" I took a long sip of ice tea.

"He worked all night and finished early this morning. Found a pinprick in Binky's neck and a strong sedative in his system. No poison. No cause of death."

My heart pounded as my eyes widened. "Sounds like the same killer. I'd like to know if it was the same sedative. Was it injected into his neck?" I leaned back as our waitress placed my meal in front of me.

John waited until the waitress served him and walked away. "The ME found traces of the sedative in his cocktail glass. I checked out the bartender. He's clean." He bit into his burger.

I swallowed a bite of grilled chicken. "Any chance Binky and Jet were partners in a shady deal with the mob?"

He reached for the ketchup. "Binky hung out with spoiled rich guys. I didn't find any mob connections."

I stabbed my fork into the salad. "The mob angle was a long shot. The deaths are clearly connected. If we can figure out the connection, we'll catch the killer."

"Both men did terrible things and got away with it. That's the connection." He dipped a fry in a small pool of ketchup. "I'm guessing some of their victims got together and hired a pro."

I paused with my fork halfway to my mouth. "A hit man?"

"Gwen, I've worked plenty of murder cases. Both of these have the earmarks of professional hits—deaths that appear natural with no evidence of the killer. I'll ask around if a heavy hitter's in town." He focused on finishing his burger.

"I know I'm new and a little naïve, but I'm confident if we keep digging and go by the book, the killer will end up behind bars along with the people who hired him."

He looked skeptical as he summoned the check. "I hate to burst your bubble, but I've seen lots of bad guys walk, even though the cops did everything by the book. We have no cause of death, no murder weapon, and no suspects. See if you can turn up evidence proving their victims communicated with each other. If we can find a link there, we can squeeze them and see who caves." He dropped money on the table and stood.

I rose to shake his hand. "Thanks for your help. I'll let you know what I find on the victim angle. Call me if you hear anything about a hit man."

***

Disappointment marred the next two weeks. I couldn't find any evidence that the rape and fraud victims had plotted to hire a hit man. John's confidential informant reported no hitters in town. Every investigative avenue dead-ended. Still no cause of death for either man.

I was batting zero when I headed for the grand ballroom at The Breakers on Saturday night. It was the season's most popular charity ball. I was ushered into a seat next to Aunt Liz at the guests-of-honor table.

"Thanks for inviting me. I love seeing all the beautiful gowns." I kissed her cheek.

She squeezed my hand. "Gwen, darling, we wouldn't dream of coming without you. You look lovely in that rose Versace."

Uncle Clive raised his glass of Ruinart Blanc de Blancs Champagne. "To our dear Guinevere, the most beautiful girl in the room." He tapped his glass against mine and Aunt Liz's. "How is your murder case progressing?"

"It's a dead end. Not a good way to launch my detective career." I glanced around the room. "Have you seen my designer friend, Cam Altman?"

She smiled. "Yes, dear, he's floating around the room, fussing over all his clients."

An hour later, I refreshed my lipstick in the ladies-room mirror before returning to the table. My relatives had disappeared, no doubt circulating among the five-hundred guests. Quite the social butterflies. I scanned the room and spotted Cam gliding toward me dressed like eighteenth-century royalty.

"OMG, Gwen, your aunt and uncle are divine! I'd love to get my hands on that extraordinary antique brooch and matching ring the duchess is wearing. I've never seen anything like them—gold and crystal with rubies and sapphires."

"Aunt Liz wears them everywhere." I hugged him. "You look dashing, Cam. What's new in the fashion world?"

"Oh, you know, the other designers kiss my face and stab my back—business as usual. My line of antique-style jewelry and gowns is all the rage." He pointed at a woman in a satin-and-lace cream gown. "That's one of my creations. Isn't it fab?"

"It's lovely. Did you design the matching pearl-and-diamond necklace and earrings?"

"I design all the jewelry for my unique gowns. My clients love dressing like Renaissance royalty." He touched his hand to his lips as he gave me the onceover. "I could make you look like a princess. I see you in an emerald satin gown with a diamond-and-emerald tiara and matching earrings. The corset bodice would accentuate your robust cleavage and help you snare a rich husband. We should do something soon, girlfriend. You're rapidly approaching old-maid territory."

"Thanks, Cam, but I don't want to blow my trust fund on diamonds and emeralds. My new job is my top priority. I'll focus on catching a husband after I collar some major criminals."

"Oh, Gwennie, I know who you're hunting. He's long gone, dear. Forget him and enjoy life. Your parents would want you to move on."

"And let that murderer destroy more families? Never. I'll get him. You'll see. But first I have to catch the person who killed Jet Donley and Binky Worthington. I don't want to fail on my first case."

Cam shook his head and scanned the room. "Here comes the duchess. I'll have another chance to gush over her jewelry."

Aunt Liz beamed and clasped his left arm. "Cam, darling, you simply must design a gown for Gwen. Your creations are superb."

"We were just discussing that very thing. Unfortunately,

your niece is more interested in catching criminals than a husband." He focused on her brooch. "Your jewelry fascinates me. May I remove your brooch for a closer look?"

She placed her hand over the large antique pin. "Sorry, darling, Lloyds of London has strict rules. It must remain on my person or locked in my safe if I wish to keep my insurance. The brooch and ring are centuries-old heirlooms."

Cam glanced over my shoulder. "Oooo, hottie alert! Check out Mr. Tall, Dark, and Handsome behind you."

"That's Lance Logan," my aunt said as I turned. "He's a detective with the Palm Beach Police. I met him earlier this evening. Would you like an introduction?"

"Yes, indeed." Cam grabbed my arm. "Come along, dear Guinevere, and meet your Lancelot."

"Geez, Cam, dial it down a few clicks. You're salivating." I pulled my arm free. "He's probably married anyway."

Aunt Liz turned to me. "No ring on his left hand. I checked earlier."

Cam grinned at her. "Well done. I love a woman with an eye for details." He shifted his glance to me, giggling. "FYI, I can have your dress ready in time for a June wedding."

I rolled my eyes. "Let's get this farce over."

Just then, the object of Cam's desire smiled at my aunt.

She stepped forward. "Lance, darling, I want to introduce my niece and her friend." She half-turned to me. "Detective Gwen Stuart, meet Detective Lance Logan."

I extended my hand and looked into the bluest eyes I'd ever seen. "Pleased to meet you."

He lifted my hand to his lips, his eyes piercing me like a laser beam. "The pleasure is mine. Are you a private detective?"

"No, I'm with the Wellington Police. I understand you're with the Palm Beach Police."

Cam cleared his throat and looked expectantly at my aunt.

"Lance, I'd like you to meet Cam Altman. He's with the fashion police."

The men shook hands as Cam said, "I'd arrest you for stealing James Bond's fabulous tux, but you look better in it than he did."

"Thank you, I ...." Lance pulled out his vibrating cell phone and read the text. "Excuse me, duty calls. It was a pleasure to meet you both." He smiled and walked to the exit.

Cam smirked at me. "That smile was for you, girlfriend. I'm thinking satin and antique lace with lots of pearls for your wedding gown."

My gut told me Lance's call was connected to my case. "I'm going after him."

"You go, girl."

I rushed outside and saw Lance heading for the oceanfront walkway that ran along the seawall behind the hotel. He followed the brick path north sixty feet and stopped at a bench where a man sat slumped against the seatback. Two uniformed officers were taping off the area.

I caught up with him. "Check his neck for a tiny puncture wound."

He spun around and thrust his hands on his hips. "Excuse me? You look like you've been a detective for maybe five minutes, and you're telling *me* what to do? This is my case. Go back to the ball." He turned away.

"Is he a wealthy criminal who escaped prosecution and appears to have died of natural causes?"

He hesitated before facing me again. "What if he is?"

"I'm working the Jet Donley/Binky Worthington cases—wealthy criminals with no obvious causes of death. Both men had pinpricks over their right carotid arteries."

Before he spoke, the medical examiner arrived. "Check his neck for a needle puncture near a carotid artery," Lance told him.

The ME examined the man's neck with a bright light and a magnifying glass for about a minute. "Yep, found a puncture mark over his right carotid. Are you thinking poison?"

Lance glanced at me.

I shook my head. "Not poison. His condition mirrors two recent murder victims. They both had non-lethal doses of sleep sedatives in their bodies."

The ME arched an eyebrow. "Who are you?"

"Detective Gwen Stuart, Wellington PD," I said.

"All right then." The ME checked the body. "No injuries or signs of a struggle. Liver temp indicates he died about an hour ago." He bagged the man's cocktail glass and cigar. "I'll check these for toxins. Is this a high-profile case?"

Lance nodded. "He's Barrett Branson, a wealthy Palm Beacher and alleged pedophile. He escaped prosecution several times by buying off the parents. Somebody did the community a big favor here." He turned to me. "Eh, Gwen, wasn't it? Sorry about earlier. Looks like our cases are connected. Let's plan to meet after the autopsy to compare notes."

I stared into his handsome face for a long moment, giving him time to regret his earlier snap judgment of me, then pulled my card out of my purse. "Apology accepted. Call me when you're ready."

I walked back to the ball feeling superior for the first time since I made detective.

***

The next morning, I switched on my police computer and read the files on Barrett Branson's numerous pedophile arrests. Each case was dropped shortly after the parents of the alleged victims suddenly became millionaires. The pattern of payoffs was obvious, but the district attorney couldn't prosecute Branson without the victim's cooperation. The injustice churned my stomach.

My cell phone rang.

"Hello, Gwen, it's Lance Logan. The autopsy results are in. Can you meet me at The Colony for dinner tonight at seven o'clock?"

I did a quick mental scan of my schedule. "Ah, yes, Lance, seven o'clock should work."

"Good, see you then."

A hint from the autopsy report would've been nice. He must be the strong silent type. He must have money too. Meals at The Colony were expensive, even if we split the check. I flashed back to his brilliant blue eyes. Then I reminded myself this was for police business, not romance. That didn't stop me from agonizing over what to wear. I wanted to see approval in his sexy eyes.

Down, girl.

Rod approved my dinner meeting, and I spent the rest of the day organizing my notes. A clever theory to impress Lance with my detective skills eluded me. Guess I'd have to depend on my electric-blue cocktail dress. I convinced myself my usual detective attire wouldn't be fancy enough for The Colony.

It was exactly seven o'clock when I strolled into the restaurant where Lance waited for me at a secluded table in a dark corner. His navy suit fit perfectly on his tall, muscular physique as he rose to pull out my chair. Whoa, he looked like a movie star. I sucked in my breath and attempted to control my heart rate.

"Good to see you again, Gwen. You look amazing in that dress." He gave me a dazzling smile.

"Lance, you look dashing in Armani. We don't look like detectives, do we? Then again, this is hardly a restaurant for cops."

"I'm trying to make amends for being a bit of a jerk at The Breakers. I shouldn't have judged your detective skills based on your youthful appearance. Care for a glass of Bordeaux?" He signaled the waiter.

The waiter deftly poured us glasses from a bottle of vintage Pavillon Rouge du Chateau Margaux and presented us with menus.

"Wow, dinner at The Colony and a legendary wine. This is too much. I already accepted your apology at The Breakers. Let me split the check with you." I took a sip of the divine wine.

"No way. You're my guest tonight. Don't worry about wiping out my bank account. My lucrative stock portfolio makes up for my meager detective salary. Relax and order whatever you like."

"You're too nice, thank you." I glanced at the jazz quartet across the room. "I love the mellow music here."

"It helps me unwind. That triple murder case has been vexing me. Palm Beachers aren't known for their patience." He breathed in the wine's bouquet and drank the ruby liquid.

I gazed into his intense blue eyes. "Dare I ask what Branson's autopsy turned up?"

"Same as the others, but this time the coroner figured out what killed him. Air embolism caused by injecting air into the carotid artery." He sat back and waited for my response.

"Brilliant—instant death with no obvious cause. The killer must be a clever pro."

"The coroner suggested we look for someone with medical expertise. Too bad we didn't find a hypodermic syringe at the scene."

I pulled out my case notes. "This is a list of Jet's, Binky's, and Barrett's victims and their family members, including their occupations." I scanned the list for medical personnel. "The father of one of Jet's victims is a brain surgeon. I see a veterinarian and two nurses among Binky's victims. The mother of one of Barrett's victims is a phlebotomist." I handed him the list.

"Looks like we hit the mother lode." He stared into space, then smiled. "I wonder if they got together and agreed to a *Strangers on a Train* scenario."

"Like Hitchcock's movie? Two strangers meet on a train, discover they each want someone dead, and agree to commit murder for each other. No one would suspect them of killing someone they didn't know." I pondered the idea a moment. "A simple yet brilliant plan, just like the murder method."

Lance turned his sexy eyes on me. "Well, now that we know who to investigate we can dispense with the cop talk for now. Would you like to enjoy some decadent red meat with our delicious red wine?"

"Sounds good. What do you suggest?" I scanned the steak section on the menu.

"How about chateaubriand béarnaise for two?" He signaled the waiter.

"That's my favorite beef entrée, and the Chateau Margaux will complement it perfectly. I'm in gourmet heaven. How is it you know my favorite wines and foods?"

"A lucky coincidence. They happen to be my favorites too. I

guess we have a lot in common." Lance gave our order to the waiter.

We enjoyed a scrumptious meal, fine wine, and lively conversation. Turned out we did have a lot in common. The climax was when he walked me to my car and gave me a gentle kiss I'll never forget.

Maybe a girl can catch criminals and a husband simultaneously.

***

Lance and I pursued the *Strangers-on-a-Train* suspects each day with the same zeal we pursued each other at night. Our days were strikeouts, but our nights were home runs. We couldn't find any evidence the medical professionals had ever met or communicated with each other. They all had rock-solid alibis. We were left with no leads.

The Palm Beach social season was over, and my aunt and uncle returned to their castle in England in mid-April.

I sat at my desk in the cop shop and stared at the files, trying to spot something I'd missed, when my cell phone played, "If I Could Turn Back Time" by Cher. Cam was calling.

"Hey, girlfriend, how's it going with Mr. Hottie? Should I get started on your wedding gown?"

"It's going great, but it's too soon for wedding bells. What's new with you?"

"I was researching antique jewelry, and I found a drawing of your aunt's fabulous brooch. Turns out it dates back to the reign of King Arthur. Legend claims Merlin himself created the brooch and matching ring with magical properties. King Arthur asked Merlin to forge the enchanted jewelry for his queen's protection after Queen Guinevere was kidnapped by Mordred and rescued by Sir Lancelot."

"I had no idea. How do they work?" I tried to visualize her ring and brooch doing something magical.

"Unfortunately, I couldn't find anything on that, and I'm dying to know. Would you be a dear and ask your aunt?"

"I'll ask her, but chances are the secret was lost centuries ago."

"Well, you know what they say, 'Nothing ventured ....' Anyway, call me after you talk to her. TTFN."

I checked the time. Almost 11:00 p.m. in England, too late to call my aunt.

The next morning, I was assigned a robbery investigation and forgot to call her.

***

The more time passed, the more I became obsessed with solving the triple homicides. A month later, I was slowly scrolling through the case files mid-morning when my cell played, "God Save the Queen." It was Uncle Clive.

"Gwen, Liz has become quite ill. She may not last long, and she's asking for you. Can you come right away?"

"Yes, of course, I'll catch the Miami-to-London flight tonight. I'll call you when I know my arrival time." I booked the British Airways flight to London online and waited for the printer to spit out my boarding pass. How had Aunt Liz changed from vibrant to terminal so quickly? She was only seventy-five. Surely the doctors were mistaken.

The police captain was very understanding and told me to take as much leave as I needed. What a relief. My next call was to Lance.

"I have to cancel our date. Aunt Liz is seriously ill, and I'm flying out tonight."

"Sorry about your aunt, sweetheart. I'll drive you to the airport. What time should I pick you up?"

"We'll need to leave at three o'clock to avoid rush hour traffic on I-95. Thank you for taking me." I hung up and drove home.

***

The next morning, I awoke to the scent of warm croissants and coffee in the first-class section. My flight landed in Heathrow on time, and Uncle Clive's chauffeur was waiting for me in the arrivals area outside of Customs. He ushered me into the back seat of the Bentley and deposited my luggage in the trunk. I fell asleep on the way to the castle.

My uncle awakened me with a kiss on my cheek. "Thanks for coming, Gwen. I fear I'm losing my dear Elizabeth. The doctor said her heart is failing, and there's nothing he can do." He looked sad and exhausted. "She's been asking for you."

"I'd better see her right away." I hugged him and followed him into the centuries-old castle perched on a hill overlooking Colchester.

In a large bedroom on the second floor, a massive antique four-poster bed seemed to swallow my frail aunt. An oxygen mask was strapped to her face.

I sat on the edge of her bed and took her hand. "Aunt Liz, how are you?"

She pulled the mask off and spoke in a weak voice. "My dear Gwen, we need to talk." She turned to her husband. "Leave us, darling. We won't be long." She gave him a reassuring smile.

Uncle Clive squeezed my shoulder. "Look after her. I'll wait outside." He walked to the heavy oak door and gently closed it.

Aunt Liz pointed at her nightstand. "Open that drawer and hand me the small red leather box with King Arthur's royal seal."

When I handed her the box, she pulled out her ring and brooch.

"Gwen, I haven't much time, so listen carefully. You're next in line for the secret weapon passed down from Queen Guinevere." She pulled a leather pouch filled with white powder from the box. "This is a powerful sedative." She pressed the center ruby on her ring and the jeweled top popped open. "Fill the ring with this powder and snap it shut. The sedative is tasteless and dissolves instantly in a beverage. Use it to immobilize your target."

"Aunt Liz, what are you talking about?"

"Patience, my dear." She held the antique brooch, pressed the ruby center, and withdrew the crystal tube that ran horizontally through it. A gold needle was connected to one end of the crystal syringe, and a ruby was embedded in the handle. "This is Guinevere's lance. Use it to inject air into your target's carotid artery. Death is instantaneous. Choose only criminals of great evil who have escaped justice."

I was shocked. "Aunt Liz, did you murder the three Palm Beach men?"

"No, dear, I fulfilled my sacred duty and executed them. Now it's time to pass the honor to you. Will you accept your inheritance?" She slid the crystal syringe into the brooch, placed it in the box with the ring and pouch, and offered it to me.

My mind reeled. "Did my mother know about this?"

"The woman who wields Guinevere's lance must bear the burden alone. I couldn't share the secret with my younger sister or with my dear husband. I told you because you're the heir. I realize this must come as a shock, but surely you know this is your destiny. You've always been keen for justice. You're the perfect woman to wield the ancient weapon designed by Merlin himself."

"Aunt Liz, I swore an oath to uphold the law. I can't go around executing criminals."

She sighed. "There's something else. I know who murdered your parents. My private detectives have been following his trail of crimes. They're sure it's him, but they don't have enough hard evidence for the police. If you accept Guinevere's lance and agree to continue the noble commission, I'll give you his name and address."

"And if I don't accept? You'll allow the man who killed my parents to remain free?"

"No. If you refuse, I'll pass the box to your cousin, Juliet, and send her after him. The authorities will never prosecute him. He tossed the gun and shipped your parents' car to a foreign country years ago. You told the police he wore a ski mask, so you can't pick him out of a lineup."

"I'd recognize his evil eyes. They're burned into my brain."

"You're a cop. You know that's not enough for a conviction. Meanwhile, he continues to destroy families. Guinevere's lance must put an end to him. Shall I give the sacred weapon to your cousin?"

I couldn't imagine meek little Juliet becoming an executioner, especially using a weapon as up close and personal as the crystal syringe. I flashed on the horrific carjacking scene and felt the searing pain of the bullet ripping through my midsection. I looked once again into his evil eyes and heard his sick laughter. How many people had he killed? How many more families would he destroy if I refused my inheritance? Justice demanded action.

I knew what I had to do.

***

It's been three months since Aunt Liz's funeral. I traded my fancy roadster for an SUV and a pile of cash. Lance popped the question. The wedding will take place in early December after hurricane season and before charity-ball season. Cam designed a wedding gown fit for a queen, and Uncle Clive will walk me down the aisle.

But first I'll fulfill my sacred duty.

The address Aunt Liz gave me was in North Miami. I spent most of my free time tracking the killer's movements and planning my mission. He frequented a sleazy bar in Hialeah. I decided to meet him there.

On a warm foggy night, I sat next to him at the bar and pretended I'd had too many glasses of Chianti as I smiled at his acne-scarred face. I whispered naughty suggestions in his ear to distract him while I dropped the sedative into his bourbon. With a saucy swagger, I strolled to the restroom in the dimly lit dive.

Alone, I stared at my reflection in the bathroom mirror. My long black wig looked real, and I barely recognized myself. The fancy brooch, pinned to a red sash tied around my waist, added a touch of class to my low-cut top and tight mini-skirt. I took one last look at the stranger in the mirror.

The middle-aged murderer with straggly brown hair and tanned leathery skin waited for me at the bar.

I nibbled his ear. "Finish your drink and take me to your

place."

He downed his bourbon and led me to his car. I sat inside and took a deep breath as he slid behind the wheel, fastened his seatbelt, and passed out.

I studied his face. The evil eyes that had haunted my dreams were closed in deep slumber. Twelve years of repressed anger and hatred boiled to the surface. My right hand rested on the ancient brooch. A fierce passion for justice, inherited from noble women across the centuries, burned inside me. I drew Guinevere's lance and sent the murderer to Hell.

There were no security cameras, but I kept my head down as I wiped the door handle and walked two blocks to my SUV.

During my drive home, I pulled off the road, opened the door, and vomited.

Not because I had slain the dragon—because my lips had touched his ear.

CLEM'S GENERAL STORE

D.M. Littlefield

George was the first to arrive after I unlocked the door to my general store this mornin'. He's a widower college professor who caused quite a stir with the single ladies when he moved here after retirin' last June. I ain't heard him profess nothin' yet, so I cain't rightly tell if he's good at it.

My store stocks everything from groceries, hardware, clothing and sundries, to farm supplies and more. My wife, Tillie, runs the little post office inside. Our slogan is: If We Don't Have It, You Don't Need It. It's also the joint where all the hill-country folks gather 'round to socialize.

Gus's two-pump gas station is across the street next to his repair shop. His sign says: I Can Fix It. Gus fixes everything, from all kinds of machinery to household stuff. He's our folks' last hope when duct tape won't do the job.

You cain't rightly call three buildin's a town, but we needed to have a sign for the lost souls who wander off the main highway and end up here on Futility Lane. Long ago, someone named this dip in the road Uncertain, West Virginia.

So, anyhow, a bunch of our good ole boys ambled in this mornin' to catch up on all the local news.

Bubba and Otis were playin' checkers when Tillie yelled, "Hey, Bubba! Come and get this big parcel someone sent ya."

He pushed his chair back, ran his hand across his ruddy face, snapped his suspenders, spat in the spittoon, and strutted over.

"It's from my ma," he said, beaming.

Everyone crowded around while he opened it. He lifted out a boy's coat with a note pinned on it and read it out loud.

"This coat is for little Billy for when he starts school. I cut the big buttons off it on account of they'd make the box heavier and cost more to send. Tell Earlene not to worry. I put them buttons in the left pocket. She can sew 'em on later." Bubba grinned. "That's Ma, always thrifty."

I smiled and nodded.

Rufus rushed in, out of breath. "Somethin' awful happened! Y'all know my brother Zeke's beat-up pickup with no glass in the side windows and wire coat hangers holdin' the doors shut? Well, he took my four cousins fishin'. My oldest cousin sat in front with him while the other three sat in the truck bed.

"When they was in the middle of the wooden bridge agoin' over the lake, the left front tire blew out. The truck swerved and crashed through the railin' and inta the water. Zeke and my cousin in the front seat swum out through the windows. The other cousins darned near drowned afore they got the rusty tailgate down."

"I'm glad they're all okay," I said.

Hank stomped in, his blue eyes a blazin'. He pushed his straw hat back and shouted, "You won't believe what our stupid gov'ment is fixin' ta do!"

"What?" I asked.

"I jus' came from a meetin' of ranchers and those stupid gov'ment guys. After years of us ranchers usin' the tried and true methods of trappin' or shootin' the damn coyotes and wolves, they want to capture 'em, castrate the males, and let 'em loose again. Well, ever'body got into an uproar and started hollerin' until big John from over by Guthrie's Gulch stood up.

"You coulda heard a pin drop. He scowled and strode over to the gov'ment guy. Big John stood toe to toe with him, tilted his Stetson back, and glared down at him. In his deep drawl, he said, 'Son, I don't think you understand the problem. Those critters ain't screwin' our animals, they're eating 'em.' He shook his head in disgust and strode out the door. We followed him and cheered."

Everbody nodded in agreement.

Young Jamey moseyed on in. "Howdy, Clem. I'll be here fer a spell. Gus won't have my pickup done 'til later, so I wanna buy that book of good ol' country stories I was readin' yesterday. That there woman writes them stories like she's from 'round here, but she must be married to a foreigner 'cause her name's Ann Onymous. It sounds Greek to me."

"Sure, Jamey. What's Gus fixin' on your truck?"

"Oh, he ain't fixin' nothin'. He's makin' an improvement."

"Whadaya mean?"

"Gus is puttin' a new gas tank in my truck."

"Was the old one leakin'?"

"Naw, but it cost too much to fill that big ol' tank, so I'm havin' him take it out and put in a smaller one." Jamey grinned and tapped his head with his finger. "Smart, huh?"

"Silas is smart too," I said. "Tell 'em how you solved your wife's problem."

Proud as a peacock, Silas leaned back, flicked the toothpick out of his mouth, and hooked his thumbs under the straps of his overalls.

"Well, sir, whenever we go away for a day or two, Purdy hides her precious stuff in the house. Bless her little ol' pea-pickin' heart, she cain't find it when we come home on account of she fergits where she hid it.

"Purdy drives me nuts, always worryin' about someone breakin' in the house and stealin' her precious stuff. Well, sir, I told her to write a note sayin' where she hid her stuff afore we leave and put it on the refrigerator. Problem solved." Silas grinned.

"I wish I coulda solved gettin' a speedin' ticket that easy," I said. "A state trooper pulled me over and gave me a lecture on speedin'. He riled me the way he was throwin' his weight around. Well, he finally gits to writin' the ticket while he keeps swattin' at the flies buzzin' 'round his head. Friendly like, I say, 'Y'all havin' a problem with them circle flies?'

"He stopped writin' the ticket and says, 'Well, yeah, if

that's what they're called, but I never heard of circle flies.'

"I said, 'Well, sir, circle flies hang around ranches, circlin' the back ends of horses.'

"'Oh,' he says and goes back to writin' the ticket. A few seconds later, he says, 'Are you callin' me a horse's ass?'

"I said, 'No, sir, I have too much respect for the law to do that.'

"He says, 'Good,' as he gives me the ticket.

"As I drove away, I said, 'It's hard to fool them flies though.'"

Everyone snickered and agreed with me.

At closin' time, me and Tillie were lockin' up the store when my agent in New York phoned and said my book, *Country Stories,* had made the best-sellers list. I told 'im I was writin' a second book and wanted to keep usin' my lucky pen name, Anonymous.

SIDE EFFECTS

D.M. Littlefield

James gasped at Ron's abrasions, bruises, black eyes, and bandaged nose. "Wow! What does the other guy look like?"

"There was no other guy." Ron frowned and limped toward James's lawn chair.

"You mean your little wife did all this damage?"

"No, but she caused it. It's a long story." Ron stood in front of him.

James patted the chair beside him. "I'm retired. I've got time."

He gently lowered his battered body into the cushioned chair and heaved a sigh. "Mary constantly nagged me to stop smoking and kept showing me photos of smokers dying of lung cancer. She waved a tally of my cigarette purchases in my face and said we could afford to take cruises if I stopped smoking. To shut her up, I agreed to quit."

"How did that go?" James leaned forward.

"The first week I was so irritable and short-tempered, even I didn't like me. Mary dragged me to the doctor. He gave me pills to ease my withdrawal symptoms."

"Did the pills work?"

"No, and a rash broke out all over my body. The itch drove me nuts. I tossed and turned in bed so much Mary moved to the guest room. The constant headaches from lack of sleep caused me to become argumentative and hostile. So back to the doctor we went. He gave me sleeping pills and lotion for the itch."

"Did they help?"

"A little, but the pills gave me vivid dreams. Last night, I dreamed I could feel the wind in my hair while driving my convertible 100 mph on the Florida Turnpike. I heard a police siren and pulled over. A state trooper approached my car and asked for my driver license. I reached for the wallet in my pants pocket and discovered I was wearing nothing but boxer shorts. The officer ordered me out of the car."

"Sounds like quite a dream," James said.

"When my bare feet hit the rough pavement, I realized I wasn't dreaming. My confusion and bizarre attire made the officer think I was drunk. He ordered me to walk a straight line. I fell face-first on the asphalt and was knocked out. I awoke in a hospital bed and called Mary to tell her our car was impounded. I asked her to call a cab and bring some clothes and our checkbook to the hospital as soon as possible."

"I bet that upset her," James said, shaking his head.

"After she paid my medical expenses, I told her we needed to hire a lawyer to defend me against charges of speeding, indecent exposure, driving without a license, driving under the influence, and not wearing a seat belt. The look in her eyes told me she was mentally adding up all the expenses.

"Mary sighed, rolled her eyes, and said, 'I surrender.' She opened her gigantic purse and handed me my confiscated pack of cigarettes and my old Zippo lighter."

SINK OR SWIM

S.L. Menear

My love affair with aviation started in 1965 when I was fifteen. My brother often took me flying in a two-seat Piper Cub before he shipped out on a US aircraft carrier three years later. I was hooked but couldn't afford lessons.

After college, I began a career as a Pan Am flight attendant because that was the only way for a woman to fly with a major airline in 1971. I was based at JFK International Airport until the mid-1970s when I transferred to Miami and joined the Pan Am Flying Club. Three months later, I earned my private pilot license. I harbored an impossible dream: to fly jet airliners.

When I began my quest, there were no female pilots with major airlines. I spent the next few years earning an instrument rating, commercial pilot license, multi-engine rating, and flight and ground instructor certificates, and logging flight time instructing and flying charter flights. After enough flight experience and a perfect score on the Airline Transport Pilot written test, I was the first woman pilot hired by Suburban Airlines, a small regional carrier that was part of the Allegheny Commuter network. I was their only new hire in 1979.

Commuter airlines were far less regulated back then. With no budget for flight simulators or flight training, the chief pilot employed the sink-or-swim method. He taught a half-day ground school for the two airplane types, Twin Otter and

Shorts 330 prop jets, and then gave me one hour of flight training followed immediately by the flight tests with a nasty, chauvinistic FAA examiner sitting behind me in the jumpseat. The fed wasn't his choice.

I passed the flight test in the Twin Otter. While I waited to take off for my test on the Shorts 330, an airplane landing gear-up crashed right in front of us, but no one was injured. The fed onboard was also an accident investigator. My chief pilot suggested we drop him off so he could investigate the crash. The fed made more veiled threats against female pilots and said the wreck would still be there when we finished.

I had to fly all the flight maneuvers perfectly so the fed wouldn't have an excuse to fail me. It's a good thing I passed because by the time we were finished, my boss looked like he was about to punch out the fed. It felt good to have somebody on my side for a change.

I loved my job as a commuter airline pilot flying Shorts 330s and 360s (they looked like Winnebagos with wings) and STOL (Short Take Off and Land) Twin Otter prop jets. The airplanes didn't have autopilots. That was my job. On a typical day, I flew several short roundtrips from my base in Lancaster, PA, to Newark, NJ, Allentown, PA, and La Guardia Airport in NYC in the Shorts. Afterward, I switched to the Twin Otter for a late trip to JFK International Airport or Philadelphia.

The Twin Otter was the most fun because it could take off and land in very short distances and cruise at a decent speed. My copilot job exposed me to bad weather, hundreds of instrument approaches, and lots of landings, so I was well prepared when the time came to apply to USAir (later changed to US Airways) a year later.

Thanks to recommendations from my old boss at Pan Am and my chief pilot at the Allegheny Commuter, I was granted an interview with USAir right before their big hiring wave in 1980. My first hurdle? A flight test in a DC-9 simulator. I'd never flown a jet airliner or a flight simulator. Back to sink or swim.

The DC-9 simulator flew like most airplanes, but everything happened faster because it simulated a jet. My instrument skills were excellent from all my bad weather experience, so I passed the flight test, even making a smooth landing. What a relief!

Next, I was grilled in a conference room by six senior captains who barraged me with questions that would be illegal today. I managed to convince them they could count on me to do a good job and not be a "pain-in-the-ass whiny broad like the first one they hired who quit when her husband complained she was gone too much."

I assured them if my husband disapproved, I'd find a new husband, which would be far easier than landing a pilot job with a major airline. They laughed. I won them over and endured six hours of the strangest written tests I've ever taken. I still wonder why the recipe for quiche, whether red or chartreuse was easier to spot from a distance, or if men were smarter than women were typical questions on that six-hour PILOT test. Maybe they ran out of aviation-related questions but needed to keep the test going long enough to see if they could wear down the applicants.

They saved the flight physical for last, but that was easy, except for the one-hour interrogation by the doctor. He asked the same questions the senior captains had asked. I guess they planned to compare notes later.

I was the only woman in the first new-hire class of ten pilots, and most of the men were captains' sons. We were all trained to be BAC 1-11 copilots, which involved some exciting late-night training in the airplane because the simulator was too primitive, using visuals from a video recorder that operated above a toy train board with model towns, rivers, hills, and an airport to give us a view out the cockpit window.

My training partner had been a Navy fighter pilot, and our instructor had been an Air Force fighter pilot and the first Thunderbird—absolutely fearless, until we practiced the stalls. At 15,000 feet, the instructor's voice filled with tension as he reminded me our jet would lose 15,000 feet in the first turn if it entered a spin. Translation: If you screw this up, Sharon, we're all gonna die!

Everyone survived.

After three months in the British airliner, I moved to copilot on the B727, the queen of the fleet at that time. Normally, a new pilot would stay on the initial airplane for the first year, but the chief pilot asked me, and the pilots hired with me, to upgrade to the 727 so they wouldn't have to put pilots directly from a new-hire class into their biggest airplane. Apparently, he didn't consider three-months experience to be "new."

Pilots received one week of 727 ground school followed by written and oral exams, then six days of flight-simulator training, involving every emergency imaginable, followed by the flight check. We also got some fun late-night training in the 727 because the simulator wasn't approved for everything. The reason all training flights were conducted late at night was because the airplanes were used for passenger flights during other times.

After a few years on my favorite, the 727, I flew copilot on the DC-9 and B737 to prepare me for upgrading to captain. That was because the copilot position on the 727 was too easy. The flight engineer did the preflight walk arounds and handled all the aircraft systems. All I had to do was fly the airplane or talk on the radio. The fun stuff.

No flight engineers on DC-9s and B737s, hence more duties and daily experience with the electrical, hydraulic, fuel, and air-conditioning systems. Also exterior preflight inspections, rain or shine.

After six years as copilot, I earned my fourth stripe and flew as captain on the BAC 1-11s, then later the DC-9s, and finally the B737s.

During my twenty-year airline career, I also flew antique, military, and exotic experimental aircraft on my days off. I helped my husband restore antique airplanes and build experimental aircraft. My favorites were the fully aerobatic German *Bücker Jungmann* biplane, Italian SIAI Marchetti SF260, Glassair III, Swearingen SX300, Russian Yak 52, and Piper Cub Special.

Years of high-adrenaline activities finally took their toll. I developed a rare eye disease called central serous retinopathy

(CSR), which damages the center of vision when the patient experiences any kind of stress, especially something that produces an adrenaline response.

I had to take an early retirement. It took three years for me to accept I needed to stop doing all the exciting things I'd loved most of my life, not just the flying. No more riding my stallion or my motorcycle. No more surfing, snow skiing, or scuba diving.

No more fun.

Lost, I almost drowned in another sink-or-swim situation.

My dear mother rescued me by convincing me to become an author, urging me to draw from my experiences to write action thrillers. It took me four years to learn how to write novels well enough to get a publishing contract.

My first book, *Deadstick Dawn*, which features a young female airline pilot, won the Royal Palm Literary Award for Best Unpublished Thriller. Two years later, it was published by Suspense Publishing in August 2013.

Deadstick Dawn is Book One in my Samantha Starr Series. Book Two, *Poseidon's Sword*, was published in 2015, Book Three, *Blaze, in 2017*, and Book Four, *Stranded,* in 2018.

Good thing my parents taught me how to swim.

UNBELIEVABLE

D.M. Littlefield

Tracie Scott smoothed her long red hair as she stepped off the elevator into the elegant hotel lobby in lower Manhattan. Her red stilettos clicked on the polished marble floor as she strode toward the front desk.

The reception clerk nudged the man beside him who was focused on the computer monitor. "Look, here she comes, the beauty I was telling you about."

The man looked up. "Wow, you didn't exaggerate. I like her thick shiny hair." He sighed. "I'd love to meet her."

A bellboy overloaded with a mountain of packages collided with Tracie, and three packages fell to the floor.

"Geez, I'm sorry," he said.

"No problem, let me help you," Tracie said in a sweet Southern drawl.

She set her Prada purse on the floor to gather the errant packages and rearrange them in his arms so he could peek through. "Can you see all right now?"

The bellboy blushed. "Yes, miss, thank you."

"You're welcome." Tracie smiled, picked up her handbag, and strolled to reception.

She handed the clerk her room key. "Good morning."

"Good morning, miss," both men said in unison.

"Wish me luck. I have an appointment with the editor-in-chief at Black Stallion Publishing. I sure hope she decides to publish my book."

"What kind of book is it?" a clerk asked.

She leaned close to read his name tag, her long lashes fluttering over her emerald-green eyes. "You'd like it, David. It's an action thriller."

Both desk clerks' eyebrows arched. Guests rarely addressed them by name, more often treating them like invisible servants.

David nervously straightened his tie. "Sounds like a winner. I'll be rooting for you."

The other clerk stepped forward to flash his name tag. "I'm Jack. Tell us more about your book."

"Well, Jack, the story is set in the hill country of east Texas. Islamic terrorists hide in an abandoned ranch house and build suicide bombs they intend to use to exact revenge for al-Qaeda by blowing up former President Bush while he's at home on his ranch. A beautiful young woman married to a Texas Ranger stumbles upon the terrorists while searching for her lost horse on the ranch land. The ranger races to rescue his wife and thwart the bombers before time runs out." She smiled. "My book is very fast-paced."

"Sounds exciting. What's the title?" Jack asked.

"*Texas Terror*. Thanks for asking." Tracie tilted her head and offered her hand. "I'm Tracie Scott, pleased to meet you. Folks back home in Texas said New Yorkers weren't friendly. I'm glad ya'll proved them wrong." She brightened the room with her smile as she waved good-bye.

Both clerks sighed as she sauntered off, her red hair gracefully bouncing against her shapely form.

Harry Stone, head of hotel security, glanced over his broad shoulder as he joined them. He plucked the unlit cigar from his mouth, leaned against the counter, and grinned. "That girl's a real bright spot in this bleak city."

Tracie swept through the revolving doors into the sunlight. She smiled at the doorman in his red uniform with gold braid when he asked if she wanted a cab. "No, thank you, Mike. It's such a nice day, I think I'll walk. Black Stallion Publishing is only four blocks that way, isn't it?" She pointed to her left and showed him the business card.

He glanced at the address. "Yes, miss, but they're long blocks."

"I don't mind. I have plenty of time."

She was only twenty yards from the hotel when a disheveled young man leaped out from the shadows of an alley and grabbed her Prada purse. Though startled, she clutched it to her body.

He glared at her with glazed, bloodshot eyes. "You'd better let go, lady!"

"No!" Tracie yelled. "My friend loaned it to me."

He yanked on the handbag while she screamed for help and kicked him.

"Ow!" He pulled a switchblade from his jeans pocket, flicked it open, and stabbed her.

When the doorman saw the glint of a knife plunging into Tracie's abdomen, he shouted for the bellboy to call 9-1-1 before running to help her.

She collapsed as her assailant bolted down the alley. Mike knelt beside her and pressed his linen handkerchief against her bleeding wound. Her eyes fluttered closed as a crowd gathered.

***

Sirens wailed as police cars arrived, followed by an ambulance. An unmarked car with a pulsing dashboard light skidded to a stop alongside them. A tall, muscular detective stepped out and asked the police to move the crowd and clear a path for the paramedics. He knelt beside the redhead and looked for identification. No handbag. He swore under his breath as he stood to make room for the stretcher and gazed at her face. Too beautiful to be a Jane Doe.

He flashed his badge at the crowd. "Can anyone identify this woman?"

"Her name's Tracie Scott," Mike said. "She's staying back there at the Grand Hyatt Hotel. The desk clerk can give you more information. I heard her screaming and ran over. She fought like a wildcat when the creep tried to grab her handbag.

He stabbed her in the gut and ran into the alley with her handbag."

After the paramedics finished working on Tracie, they lifted her onto a stretcher.

One of the medics turned to the detective. "It doesn't look good. She's lost a lot of blood." He glanced at his partner. "Start an IV, and I'll notify the ER we're on our way."

Tracie moaned in pain. "Get Prada handbag ... behind dumpster ... Manny's Smoke Shop."

The detective leaned down. "Wait! What's she saying?"

"She won't be saying much more if we don't get her to the hospital," a medic said.

The detective tilted his ear close to her mouth. "Can you repeat that?"

"Get handbag ... behind dumpster ... Manny's Smoke Shop."

Tracie lost consciousness. The medics shoved the stretcher into the ambulance and raced off with their siren wailing.

The detective scribbled on his pad as he asked the doorman, "Did anyone chase the assailant?"

"No, I was trying to help her, but I can describe the creep," Mike said.

"Good, let's have it." He took notes as he followed the doorman into the hotel to talk to the desk clerks.

When the detective told them what happened, they looked crestfallen.

"Oh no, not her! She's just a sweet, small-town girl from Tyler, Texas," David said.

"She's here because she wrote a novel, *Texas Terror*," Jack said.

"She was here to meet with an editor at Black Stallion Publishing," Mike said.

The detective wrote it all down and asked for her room key. He hoped to find an easy way to notify her family.

After searching Tracie's room, he ran his fingers through his thick black hair. "Damn, nothing useful here." His intense blue eyes filled with concern as he contemplated the impression she had made on the hotel staff. They obviously were concerned about her. Too bad they had only her business address and not her home phone.

He ordered a cup of coffee in the hotel coffee shop and sipped it while reviewing his notes.

Harry Stone from hotel security settled next to him. "Good morning, Mark. I hoped you'd get this case." He smoothed his thick gray hair. "That little gal from Texas needs the best man on the job. Think she'll be all right?"

"I don't know, Uncle Harry. The medics were worried about blood loss. Can you tell me anything about her?"

Harry tilted his chair back, smiled, and removed the cigar from his mouth. "Well now, after twenty years in this business, I've learned how to read people by their body language, behavior, and especially their eyes. A person's eyes reveal their soul. That sweet girl has the most honest green eyes I've ever seen."

"That's nice, but do you have anything more concrete?"

"Most people give me a dirty look when they see a cigar in my mouth, even though it's unlit. You know I gave up smoking years ago, but I still like the taste. In the elevator with me, she smiled and said my cigar brought back fond memories of her Uncle Bob, who taught her how to ride horses on his ranch."

Mark rolled his eyes. "Is there anyone in this hotel who isn't charmed by Tracie Scott?"

He grinned at his nephew. "Well now, I don't know. How about you?"

"Aw, Uncle Harry, give me a break. You're always trying to play matchmaker for me." He held his palms up. "I admit she's beautiful, but I'll know when the right girl comes along. I plan to pick her out myself."

"Point taken. Please keep me informed on Tracie's condition. The hotel staff will want to know as well." He reinserted his cigar and drifted off into the lobby.

Mark paid his tab and left. He lamented it might be days before he could talk to Tracie, if she survived. His only lead was her whispers about Manny's Smoke Shop. He drove around the block, found the shop, and parked in the alley behind it.

"Bingo." He found a large handbag wedged behind the

dumpster and looked inside. No wallet. Just lipstick, a brush, a notepad, and a business card with Tracie's name, address, and phone number.

He shook his head. How did she know her handbag was behind the dumpster? She was losing consciousness and couldn't have seen her assailant throw it there.

Mark drove to the hospital to check on Tracie's condition before notifying her family. She was still in surgery, so he settled into the waiting room.

Twenty minutes later, a surgeon strode into the room. "Who's here for Tracie Scott?"

"Detective Mark Evans." He flashed his badge. "Is she going to be all right? I need to notify her family."

The surgeon nodded. "The wound was deep, but she'll pull through. She lost a lot of blood and needed transfusions. She's in recovery, but she'll be unconscious for a good while. I suggest you come back tomorrow. We'll keep a close watch on her. You can tell the family her prognosis is good, barring infection."

Mark called his Uncle Harry with the good news and asked him to direct a hotel maid to pack Tracie's suitcase. Harry could store it in his office after closing out her room.

***

The next morning, Mark visited Tracie and flashed his badge. "Hello, I'm Detective Mark Evans. How're you feeling?"

"Weak and sore but happy to be alive." She forced a smile.

"Do you mind answering a few questions?"

"No, I just hope you can find the Prada handbag. It belongs to my friend, Brittany. She's a fashion diva and insisted I borrow her purse. She thought it would impress the editor." Concern clouded her green eyes.

"Don't worry, I found the handbag. I guess the perp didn't know its value, or it was too big to hide, so he threw it away. Oh, and I called Black Stallion Publishing and explained what happened to you. They were very understanding and send their best wishes."

Tracie's eyes welled with tears of joy as she smiled at the good news.

"I also found your author business card and called the phone number but only got your answering machine. Is there anyone you want me to notify?"

"No."

"No?" He raised his eyebrows. "No parents?"

"No, not living"

"I'm sorry. What about a husband or boyfriend?" *Why was he hoping she'd say "no?" Am I falling under her spell?*

"No family, husband, or boyfriend." She blushed. "Still looking for Mr. Right."

He exhaled. "Did you have any valuables in the handbag?"

"Just fifty dollars in my wallet."

"That's it?"

"My credit cards are in the hotel safe."

"I found your handbag where you told me to look. How did you know it was there?"

She looked away as she fingered the binding on the blanket. "You wouldn't believe me if I told you. It's … it's … unbelievable."

He pulled up a chair and perched on the edge. She looked confused, uncertain. He'd seen that look before … a mixture of skepticism and wonder. The way people looked when watching a magician perform feats of magic.

His deep voice softened. "Miss Scott, since I've been on the force, I've seen lots of things I thought were impossible. Tell me, what do you think is unbelievable?"

She shook her head, still avoiding his eyes. "No, you'll have them transfer me to the psychiatric ward."

"That's not my call, and I wouldn't do that anyway."

She gazed into his eyes. "Please … I don't want to talk about it."

"All right, we'll let that go for now. Can you describe your assailant?"

She took a deep breath. "He was white, skinny, about six-four, and had a scraggly brown ponytail and bloodshot eyes." She bit her lip and looked up at the ceiling, trying to recall more. "And he had a dagger tattoo on his neck below his right ear."

"That's a pretty good description. When you're up to it, I'd like to bring my laptop and show you some mug shots. You might recognize his photo." He pulled out his card. "Oh, the hotel staff and my Uncle Harry, who's head of hotel security, said to tell you to get well soon. Harry checked you out of the hotel and stored your luggage in his office."

Tracie's eyes glistened. "That's so kind of him to do all that. Please tell him I appreciate it and thank all of them for caring about me." As she took his card, she grasped his hand in both of hers. "I want to thank you for all your trouble ... finding the handbag and calling my editor."

His heart raced as he felt her hands tighten. A smile creased his face as he left her room.

***

Mark visited her over the next three days. Tracie looked forward to seeing him and began to feel more at ease as they shared their life stories. He told her he'd been shot once during a robbery and experienced a weird feeling of floating above his body.

Her green eyes widened, and she gasped. "That's what happened to me after he stabbed me! I seemed to float behind him as if running after him, but I felt weak and so odd. I saw everything he did after he ran away. I tried to pick up my handbag behind the dumpster, but my hands went right through it."

Spellbound, he leaned forward. "Go on, what happened next?"

"I was whisked back to the sidewalk where I floated above the crowd, but I didn't realize it was my body lying there. When I saw all the blood and *my* face, I couldn't make any sense of what was happening. I heard everything that was said and wondered if I had died. When the medics started the IV, it pulled me back into my body. That's when I felt the pain and told you where to find my handbag. It's still hard to believe it really happened."

He took her hand in his. "Believe it. I had a similar experience." He smiled. "It seems we have a lot in common, Tracie. Both my parents are deceased, and I live alone. The only family I have is my Uncle Harry and Aunt Grace. You've made quite an impression on my uncle. He wants me to bring you home to meet my aunt as soon as you're released from the hospital."

"Your uncle is very kind. I'd love to thank him and meet his wife."

***

The next morning, Mark carried Tracie's suitcase and his laptop to the hospital. After thirty minutes of searching, she found the picture of the man who stabbed her. In fact, he'd been arrested for a robbery earlier that day. Her charges were added to a long list of his crimes and bail was denied.

Tracie was discharged at 5:00 p.m., and Mark drove her to his uncle and aunt's house for dinner. Aunt Grace, who was slender with short blond hair, was a talented cook. Tracie raved about the delicious steak Diane. They enjoyed a lively conversation and Harry's stories about his unusual cases.

Tracie stifled a yawn and glanced at her watch. "Sorry, I haven't recovered my stamina yet. I enjoyed spending time with you, but it's getting late, and I have to get a room at the hotel."

"You'll do no such thing," Grace said. "We have a nice guest room. We'd enjoy your company and want to hear all about your book."

"You're too kind. I couldn't impose like that. We just met."

"I'm a good judge of character," Harry said. "We feel as if we've known you a long time. Please stay."

Grace nodded. "Please, say yes."

Mark raised his eyebrows, waiting for her reply. "You'll feel right at home here, and Aunt Grace will take good care of you while you recuperate. She's a retired nurse. Why don't I go and get your luggage out of the car?"

Tracie blushed. "All right, if you're sure I won't be too much trouble."

"Actually, I'm looking forward to having a real live author in the house," Grace said.

"Thanks, but I need to go to the hotel first to pay my bill and thank the hotel staff for their help."

"Okay, but we won't stay long," Mark said. "You've had a busy day, and you need rest."

"Dear, your room will be ready when you return." Grace hugged Tracie.

***

Grace and Harry watched through the window as their nephew helped Tracie into his car.

"Did you notice Mark couldn't take his eyes off her all night?" Grace said. "I think he's falling in love with her."

Harry nodded and turned to his wife. "Yep, she seems perfect for him, and I deserve all the credit."

He grinned and puffed out his chest. "Mission accomplished."

WHAT'S GOING ON HERE?

D.M. Littlefield

Something always went wrong when my husband, Don, was out of town on business.

Today my washer wouldn't go into a spin cycle. Don wouldn't be home for two days, so I looked at the Yellow Pages online and called Big John's Plumbing Service. It was a rainy day, and my five-year-old son, Bobby, was playing with his three-year-old sister, Annie, upstairs. I was explaining my problem to the plumber on the phone when Bobby wandered downstairs and tugged on my blouse.

"Mom, Mom, Mom, I don't want to play house with Annie anymore. It's too boring. I want to watch my favorite cartoons."

I heard Annie crying upstairs and gave Bobby a stern look. I blocked his persistent hand as I continued my conversation with the plumber.

"Yes, that's my address. When can you be here? Thirty minutes? Great." I hung up and walked upstairs with Bobby to see why Annie was crying.

"Bobby, you know you're the man of the house when your dad is away. I need you to stay with Annie until the plumber gets here. Then you can watch your cartoons."

"It's no fun being man of the house if I only get to boss her. Dad watches football games whenever he wants. If I'm the man of the house now, why can't I watch cartoons?"

"I don't have time to argue with you. Stay with Annie until I show the plumber the washing machine and breaker box."

I picked Annie up, dried her eyes, and hugged her.

She snuffled. "Bobby's bad. He won't play with me."

I stroked her long blond curls. "Don't cry. I'll play house with you in a little while. Be a good girl and play with your dolly. Bobby will stay here until I come back." I walked past Annie's five-foot-square plastic playhouse and handed her one of her dolls.

After locking the expandable security gate on the playroom, I walked downstairs. I was making lunch when the doorbell rang.

A burly giant of a man held out a hand almost the size of a frying pan, smiled, and said in a deep voice, "I'm big John, the plumber. I can fix anything that needs fixin'."

I looked up at him with awe and shook his callused hand. "Thanks for coming. I'll show you the utility room. My washer is near the breaker box."

His tool belt clanked as he swaggered down the hall. He reminded me of a confident gunfighter on his way to a showdown as he grabbed a wrench and twirled it like a gun before holstering it without a glance. When he knelt at the washing machine, his weighty tools pulled down the back of his pants and revealed more than I wanted to see.

I backed out of the room. "If you need me, I'll be upstairs."

Annie was crying as Bobby shouted, "I told you not to put your doll in the kitchen cabinet! Mom, she doesn't do what I tell her. Can I watch my cartoons now?"

I knew he wasn't talking about our real kitchen cabinet. Annie's playhouse was equipped with built-in cabinets and a mock stove and refrigerator.

"Yes, Bobby, I'll take care of this," I said after climbing the stairs. I turned to Annie. "Come out of the dollhouse, and I'll get the doll for you."

She walked out, and I got down on my hands and knees to stick my head through the Lilliputian door. My shoulders barely fit.

After backing out, I rolled onto my back and squeezed

inside up to my waist. The cabinet door wouldn't budge. I gritted my teeth and pounded on it so hard that I smashed a hole and cut my hand.

The hole wasn't big enough for the doll, and every time I tried to retract my hand the jagged plastic cut it. Blood trickled down my wrist. I tried to pry away the plastic with my other hand.

Nope. I was officially stuck.

I yelled for Bobby, but he couldn't hear me over the loud TV.

I guess the plumber will rescue me when he wants to be paid.

"Mommy, come out and play with me."

"Annie, I'm stuck in here. Look at your picture books while you wait."

"I don't wanna look at books. I wanna play house with you. I'll climb in the window."

"No! There isn't room."

Annie peeked through the window. "Where's my dolly?"

"She's in the cabinet."

"You couldn't get her out?" She started to cry again.

"We'll get her out when Daddy comes home. Now be a good girl and use your crayons to draw a picture for Daddy. You can surprise him on Saturday."

She snuffled. "Okay." She walked to the desk.

I heard heavy footsteps and John's voice in the upstairs hallway. "Missy, your washer is fixed."

"Help me!" I yelled. "I'm stuck in the playhouse."

He walked into the room. "Stay calm. I'll get you out in a jiffy."

I heard him circle the playhouse. "I can't see where you're stuck from out here or through the little window. I'll have to stick my head inside."

He knelt at the open door, straddled my legs, put his hands on the floor, and leaned forward.

As he eased his head inside, he looked dizzy. "My blood sugar—I forgot to eat."

He collapsed on me with his face over my breasts.

***

Don Mason smiled. He was happy his business trip had gone so well that he could return home two days early. He missed his lovely wife, Judy, and his two children.

When he grabbed his suitcase from the car, he noticed a plumber's truck parked at the curb between his house and the neighbor's. He planned to yell surprise when he walked in, but no one would be able to hear him over the TV blasting in the living room. He went to turn it down and saw Billy watching cartoons. "Bobby! Turn the volume down. Where's your mother?"

"She's upstairs playing house with the plumber."

Don frowned. "What did you say?"

"She's upstairs playing house with the plumber."

He raced upstairs with his suitcase and threw open the master bedroom door. Empty. He dropped his suitcase and ran to the children's bedrooms. Empty too.

From the doorway of the playroom, he shouted, "What's going on here?"

Those were Judy's shoes! The uniformed plumber, complete with tool belt, was straddling his wife on the floor with his head atop his wife's breasts inside the playhouse.

"Don?" she yelled. "Thank God you're home! Bobby didn't hear me because of the loud TV. Call 9-1-1. I'm stuck in here. The plumber tried to free me, but he passed out from low blood sugar."

Don grabbed the plumber's ankles. "I'm not calling anybody until I haul his ass off you!"

CRUISE CAPADES

S.L. Menear

I used to be a competent and sharp-witted person—exactly what one would expect from one of the world's first female airline captains. When I retired from flying airliners, I assumed nothing would change.

I was wrong.

Now fatigue affects me in ways it never did before. After a late night of packing and leg cramps that disturbed what little sleep I might have enjoyed, my octogenarian mother and I embarked on a fourteen-day cruise through the Caribbean.

We boarded the *Constellation* at 11:30 a.m. in Miami and dived into the lunch buffet while waiting for our cabin. Our three previous vacations on Celebrity Cruises were aboard their new ultra-luxurious Solstice Class ships. We were assured this older Millennium Class ship had been refurbished to be in line with the newer ships. Maybe we would've agreed if the new ships hadn't spoiled us. We booked it because of the two-week itinerary available only on this ship.

When we entered our so-called suite, we were dismayed by the tight quarters and tiny bathroom. There was barely enough room to stow our belongings. I couldn't walk around without banging my shin on a bed corner or bumping into something. My coordination wasn't at its best after a sleepless night, so the bruise count was mounting.

We somehow stowed everything away by 3:00 p.m. and

decided to enjoy siestas before the 4:30 sail-away party. My nap in our balcony deck chair was interrupted by a loud persistent announcement. In my exhausted stupor, I couldn't understand the heavily accented voice. I managed to catch a few words: mandatory drill, muster station, and life jackets. It was 4:00 p.m., and my foggy brain recalled doing this on every cruise before departure. Too bad I didn't remember the salient details of previous musters.

I studied the plaque on the door, located our muster station on the map, and noted pictures of passengers wearing life vests. Mother and I dutifully donned our life jackets. The stiff design clamped around us like neck braces for crash victims.

I stepped into the hall and learned something interesting about people for whom English is a second language. If what you say to them doesn't match the situation and how you look, they focus on what they see and tune out your words.

I encountered a steward and reminded him to separate our beds. He looked confused, so I made hand gestures. He fixated on my straitjacket life vest and assumed I was asking how to remove it. I assumed he didn't speak English because even though I kept saying, "Beds. Separate the beds," he kept saying, "Yes, pull apart front and lift over head."

I gave up, and Mom and I headed for the stairs. We were greeted by laughing crew members who cheerfully informed us life jackets were not required for the drill. So Sharon Stupid and Dottie Dimwit dashed back to our cabin to stow the life vests before reporting to the muster station. By the time we arrived, the only unoccupied seats were tall bar stools.

My mother loses all coordination when she's tired, and I seem to be headed that way. Sitting on the barstool should've been a simple maneuver, but Mom looked like a two-year-old trying to climb into a big girl's chair. She succeeded on her third try. By then, the crowd was staring.

Mom and I get the giggles when we're tired. We looked at each other, remembered the stupid stuff we'd just done, and giggled uncontrollably. Fortunately, it was New Year's Eve, and everyone assumed we were harmless drunks rather than incompetents.

We attended the sail-away party on the top deck, followed by dinner, a show, and the countdown-to-midnight party and New Year's celebration with plenty of the Paso Robles Midnight merlot for *moi*.

Back in our microscopic cabin, we collapsed into our separated beds, which I had finally arranged with an English-speaking crewmember. We planned to skip breakfast and sleep in.

That didn't work out.

***

Even though a Do-Not-Disturb sign was displayed on our door, I heard persistent knocking early in the morning. I opened the door and smelled smoke. A crewmember said we must evacuate the room and proceed to our muster station. I stumbled to Mom's bed and told her to get dressed quickly. Silly me, we couldn't do anything fast in such tight quarters.

I wish I could say that I took command of the situation and made sensible decisions, but no. Apparently my brain only switches to pilot mode when I'm in an airplane, and my airline captain days are long gone.

I'm a writer now. So is Mom.

Did we grab our diamond jewelry and warm clothes for the life boats? No. Did we take our money, passports, water bottles, or life vests? Nope. We threw on shorts and T-shirts, slipped on sandals, and grabbed our laptops.

We were almost out the door when Mom said, "Wait! We forgot our Kindles!"

We shoved the Kindles into the laptop cases and hurried to the muster station, confident we had saved what was most important.

We knew we couldn't eat our Kindles or drink our computers, but our manuscripts were in the laptops, so no way would we leave without them. When we arrived at the muster station sans life vests, hugging our computer bags, we once again drew the attention of the crowd and crew. As our stupidity became apparent, Mom and I looked at each other and giggled uncontrollably. Fortunately, the group assumed we were still drunk from New Year's Eve.

While waiting for the crew to douse the small fire in the breakfast buffet and evacuate the smoke, I began writing this account of the first twenty-four hours of our fourteen-day cruise. I could hardly wait to discover what stupid things I'd do next. Too bad I left the sensible part of my brain in the Boeing cockpit.

My next blunder was sitting next to the only man at our dinner table for eight. Frail and balding, he appeared to be in his seventies. I attempted to engage him by inquiring if he'd served in the military.

"I served in the Canadian military as part of a U.N. peace-keeping mission in Palestine in the sixties," he said.

"Sorry, did you say you were in *Palestine* in the 1960s? Did you mean Israel?" I asked, trying to be helpful.

His voice increased by about twenty decibels. "No! I mean the *nation* of Palestine. They still have their own country."

"Really? Where? I don't recall seeing it on a recent world map."

"It's there! They have their own government leaders and everything."

"Then why are there Palestinian refugee camps in Lebanon? Wouldn't they rather live in their own country if it still exists?" I asked. Big mistake.

He blasted into a loud tirade about the Jews stealing Palestine. All the women at our table glared at him, siding with me. A woman from Texas reminded him the land had belonged to Israel thousands of years before the Palestinians took it over.

Spittle spewed from his frothing mouth as he raged on about how wrong we were. He finally stopped yelling when his wife gave him the evil eye.

I never sat near him again. I try to learn from my mistakes.

***

The next night, I savored Wild Horse merlot and listened to a talented young man play guitar and sing on the afterdeck. A man resembling a scrawny old rooster danced alone in front of the singer. He wore swim shorts, a sleeveless shirt, and flip flops while everyone else was dressed in formal evening attire.

His dancing was the strangest I'd ever seen. He looked like he was constantly getting zapped by a Taser as he jerked and contorted his body. It was apparent large quantities of alcohol were involved. He almost fell several times. Then he dragged a woman onto the dance floor and grabbed her every time he lost his balance.

The spastic dancer entertained the crowd through several songs before he staggered over to me and said, "Come on, baby, you know you want to!" He tried to pull me out of my chair.

That's when the Russians came to my rescue.

According to our cruise director, there were eighty-two passengers from Russia. I noticed the men were tall and broad-shouldered with deep voices. After all those years of repression, they were making up for lost time in the fun department. A giant Russian bear pulled the rooster away from me and crushed him against his chest in a silly man-on-man slow dance. His buddies shared a good laugh. When the dance ended, the rooster stumbled away in a daze.

When I smiled at the Russian and said, "*Spasibo*," he bowed.

As Mom and I headed downstairs for the evening show, she did something completely unexpected. I sensed she wasn't behind me when I reached the bottom of the two-story stairway. When I looked up, she was still at the top.

"Stay there and catch me!" she shouted as she hiked up her black chiffon gown, swung her leg over the railing, and proceeded to slide down.

Mom was eighty-five and a non-drinker, so you can imagine my surprise.

"Slow down! There's a painful-looking lip at the end of the banister!" I managed to stop her before she reached it.

"Mom, what the hell?" I said when she climbed off.

"It was on my bucket list," she said with a defiant look.

"Well, okay then. Dare I ask what else is on your list?"

"I'd like that darn fairy book I worked on for twenty-five years to be published!"

"*Journey into the Land of the Wingless Giants* will be published in 2012. That's a promise," I said as we strolled into the theater.

***

The following day, I met the handsome captain of the ship, Alexandros Andreas, in his fancy uniform. He was from Greece—aren't they all? I convinced him to give me a tour of the bridge. Afterward, he invited me to join him for a private dinner.

Cruise ship captains are treated like kings. His steward served us steak Diane and new potatoes with a bottle of Chateau Lafite Rothschild. I must admit I was impressed. And the decadent chocolate parfait was the perfect finale.

Over the next several days, we enjoyed each other's company.

As the cruise neared its end, Alexandros confided in me that he was deeply depressed. "If you don't sleep with me, I'll end it all and sink the ship."

That night, I saved the lives of thirty-five hundred people.

Twice.

MELANIE

D.M. Littlefield

"Tom!" I shouted and waved.

He hurried to my table in the restaurant. I stood to give him a warm hug. He had been away for eight weeks on a business trip and European castle tour. Of course, I wanted to hear all about his trip, but I was excited and anxious to tell him about my own amazing experience.

"Did you see any ghosts in the castles?"

"No, but the tour guide assured us the castles were haunted." He grinned. "Let's order lunch. I'm hungry."

Soon the food was served, and we exchanged small talk while enjoying our meals.

"Okay," Tom said after we finished eating, "you can stop with the pleasantries and tell me what's on your mind before you burst."

I leaned forward. "It was the most amazing thing that has ever happened to me. For the past six weeks, I lived on a beautiful historic estate in Savannah, Georgia and substituted for my Aunt Sue as a governess while she recuperated from a car accident."

"Is she okay now?"

"Yes, thank God. She's back to taking care of precious little Cindy, who'll be four years old next month. She's a sweet child. I miss her."

"Tell me everything." He arched his eyebrows and crossed

his arms.

"Okay." I took a sip of my ice tea. "A nice middle-aged chauffeur named George met me at the train station. As we drove through the iron gate of the mansion, I was impressed by the huge oak trees that flanked the drive. It was like driving through a long green tunnel as the boughs overhead blended together with dangling Spanish moss.

"The grounds of the estate are extensive and well kept. George told me he felt sorry for the little girl because her mother had died giving birth to her. Cindy's father, a wealthy businessman, travels extensively and is seldom home."

"That's sad. Sounds like she's essentially parentless."

"The little girl only has the servants to keep her company, so she invented an imaginary playmate named Melanie. Aunt Sue and I played along to keep Cindy happy."

"Sorry, but there's nothing exciting about this. What aren't you telling me?" He leaned forward.

"Hold on, I'm getting to it." I took another sip of ice tea. "The mansion reminds me of the movie, *Gone with the Wind*. It has six huge white columns in front of its three stories. French doors open onto large verandas on each floor. The view from my room was spectacular." I sighed. "Mrs. Stevens, the housekeeper, is the stern type. She manages all the help and doesn't put up with, as she called it, imaginary nonsense."

"Describe Cindy. Is she a troubled child?" He sat back and sipped his beer.

"She's shy and small for almost four but pretty with long blond hair and blue eyes. She reminds me of the Precious porcelain statues I've seen in the Hallmark shops. When I met her, she hid behind the housekeeper. Mrs. Stevens pulled Cindy in front of her and said, 'This is Cindy. She has an imaginary friend named Melanie. Cindy never does anything wrong, but her friend, Melanie, does. Isn't that right, Cindy?'

"The little girl lowered her head and said, 'Yes, Ma'am.' I felt sorry for her. It didn't take long for me to win her over. You know I'm good at that, don't you?" I grinned at Tom.

He nodded and smiled. "Yes, we all know you're charming."

"So Cindy took my hand and led me to my room upstairs next to hers. The chauffeur followed us with my luggage. Cindy showed me her bedroom and the connecting playroom filled with toys, dolls, and books. It was furnished with a table, chairs, and two children's rocking chairs. The new rocker was by the bookcase, and the antique rocker was placed in front of the French doors. I pointed at it and asked her if she liked to look outside while she rocked in the chair. She said, 'No, that's Melanie's rocking chair. She doesn't like anyone to touch her things. Besides, mine's newer.'"

"If she's an only child, why are there two rocking chairs?"

"Good question. I wondered the same thing."

"Did you discover the answer?"

"Ah, yes. Cindy loved having someone read stories to her, and shelves of children's books lined the playroom. I enjoyed my time with her, and we got along fine.

"One day, Mrs. Stevens accused Cindy of not putting her toys away before she went to bed. But I told Mrs. Stevens I had helped her put them away. She glared at Cindy and said, 'Am I supposed to believe Melanie played with your toys while you slept? Don't lie!' Cindy's lip quivered, so I put my arm around her."

Tom's face reddened. "What a bitch!"

"She sure was. Mrs. Stevens glared at both of us and stomped out of the room. I pulled a book from the shelf to read to Cindy and found an antique music box hidden behind it. The lid had an inlaid picture of a lovely woman asleep in bed. The label inside said the song was 'Beautiful Dreamer' by Stephen Foster, one of my favorites. I didn't see the key to wind it up, so I asked her if she had it. She claimed she'd never seen the music box before, so I set it back on the shelf and read her a story as I held her on my lap.

"That night I couldn't sleep, wondering if Cindy walked in her sleep like I had done when I was a child. In the wee hours, I heard faint music. My French doors to the veranda were open, and so were the ones to her bedroom and playroom. I put on my robe and slippers and tiptoed into her room. She was sound asleep. The music was coming from the playroom—the music box playing 'Beautiful Dreamer.'"

Tom raised his eyebrows. "So what happened next?"

"I slowly turned the doorknob to the playroom and opened it without a sound. A little girl bathed in moonlight was rocking in the antique chair in front of the French doors. She had long brown hair and wore an old-fashioned dress with a pinafore. She was holding the music box and staring out across the lawn toward the old wishing well.

"When I gasped, she vanished, and the music box clattered to the floor. You see, Melanie wasn't imaginary after all. She was a little ghost from the past!"

WIFE WANTED

D.M. Littlefield

Twenty-eight and homeless, Stacie drove her SUV loaded with all her belongings to a park in Boca Raton. It was her favorite place to relax. She bought an assortment of muffins for breakfast and pondered her dilemma while watching the dogs catch Frisbees. She missed Lady, her German shepherd, who had died a month before she moved to Florida two years ago.

She grabbed the bag of muffins and munched on one as she leaned against the car door. Perplexed, she stared at an unusual sign on the front lawn of a stately two-story home across the street.

She turned toward whistling in the park and saw a big German shepherd prancing in front of a tall, muscular man carrying a Frisbee. When the dog saw her, he grabbed the Frisbee, ran to her, dropped it at her feet, and sat up to beg. She laughed.

The man smiled. "He has a nose for goodies and can spot a soft touch a block away."

She leaned down to pet the dog. "I love dogs, especially German shepherds. Is it okay if I give him a muffin?"

"Sure, Barf will like it."

She raised her eyebrows and chuckled. "His name is Barf?"

The man's brown eyes twinkled as he smiled and ran his hand through his dark hair. "Yeah, when he was a puppy, he ate everything that wasn't nailed down. Then he barfed most of it back up."

She smiled as she fed Barf a muffin and then held the bag out to the man. "Would you like one? I bought six. They're delicious."

"Thank you." He took one, leaned against her car, and bit into the oat muffin.

"Do you know who lives there?" Stacie asked, pointing at the house with the sign.

He nodded. "Mark Taylor. I know him well."

She crinkled her nose. "What's with the sign? Is he weird?"

He shook his head. "His dates don't seem to think so."

She bent down to pet Barf again. Her long dark-brown hair fell off her shoulder and hid her face. "Since you know him, maybe you can give me some advice. I'm desperate."

When she stood back up, her blue eyes pleaded for understanding. "I had to move out of my furnished apartment this morning. Two weeks ago, I gave my landlord and my boss notice that I had accepted a job in Atlanta. Yesterday, Atlanta rescinded their offer because of the recession, so now I don't have a job or a place to live."

The man shook his head. "Bummer." He waved for her to follow. "Come on, I'll introduce you to Mark. I'm sure you can work something out."

When she hesitated, Barf nudged her forward.

The man smiled. "Looks like you already have one good reference."

He rapped the brass knocker on the front door of the two-story mini-mansion. No one answered. "He's probably in the shower. Let's go in and wait for him." He led her into the living room, and they sat next to each other on the sofa.

"What's your name?" he asked.

"Stacie Sinclair."

"I'm Mark Taylor, pleased to meet you." He kissed her hand.

She gaped and sputtered, "But … you … I … don't understand." Her eyes widened as she stared at him. "You seem nice and are quite handsome. You can probably get any woman you want. Why would you put a Wife Wanted sign in your yard?"

He grinned. "Thanks for the compliment. I'm thirty, and I've dated a lot of women but haven't found one I'd want to marry. It's imperative that I be married by the end of this week, and I couldn't advertise in the newspaper. I've had the sign up for four days. None of the applicants were suited for the position, but I think you are. You're intelligent, well spoken, pretty, kind, and most important, Barf approves of you. He has good intuition about people. Are you married, or do you have a boyfriend?"

She frowned and shook her head with a puzzled look. "I date occasionally. Nothing serious. I'm on a deadline to finish the novel I'm writing in my spare time, but a deadline to get married sounds odd. What's the deal?"

Mark sighed. "I'm the district manager for Trend Corporation. The vice-president is retiring and told me the board agreed I'm the best qualified of the three men being considered for his replacement, but they prefer their top executives to be married. They vote in two weeks. That doesn't give me much time to get the license, get married, and introduce my bride to the board of directors."

"What would you expect from me as your hired wife?"

"You'd be my wife in name only. Your duties will be business related, such as dinner parties, business functions, etc. I'll pay you five-hundred dollars a week, plus free room and board. I have a housekeeper, and I rarely eat at home. I'll hire a catering service for dinner parties. And you'd have a lot of free time to finish writing your novel."

Stacie nibbled on her lip while weighing the pros and cons. This seemed too good to be true. If she had written this scene in her novel, no one would've believed it. She didn't know anything about this man, except where he lived and what he'd told her about himself. She had four days to find out if what he said was true. He seemed very nice and needed her as much as she needed him. And Barf was a definite plus.

"What about sleeping arrangements?" she asked.

"You'd have the guest suite upstairs. I'll convert the spare room next to it into an office for you. It'll be like your own apartment."

She blushed. "Where's your bedroom?"

He hid his amusement with a stern face. "My bath, bedroom, and office are downstairs. I rarely go upstairs."

She arched an eyebrow. "Rarely?"

He held up his hands. "Okay, how about *never*, after we set up your office ... unless I'm invited." He smiled. "If you agree, we'll draw up the agreement with my lawyer tomorrow. You'll have time to think about adding any stipulations."

Mark knelt on one knee and held her hand while gazing into her eyes. "Please, Stacie, will you marry me?"

Barf had been sitting in front of them with his ears alert, turning his head to look at each one as they spoke. He pawed her leg, laid his head on her lap, looked up at her with the same pleading look as Mark, and whined.

She looked at Mark. "Did Barf understand everything we just said?"

He shrugged. "What can I say? He's uncanny."

She laughed. "How can I refuse? It's two against one."

Barf wagged his tail and barked.

Mark pulled her up and hugged her. "I think this'll work out well for both of us. Let's unload your car and get you settled."

Barf gently took her wrist in his mouth and led her to the front door. When Mark opened the door, Barf ran to the Wife Wanted sign and tugged on it.

"Right! We don't need that anymore," Mark said. He pulled it up and handed it to Barf. "Take it to the trash." Barf dragged it to the back of the house.

"Will you miss having a big wedding with all the frills?" Mark asked.

"No, I wouldn't like all the fuss, but I'd like to be married in a church with my family there. My mother is a widow and lives in Texas near my two brothers and their families." She smirked. "Now they'll have to stop nagging me to get married. What day and time is the wedding?"

"The wedding has to be on Thursday. You pick the time. I belong to the Presbyterian Church. Will that work?"

"Sure. Let's have a candlelight wedding, followed by a dinner reception."

"Great! I'll make reservations at The Breakers hotel."

She grabbed his arm. "Wait! I don't have the proper attire for any of this."

"Don't worry." He patted her hand. "After we sign the agreement, we'll go shopping. I'll pay for everything—rings, wardrobe, and wedding gown."

She sighed with relief. "Thank you. I don't know if my brothers will be able to attend the wedding, but my mom can be my matron of honor. She isn't tied down with a job."

"Good!" Mark leaned down and hugged Barf. "He's my best friend, so he'll be my best man. I think he'll look great wearing a black bow tie."

***

It wasn't long before their business relationship blossomed into love. Over time, her romance novels became bestsellers, and the couple remains happily married to this day.

Author's Note: I wrote this eulogy for the funeral of a dear friend who loved flying. I'd like to take this opportunity to thank every person who ever served in the U.S. military.

SEMPER FI

S.L. Menear

He was a true American hero
Who served his country well
He fought bravely through Satan's jungle
In a Vietnamese Hell

His fellow soldiers called him Old Man
Though he was just twenty-three
Naïve new recruits faced a fate
Only Bill could possibly foresee

When offered an honorable discharge
And a ticket to fly home across the sky
He signed up for another tour of duty
So new recruits wouldn't die—*Semper fi*

On his last day in Vietnam
Bill stepped on a land mine
He awoke three months later
Saved by a force divine

Over the years, civilian Bill volunteered
With Marine Corps instructors at a base nearby
He taught left-handed soldiers how to shoot
Guns designed for right-handed men—*Semper fi*

His humor and kindness
Endeared him to everyone
His extraordinary talents
Were second to none

He transformed a pan-head Harley
Into a fire-breathing work of art
He was a loving father to his son
And daughters right from the start

Bill could always be counted on
To help a friend in need
He was a truly honorable man
In both word and deed

A Citation X Captain, he was happiest
Jetting through the sky
Until that sad and fateful day
When cancer made him die

Fly high forevermore, brave Marine
And friend. I miss you—*Semper fi.*

THE RATTLED HUNTER

D.M. Littlefield

A HUNTER GETS BIT BY A RATTLER—that was the headline in our town's newspaper, but the paper didn't git the whole story. My older brother, Clem, told me how it really happened.

Well, sir, Clem and Bubba, I mean Buford—we called my cousin Bubba 'til my kinfolks moved ta town—went huntin'. Aunt Jess, I mean, Aunt Jessica, got all uppity and gave us a long lecture about usin' their proper names.

Buford's pa was a good hunter and wanted his son ta be too, but Buford couldn't hit the broad side of a barn. So his pa bought him a shiny new shotgun, hopin' ta improve his skill an' git his nose out of the library books he was always readin'. Buford's pa asked big Clem ta teach Buford how ta hunt cuz he wasn't havin' any luck with him. So Clem took him huntin' in the forest next to our farm.

Buford brought along Snuffy, his ol hound dawg, who loved ta hunt and had a nose that jus wouldn't quit. Well, sir, after they was in the forest followin' Snuffy, Buford doubled over, grabbed his fat gut, and made a face like he was in awful pain. He yelled he needed a place to poop and ran in circles, like a chicken with his head cut off, afore he saw a fallen tree with a limb strong enough ta drape his butt over and unload.

He leaned his shotgun against the branch and almost ripped his britches in his rush ta pull 'em down as he backed up ta the fallen limb. Then he exploded and let out a loud sigh of relief.

When he caught the scent, Snuffy raised his nose and raced back ta investigate.

Buford was bent over and wiping himself with a handful of leaves when Snuffy's cold wet nose poked his behind. He yelped and leaped forward. His britches were still down around his ankles, so he grabbed onto his shotgun ta keep from fallin'. He accidentally jerked the trigger and shot a big limb he was standin' under. The heavy branch knocked him ta the ground.

As he tried ta crawl out from under it, he heard a rattlin' sound. He looked over his shoulder and saw a rattlesnake all riled up by the loud commotion. Buford clawed the ground, desperate ta git away, but his britches were tangled around his ankles, and his suspenders were caught on a branch.

Afore Clem could shoot the snake, it bit Buford on his bare behind, and he shrieked and fainted. Clem killed the snake and dragged Buford out. Big Clem heaved him over his shoulder and ran as fast as he could on home for our ma ta save him.

She took one look at his swellin' behind and said, "I ain't suckin' the poison out of there, but I'll deal with it."

Ma put kerosene on the snakebite cuz, you know, it's the wonder cure-all for us country folks. Buford swelled up a whole lot and got real sick, but he lived ta tell the tale. He found out the itchy rash on his hands and behind wasn't from the snakebite; it was from the poison ivy leaves he'd used to wipe himself.

With all the readin' he'd done, I'd a thought he'd of read up some on poison plants.

Author's Note: A dear friend gave me permission to write her true story as long as I omitted names and places to preserve her privacy.

MONSTERS

S.L. Menear

I was alone in bed, the room in pitch-black darkness, when I rolled onto my stomach and felt a jolt of fear.

I sensed someone in the room.

My irrational hope was the intruder wouldn't notice me if I froze and held my breath. Fear spiraled to panic when the bed gave way as a heavy weight crushed me into the mattress. Terror paralyzed me. I couldn't even scream.

Later, my mother found me whimpering inside a closet. She assumed I'd been sleep walking. I was three years old, and that was my first encounter with a monster.

***

Now an adult, nightmares had tortured me as long as I could remember. I also suffered night terrors—detailed, repetitive, and realistic enough to flood me with adrenaline.

As a child, I had tried to fight it by planning my dreams before I fell asleep. My vivid imagination would conjure storylines of adventure, romance, humor, and the requisite happy ending. I desperately hoped my subconscious would harness the pleasant images in a dream sequence.

Sometimes it prevented nightmares, although sleep usually arrested my imaginary stories.

Unfortunately, the night terrors haunted me into my early fifties. The monsters attacked under the cover of darkness when I was alone. They were so terrifying my subconscious blocked their faces from my conscious memory.

***

I was thirty-six, married, and snuggling in bed early one morning when the UPS man knocked on our front door. I rolled onto my stomach as my husband trotted downstairs.

That's when one of the monsters sneaked into the darkened room.

I felt his eyes on me. My husband's muffled conversation with the UPS guy drifted in. A scream would summon him. Yet again, the familiar terror paralyzed me as the monster's weight smothered me. Then, the blessed blackness, like so many times past.

Why did this keep happening to me? Why did no one protect me? Why couldn't I protect myself? Had I done something to deserve this?

My self-esteem had become a victim.

***

The next year, I was alone in bed late at night, after the divorce. As usual, I was restless, often surfacing from sleep. I rolled onto my stomach and froze. Did I hear someone?

I stole a glace. A dark shadow loomed. I prayed I was dreaming as I reached for the pistol under my other pillow.

Too late.

The monster's heavy weight imprisoned me as he breathed on my neck. The terror, overwhelming. This time I managed to squeeze out a squeak.

Paralysis.

Blackness.

***

By age fifty, I had lost hope for any refuge from my night terrors. I didn't know why the monsters were so relentless or how to stop them.

Five decades of this.

I tried not to think about it and never told anyone because I didn't know who the monsters were or how to explain it.

My secret horror. My secret shame.

In my mid-fifties, I embarked on a rejuvenating journey that began with a three-week stay at a spa clinic where I cleansed my body with wheat-grass juice, vegetarian meals, enemas, salt-water pools, ice-water pools, infra-red heat, and yoga.

The program included health classes and one session with a world-renowned psychiatrist. I made an appointment with the doctor mostly out of curiosity. I didn't expect him to accomplish anything useful in one hour.

"How may I help you?" he asked.

For the first time, I divulged the monsters, the night terrors.

"I'll put you in a state of deep relaxation," he said. "We'll discover the identities of your monsters, and we'll stop them forever. No worries, you're safe here."

I didn't believe him for a second, but I decided to try it. After all, what did I have to lose? I invested my trust in him.

The psychiatrist transported me back to age three and asked me for details on what I saw. We progressed in age until all five monsters' identities had been exposed. Finally, the truth too terrible to face.

The monsters were real men—relatives—all dead now. The attacks had stopped four decades ago, but my night terrors made it seem as though they were still happening. Half asleep, half awake, my subconscious reproduced the monsters in such vivid details, I believed they were really there. I could hear real sounds, like my husband chatting with the UPS guy, while also feeling the monster on top of me, his breath on my neck. Terror.

The doctor helped me confront my attackers and express my hurt and anger over their evil abuse.

How could they?

The very men who should've been my protectors had betrayed me. Why had my female relatives done nothing to protect me? Apparently to conceal the family's disgrace.

The doctor explained the women in my extended family were trapped in shame and denial because they had been victimized too. Through understanding, I was able to forgive them.

My hour with the psychiatrist proved to be the most valuable hour of my life. It gave me the closure I needed to end my suffering.

Good-bye, monsters.

Good riddance, night terrors.

Thank you, Doctor!

MY UNCONSCIOUS MUSE

D.M. Littlefield

My brain cells weren't percolating sufficiently for an assignment from my writers group on my greatest disappointment. Only childhood downers lingered ... not getting the doll I wanted for Christmas ... unrequited love for movie star Cary Grant.

To spark my imagination, I perused some magazines. An article in *Poets & Writers* magazine recommended meditation to quiet the mind from distractions and facilitate communication between your muse and subconscious. The author suggested sitting cross-legged on a floor pillow and counting to ten to clear the mind and connect.

I decided to try it, even though my subconscious was unconscious most of the time. So I grabbed the blue throw pillow off the couch and tossed it on the white tile floor in my living room. Crossing my legs Buddha style was difficult to accomplish at eighty-six, but groaning and grunting inched me into it. I took a deep breath, closed my eyes, and softly counted. When I reached seven, I shrieked from leg cramps.

When I grabbed my legs, I fell backward and rolled over to the couch. After pulling myself up, I stomped, hopped, and jumped all around the room while reaching down to rub out the cramps.

Thank goodness no one saw my impromptu version of a rodeo bronco buster. I couldn't stop the spastic contortions. It must've shaken some brain cells loose and short-circuited my brain, making me think of *Dancing with the Stars,* one of my favorite TV programs.

I knew how the three original judges would've scored my dance of pain.

Judge Carrie Ann Inaba would've said, "I realize you put a lot of effort into this performance, but you need to concentrate more on your upper body movements. Don't keep bending your head and grabbing your legs. Look up. Smile. Keep your shoulders back, and move your arms gracefully. I'm giving you a five."

Judge Len Goodman, a stickler for perfection, would've shaken his head and said, "I couldn't figure out if you were dancing the quickstep, the jitterbug, or the bunny hop. This was your worst dance. I've never seen anything like it, and I hope I never do again. I'm giving you a three."

Judge Bruno Tonioli would've stood up, waved his arms, and said, "You were very entertaining, my darling. I didn't realize someone your age could have so much energy. Your choreography was beyond description. You need to stop grimacing, though. Smile. Show us some sexy moves. Give me a sultry look. Shake your booty. I'm giving you a four."

I exhaled a deep sigh and rode off into the sunset on my charley horse.

STRESSED OUT

D.M. Littlefield

I mentally crossed off my list of the morning's to-dos. First, I'd left Muffy at the groomer's. I gave Amy a new coloring book and crayons to keep her busy while waiting at the dentist's office to get Billy's tooth extracted. Then I picked up the dry cleaning, bought groceries, and picked up Muffy.

I sighed as I drove into our driveway in Palm Beach Gardens.

My three-year-old daughter's allergies had made her cranky all morning, so I would put her down for a nap right after lunch. But first, I had to rush to put the groceries away, make lunch, throw a roast in the oven, bake a cake, tidy the house, and set the dining room table. Dave forgot to tell me until this morning that he was bringing home the new district manager for dinner. I wished he wasn't so forgetful.

I popped the trunk and turned to Billy and Amy buckled in the backseat. I handed Billy the leash. "Billy, don't let Muffy out of the car until you put the leash on her. You know she likes to run away. I'll start unloading the trunk. After you walk Muffy, you can help me carry in the groceries. We have to hurry. I don't want the ice cream to melt."

I grabbed the bags with perishables and hurried to the house. When I got to the front door, I realized I left my purse in the car with the house keys in it.

"Billy, please bring me my purse!"

Billy slammed his car door shut and stomped toward me. "Mom, Muffy won't hold still for me to put the leash on her. She's so excited, she keeps jumping from the front to the back."

I set the groceries by the front door, marched to the car with the leash Billy had handed me, and yanked on the front-door handle. It wouldn't open. The dog had pushed the driver's master lock button in her excitement to get out. Muffy's cute black-button eyes peered at me as she pressed her wet, black nose on the window. An adorable, empty-headed toy poodle, she was the canine version of a dumb blonde. All show and no know.

Tired, I slowly pieced together the calamity: My cranky daughter and our slap-happy poodle were locked in the car with the keys to the car and house. I blew out a sigh and tapped on the window at Amy, who was coloring away in her book. She finally looked at me and pouted as my tapping intensified.

"Amy, Mommy needs you to pull up on the little silver knob that's sticking up on the door so we can all have lunch."

Amy shook her blond head. "I'm not hungry."

"Amy, Mommy has a lot of work to do. We're having company for dinner, and we're going to have ice cream for dessert. If you open the door, I'll let you have some now."

"What kind?"

"Vanilla."

"I want chocolate." She bent her head and continued coloring.

I thrust my hands on my hips and leaned my forehead on the car above the window. "Ouch!" *I hope that hot metal won't leave a mark.* I kicked the tire in frustration. Another mistake. *Never kick anything in toeless shoes.* I tried to rub my toe while hopping on one foot.

"Amy Miller, do you hear me? Open the door!"

She sniffled and wiped her hand across her runny nose without looking at me.

"I know you can hear me! The next block can hear me! Open the door!"

Billy tugged my arm. "Mom, my tooth aches."

"How can your tooth ache? It's not in your mouth. It's in

your pocket to put under your pillow tonight."

Billy shrugged. "I don't know, but my friend Jimmy said you should eat ice cream after you have a tooth pulled. It makes you feel better."

I shook my head. "You eat ice cream after you have your tonsils removed, not your teeth."

"I know it'll make me feel better if I eat ice cream now. Besides, it's melting."

He pointed at the front door.

I glanced at the bags on the front step. Yikes, they were leaking. Muffy clawed at the window. Beads of perspiration were forming on Amy's face. I closed my eyes and rubbed the back of my sticky neck, visualizing the newspaper headline: Unfit Mother Abuses Children, Poodle, and Perishables.

I reached inside my pocket for my cell phone to call the police. Not there. In my purse! I kicked the tire again and stubbed my other big toe. I mentally swore. It took a lot for me to conjure profanity, and even then, never out loud. Not for the kids' ears.

This emergency called for drastic measures. *I'll ask one of my neighbors to use their phone. But who? Mrs. Perfect ... Judy Duncan, with the perfect kids who never do anything wrong?* I shook my head. I'd never hear the end of it.

What about Mr. Sims, the neighborhood curmudgeon? No! I'd get a long lecture about how kids were raised in his day when the world was a better place.

How about Mrs. Perry, the elderly widow who has taken gossip to new heights since she got her own website. No! Terrible idea.

I glanced at my watch: two o'clock. Dinner was set for five. My head ached.

As I stared down at my sore toes and prayed for a miracle, I heard a voice call out. "Are you having car trouble? Can I help you?"

A young woman pushed a twin baby stroller toward us. My eyes lit up as I looked up to heaven and mouthed, "Thank you!" Her twins weren't old enough to know right from wrong. She didn't have enough experience yet to give me a lecture on how to raise my kids, and she wouldn't have time to gossip.

"My daughter is locked in the car, and she won't open the door. May I use your cell phone to call the police?" I raised my eyebrows. "You do have a cell phone, don't you?"

"Yes." She smiled and handed me her phone.

I called the police and then my husband. He said he'd take his manager to a restaurant for dinner and suggested I order in a pizza and relax. He planned to call back in a half hour for an update.

When the police arrived, they asked questions and started using a special tool to unlock the door.

One of them grinned. "Don't worry, lady, this happens all the time. After all this, I know you'll always take your keys and purse out of the car first."

When they opened the door, Amy screamed, and Muffy jumped out and raced down the block. I stumbled and fell on the lawn when I tried to chase her.

Just another normal day in my stressed-out life.

Author's Note: For twenty-five years, off and on, my mother worked on a book about tooth fairies. I wrote a few chapters to help her finish it, but the book was born from her wonderful imagination. The following poem is about her and her beloved fairy novel, *Journey into the Land of the Wingless Giants*.

THE FAIRIES' GODMOTHER

S.L. Menear

She views the world with childlike wonder
In everything beauty she does see
The fairies all adore her
And she loves them equally
She honors their lives in the telling
Of their stories both mighty and small
And all God's children everywhere
Take delight in reading them all
The power of her visions
Keeps her forever young
With each new chapter in her life
A new adventure is begun
She's a very special person
Who is loved by one and all
And especially
She is loved by me
My friend, my mentor, my mom

DUMPSTER DIVING

D.M. Littlefield

I was savoring my morning coffee when my neighbor, Jane, knocked on my door. Weary, I sighed and limped to open it.

"Good morning, Dottie. Are you going to the condo board meeting this morning?"

"No, I don't feel like it."

"Why not?"

"I didn't sleep well after my terrible night." I rolled up my sleeves and showed Jane my arms.

"How did you get all those scrapes and scratches?"

"I'll tell you if you promise to keep it to yourself."

She rolled her eyes. "I promise."

"Okay, sit down and I'll get you a cup of coffee."

"This had better be good because I don't want to be late for the meeting."

"Oh, it is, believe me." I handed her the coffee and sat across from her.

"Yesterday, I spent the whole day cleaning out my kitchen cabinets. I filled lots of bags and piled them by the front door to take to the dumpster. I was so exhausted afterward, I had to sit down and rest."

"See, that's your problem. You don't know when to quit, and you suffer for it later. For Pete's sake, Dottie, remember you're seventy-six." She sipped her coffee and made a sour face. "Pass the sugar, please."

"You're right. Old too soon and smart too late, that's me. I fell asleep watching TV and woke up at midnight. I took a shower, put on my pajamas, and remembered the garbage pickup was today."

Jane stirred the sugar in her coffee. "So?"

"So I put the stretch bracelet with all my keys on my left wrist. I needed the mailbox key on the way back from the dumpster. I thought no one would be outside at midnight, so I went out in my pajamas and fuzzy house slippers."

Jane arched her eyebrows and shook her head.

"I opened the front door with a bundle of newspapers under my right arm and picked up a shopping bag with each hand. Somehow, I also managed to grab two garbage bags and clutch them to my chest. I was so loaded down I almost lost my balance when I pushed the door closed with my foot."

"It's a good thing we have streetlights so you could see."

"I trudged to the dumpster, laid the bags on one of the double plastic lids, put the newspapers in the proper receptacle, and threw the plastics in the other one. Then I lifted one of the dumpster lids and dropped the bags in along with my keys!"

She gasped. "No!"

"That dumpster is eight feet long and four and a half feet deep! I swore, stomped back to my condo for an old pair of sneakers, a penlight, and stepstool. I put the stool next to the dumpster and climbed inside to rummage through all that stinky mess, but then I heard whistling."

"Oh, no!" Her eyes widened. "Was it that handsome single guy I always hear whistling? I think his name is Bob Jamison. He just moved into Condo 169 near the dumpster."

I shrugged. "With my luck, who else could it be? I snapped off the pen light, crawled under the closed lid on the other side, and hid behind garbage bags in the corner. Then I covered my head with a palm branch."

Jane cringed. "Aauugh, that's disgusting!"

"I watched a big bag drop in and the lid close. He whistled as he walked away. I held my breath and waited until I couldn't hear the whistling anymore. Then I inched up the lid with my head to peek out and gulp some fresh air. My back ached as I searched through the icky garbage, but I finally found my keys stuck in a torn bag of rank kitty litter. I shook off the keys and felt so relieved until I noticed my stepstool was gone."

"Did Bob take it?"

"He must've thought it was a give-away."

"So how did you get out?"

"By using my ingenuity."

"What do you mean?"

"I stacked bags against a side to climb to the top, but then two large raccoons lifted the other lid."

"Oh my God!"

"The raccoons gave me a fierce look and hissed. Talk about motivation! I grabbed an edge, climbed up the bags, swung my legs over the side like I've seen in movies, and landed on top of Bob, who was on his hands and knees. I yelped as we rolled over. I was so embarrassed I wanted to die."

Jane shrieked, "You poor thing! What did you do?"

"I tried to apologize and explain what I was doing, but I probably sounded irrational from crying so hard. He smiled, pulled me up, and put his arm around my shoulder."

"But why was he there?"

"He explained his keys had fallen out of his pocket when he leaned over to pick up the stepstool. He didn't realize it until he reached into his pocket to hang the keys on a hook in his kitchen." I shook my head. "We both limped as he helped me home."

"Did you get your stepstool back?"

"Yes." I grinned. "And I'm taking Bob to my chiropractor this afternoon. We both need an adjustment."

"Yeah, in more ways than one." Jane winked with a smug smile.

THE WORD ARTIST

D.M. Littlefield

I'm an artist painting black images
On backgrounds of white.
My paintings gain color when
Your imagination takes flight.

I am an author, painting word pictures
Even the blind can see by touch.
Language is my palette, paper my canvas.
I use a pen, not a brush.

I hear the pitter-patter of raindrops
From clouds that weep
And write them to lull my readers
Into a peaceful sleep.

My readers awake to a sunrise
Of shining molten gold,
And I include all of nature's beauty
For them to behold.

I write about God's promise sign,
A rainbow in the heavenly mist.
As my readers inhale the fragrant scent
Of flowers the sun has kissed.

My pages describe lush meadows mantled
With silver sheets of morning dew
And include the tiny, hovering,
Iridescent-hued hummingbirds too.

My fairies admire pretty butterflies
Fluttering above the flowers with care
And watch them as they carefully search
Among the busy bees for blossoms to share.

My readers hear the lilting sound
Of the bird's sweet song
And listen as he cheerfully sings
The whole day long.

They follow the babbling brook
Into the dense green forest
And heed the loud resonance
Of the cicada's chorus.

They listen to the roaring,
Cascading, mountain waterfall
And marvel at the forests' giants,
The redwood trees so tall.

They hear the towering pines,
Caressed by the wind as they whisper and sigh,
And they watch as the bright stars twinkle
Like diamonds in a black velvet sky.

They climb the highest mountains
And find deep-blue crater lakes
And stand in the hushed silence
Of softly falling snowflakes.

They gaze at the magnificent orange glow
Of sunset before dusk diminishes light

And admire the silvery magic of moonlight
On a clear, quiet, snow-covered night.

My readers enjoy reading about beautiful
Scenes of nature I've seen everywhere.
I remind them the real-life scenes are gifts
From our Creator for all of us to share.

LUNAR MADNESS

S.L. Menear

My thriller novels are fiction, but most of the short stories I write are true and usually involve the consumption of wine. I should probably learn a lesson from that.

This one started on the deck of one of my favorite Singer Island hotels on a warm Saturday afternoon with a cool breeze blowing in off the ocean. The sea air and festive atmosphere stimulated my creative flow. My fingers danced across my laptop as I sipped ice tea and worked on *Blaze*, Book Three in my *Samantha Starr Series*.

I spent so much time writing at that hotel I was on a first-name basis with most of the staff. During lunch, I noticed a new waiter, a handsome young man named Matt. He was waiting on a table of pretty, bikini-clad college girls. Although they kept summoning him back to their table, he couldn't linger during the busy lunch hour.

Later that afternoon, a seasoned waitress stopped by my table with a shocked look.

"Hey, Sammie, what's going on?" I asked.

"I just delivered a room-service order for Matt while he was on a break. A girl about twenty in nothing but skimpy panties opened the door. She and three other almost naked girls looked disappointed when they saw me. They were expecting Matt."

"Whoa, sounds like they were going to ambush him."

"Yeah, should I tell him what he missed?"

I couldn't resist saying, "Be sure to emphasize their spectacular breasts and obvious disappointment he wasn't there."

"Heh, heh, that'll be fun. But he still has food to deliver to them. I couldn't carry it all in one trip."

"Then plan on working without him for the rest of the day."

Thirty minutes later, Sammie returned with a grin.

"What happened to Matt?"

"When he went to their room, the girls were dressed and their mothers were there."

"Whoa! He's such a nice guy, I'd hate to think what would've happened if the girls had pounced on him and their mothers had walked in. He definitely dodged a bullet."

"You've got that right." She giggled and scampered away.

I continued writing until my cousin, Linda, called to invite me for drinks and dinner at my other favorite place, The Islander Grill & Tiki Bar at the elegant Palm Beach Shores Resort, about a mile down the beach. Closer to the southern end of the island, it was only three blocks from my house.

We'd both had a stressful week and needed to unwind with a little *vino*. Okay, maybe a lot of *vino*.

The always charming manager, Larry Wertz, welcomed us and led us to a table where we could watch people on the dance floor and enjoy listening to Steve and Angela sing contemporary songs and oldies, with a few World War II songs thrown in for the Greatest Generation. Marco Berisha, who speaks nine languages, waited on us and treated us like royalty. We love him. Actually, everyone loves him, including an Italian countess from Palm Beach.

The clientele was an interesting blend of vacationers in resort wear, families with children, and local couples dressed to the nines, all enjoying the dining and dancing.

Niko Bujaj, the handsome and gregarious owner of The Islander, bought us a bottle of Ménage a Trois blended red wine and regaled us with funny stories about the resort. Little did we know we were about to become another one of his stories.

After an entertaining evening with plenty of red wine and delicious gourmet dinners, Linda and I strolled out to the ocean behind the beautiful resort.

Ankle deep in calm water warmed by the Florida summer, we gazed at the ocean sparkling beneath a brilliant full moon. I breathed in the balmy sea air and felt pure joy.

That didn't last long.

I sensed a presence on my left and turned.

A tall, handsome black man held out a cigarette. "Can you give me a light?"

If I'd been sober, I would've been startled. Instead, I said, "I'm sorry, I don't smoke."

He stood inches from me, his biceps bulging over a cropped, sleeveless tank top that stretched across his broad upper chest.

I glanced downward and froze.

His lower half was totally naked.

Holy crap, this isn't France!

As the moonlight illuminated his manhood, my inebriated brain refused to believe what I saw. Everything seemed to be in slow motion. I glanced to my right to ask Linda if she saw him too.

She was gone.

Apparently, she had bolted the moment she spotted him. Well, obviously I couldn't count on her for backup. In her defense, there wasn't much need for training on how to handle drunks or criminals in dental offices.

Before my early retirement, I was an airline captain with extensive training in dealing with drunks, hijackers, and terrorists. That might have helped had I been sober on this lovely evening. I was slow to react as remnants of my rational brain struggled to convince my intoxicated brain that the man next to me was indeed naked.

Rather than feeling frightened, I found the situation amusing. Clearly Linda was the smarter cousin. I glanced around and spied her running toward lanterns set behind three people fishing in the surf.

I faced Naked Guy. "Excuse me, my friends are waiting for

me down the beach."

I strolled to where Linda was pacing behind two women and a man fishing. As I told them about the nude man, I realized children at the resort might encounter him, so I dialed 9-1-1 on my cell phone.

Linda and I were halfway to the resort's wooden walkway when a man strode onto the beach with a radio clipped to his belt. He stood ramrod straight in a commanding stance as he surveyed the area.

My wine-addled brain assumed the police had sent him even though he wasn't wearing a uniform.

"Wow, you got here really fast," I said as we approached him. "I'm impressed."

"What are you talking about?" he asked.

"I just called 9-1-1. Aren't you a police officer?"

"I'm with the Palm Beach Shores Police, but I'm working my second job as security for the resort."

Before I could explain, two cops sped up on an ATV.

"Are you the lady who called 9-1-1?" one of them asked.

"Yes, and the naked man I reported is sitting right over there on that lounge chair."

When I pointed at him, Naked Guy turned his head and spotted us.

In order to make their case, the police had to apprehend him before he pulled on his pants. Otherwise, the courts would consider it a "he-said, she-said" legal quagmire.

So Naked Guy, who was obviously drunk or high or both, grabbed his pants and rushed to pull them on as the cops sprinted across the beach toward him.

He managed to get his pants over his ankles, but then he tripped and fell face-first on the sand.

They caught him with his pants down and drugs and a flask of whiskey in his pockets. By then, two more officers had arrived. They handcuffed and escorted him—with pants on—through the resort and out to their car, drawing the attention of guests and employees.

After watching the comical takedown, Linda and I couldn't stop giggling.

"Ladies, we'll need you to come inside the resort and fill out police reports," one of the cops said.

"Sure, Officer, but we need to use the restroom first," I said.

"Now, ladies, you're not planning to sneak off, are you?"

Apparently, all our grinning and giggling worried him. Most people take police matters more seriously. But we were tipsy, and Naked Guy's arrest was hilarious. Every time I pictured him struggling to pull up his pants while the cops charged toward him, followed by his face plant, I started giggling again—couldn't help it.

"Honest to God, Officer, my bladder is about to burst," Linda said.

"Mine too. Why don't you wait outside the ladies' room? Then you won't worry," I said with a smile.

He guarded the door while we took care of business. By the time we arrived at the table in the lobby, the police had more info about Naked Guy.

One of them said, "His excuse for trolling the beach nude was that his wife is almost eight months pregnant, and he's not *getting any* at home."

"Oh, so he thought he'd show me his junk, and I'd say I've got to have me some of that! *Really*?" I laughed.

The cops chuckled.

He handed me a form for the police report. "He'll be stuck in jail a while because his wife refused to bail him out."

At this point I should mention all the police officers involved were white men so you'll understand my next comment, which was truthful, motivated by humor (and too much wine), and not meant to disparage.

I glanced up at them and grinned. "If he was a typical example, I have to tell you it's not true what they say about the size of—"

The officers burst out laughing. Linda and I giggled.

Word of our little adventure must have circulated. As we filled out the police reports, employees strolled past, snickering.

Linda, a dental hygienist, wrote a concise clinical report:

My cousin and I were standing in the ocean when a big naked man walked up to us. I ran away. Sharon called the police.

I'm an author, so I felt compelled to write a detailed two-page report that began: *The soothing water of the summer-warmed Atlantic lapped at our ankles as my cousin, Linda, and I gazed up at the brilliant full moon ....*

ABOUT THE AUTHORS

Dorothy Metz Littlefield has been writing for over fifty years. Her first story, *When Time Stood Still*, was published in magazines and in another short-stories anthology.

Dorothy is currently writing mystery and romance novels as well as short stories. She draws on experiences from her world travels with her daughter, aerobatic flying, soaring, diving, hang gliding, horseback riding, and hot-air ballooning with her children.

Born and raised in Chicago, Illinois, she moved to Diamond Lake, Michigan after marrying her husband, Ken. They raised their two children, Sharon and Larry, in Michigan and later in Bradenton, Florida.

Dorothy was a long-time resident of Kilgore, Texas, where she raised horses on her ranch until she moved to West Palm Beach, Florida in 2002 to be near her children.

A child at heart, Dorothy wrote a children's adventure novel that includes accurate details about wildlife and numerous examples of good morals.

Journey into the Land of the Wingless Giants, the result of limitless imagination and extensive research on plants and wildlife, answers the age-old question: What do tooth fairies do with the teeth? The middle-grade novel tells the story of eight fairy children aged nine to twelve who embark on a thrilling adventure into a land of giants. Only three inches tall, the fairies will need all their skills in the use of magic to survive their dangerous quest in unfamiliar territory where almost everything is enormous and deadly.

Enchanted: A young child is kidnapped by an old hag who takes her deep into a forbidden forest. The hag's cart crashes into a tree when her horse is frightened by a grizzly bear, freeing the child.

Lost in the dark forest, the little girl meets a fairy queen. The fairy bestows an enchantment that makes all animals accept the child as one of their own. A wolf pack protects the girl and helps the fairy lead her home. Later, the girl's mother meets the fairies, and they allow her to draw their pictures. And that is how the first fairy pictures entered the world.

***

Sharon Littlefield Menear is a retired airline pilot. US Airways hired Sharon in 1980 as their first female pilot, bypassing the flight engineer position. The men in her new-hire class gave her the nickname Bombshell. She flew Boeing 727s and 737s, DC-9s, and BAC 1-11 jet airliners and was promoted to captain in her seventh year.

Before her pilot career, Sharon worked as a water-sports model and then traveled the world as a flight attendant with Pan American World Airways.

Sharon also enjoyed flying antique airplanes, experimental aircraft, and Third World fighter airplanes. Her leisure activities included scuba diving, powered paragliding, snow skiing, surfing, horseback riding, aerobatic flying, sailing, and driving fast cars and motorcycles.

Sharon has flown many of the airplanes in her debut novel, *Deadstick Dawn*, winner of the Royal Palm Literary Award, *Poseidon's Sword*, *Blaze*, and *Stranded*, Books One, Two, Three, and Four in the *Samantha Starr Series* featuring a woman pilot in fantasy action thrillers.

She and her mother, D.M. Littlefield, also co-wrote a middle-grade children's adventure novel, *Journey into the Land of the Wingless Giants* and a novella for young children, *Enchanted*.

The first novel in the Samantha Starr Series, **DEADSTICK DAWN**, won the 2011 Royal Palm Literary Award for Best Thriller. In that book, the Belfast Agreement is about to be shattered by Operation Blue Blood. One young American stands in the way, airline pilot Samantha Starr.

She is catapulted into a deadly chess match with police, assassins, and British Special Forces, all who want her dead. The fate of nine noble bloodlines depends on Samantha and a boy whose hero is a wizard.

Stranded in Scotland where she is accused of kidnapping and murder, where can she run? When a US Navy fighter pilot and a SEAL join the hunt and every choice can get her killed and start a bloody war in Northern Ireland, on whom should she rely? The line between trust and betrayal is razor sharp, and it is cut at *Deadstick Dawn*.

In **POSEIDON'S SWORD**, Book Two in the Samantha Starr Series, an 11,000-year-old prophecy plunges airline pilot Samantha Starr into an international maelstrom. While flying to exotic locales during a round-the-world charter flight, Sam stumbles upon the enigmatic key to Poseidon's Sword, an ancient weapon of unimaginable power.

Her discovery triggers a race among secret cults, arms dealers, and world leaders, intent on possessing the doomsday weapon. Old enemies and mysterious allies enter the fray, believing Sam is vital to locating and activating Poseidon's Sword.

She becomes an unwilling pawn thrust into a treacherous game trapping her crew, passengers, and family in the rivals' deadly power plays. Sam struggles to save them and thwart her evil adversaries before time runs out in this fast-paced fantasy action thriller.

In **BLAZE**, the third fantasy action thriller in S.L. Menear's Samantha Starr Series, airline pilot Samantha Starr is on the adventure of her life, an unexpected one headed for disaster. Stealth submarines, Scottish castles, Antarctic ice chasms, deep-sea dives to an underwater city near Cuba, and a secret enclave in the frigid Himalayas test Sam's survival skills.

World powers, nefarious groups, and an evil billionaire are hot on the trail of an ancient weapon of mass destruction that can only be activated by Sam's touch. Her twin brothers in the Navy join forces with two airline pilots and Sam's Scottish boyfriend in an effort to save her and half the world's population. As time runs out, will Sam make the ultimate sacrifice?

In **STRANDED**, the fourth fantasy/action thriller in S.L. Menear's Samantha Starr Series, airline pilot Samantha Starr returns in another action-packed fantasy thriller. "Sam" is back in the cockpit of a luxury jumbo jet when she meets an old nemesis turned ally, Dragon Master. His shocking revelation sends her hurtling into an international conflict over the recent discovery of ancient Atlantis.

Russia and China join North Korea and Iran in threatening America and the UK to secure the advanced scientific data hidden 2,000 feet beneath the sea. Sam's unique knowledge of Atlantean weapons and systems is crucial if the crew on the USS *Leviathan* is to succeed against overwhelming odds.

The international crisis heats up when Sam's charter flight goes missing over a remote part of the jungle in South America. A Special Forces team that includes Sam's Scottish boyfriend and her SEAL brother is sent to find her. In their race to rescue the crew and passengers, the team discovers an underground city with a terrifying secret.

As WWIII looms closer, the US goes to DEFCON 1. Dark forces kidnap Sam, forcing her into an impossible situation in underwater Atlantis. Time is running out as she struggles to outsmart her adversary and avert a worldwide disaster.

S.L. Menear's web site: www.slmenear.com
Author's Facebook page: www.Facebook.com/slmenear

All books by author S.L. Menear and author D.M. Littlefield are available in soft cover and ebooks at www.amazon.com, www.barnesandnoble.com, and on request at bookstores. Next up is **SMILES *for* SENIORS**, an anthology of humorous short stories featuring senior citizens, coming soon.

A Request from the Authors

We hope you enjoyed our short stories. May we ask a favor? Please post a review on amazon.com, barnesandnoble.com., or goodreads.com. Your brief review might help someone else decide whether they'd like to read our book. We, like all authors, live and die by readers' reviews. Please help us out so we can continue to entertain you with future books. Thank you.

    Warm regards,
    Sharon and *Dottie*

Manufactured by Amazon.ca
Bolton, ON